Sheriff's detective Katrina "Hurricane" Williams confronts deep-rooted hate and greed in the Missouri Ozarks in this riveting police procedural . . .

What at first appears to be a brush fire in some undeveloped bottom land yields the charred remains of a young African-American man. As sheriff's detective Katrina Williams conducts her inspection of the crime scene, she discovers broken headstones and disturbed open graves in a forgotten cemetery.

As Katrina attempts to sort out a complex backwoods criminal network involving the Aryan Brotherhood, meth dealers, and the Ozarks Nightriders motorcycle gang, she is confronted by the sudden appearance of a person out of her own past who may be involved. And what seems like a clear-cut case of racially motivated murder is further complicated by rumors of hidden silver and dark family histories. To uncover the ugly truth, Katrina will need to dig up past crimes and shameful secrets that certain people would kill to keep buried . . .

Visit us at www.kensingtonbooks.com

Also by Robert E. Dunn

A Living Grave
A Particular Darkness
A Dark Path

Published by Kensington Publishing Corporation

A Dark Path

A Katrina Williams Novel

Robert E. Dunn

LYRICAL UNDERGROUND
Kensington Publishing Corp.
www.kensingtonbooks.com

First Electronic Edition: August 2018
eISBN-13: 978-1-5161-0654-7
eISBN-10: 1-5161-0654-7

First Print Edition: August 2018
ISBN-13: 978-1-5161-0656-1
ISBN-10: 1-5161-0656-3

Printed in the United States of America

For Letha Pearl

Chapter 1

Burning is not the best way to dispose of a body. It's hard to get a fire hot enough, long enough, to burn through the layers of fat, muscle, and bone to destroy all the evidence you need gone. It doesn't smell very good either.

Before it ever got to me, the situation had worked through a few preliminary steps. First, the pair of teens who discovered the fire debated calling it in. They had been parking and fooling around in a secluded spot off a rutted dirt track—usually used by fishermen going to the lake. I imagine it was a tough debate among hormones, responsibility, and fear of angry parents. They told me later they would have let the blaze go if the boy's father hadn't been a volunteer fireman.

After a brutally stormy spring, the summer had been hot and dry. Over recent weeks, the Ozarks had fallen into a deep drought. Lake levels were way down, crops were withering, and small fires were whipped into big ones by even the smallest breeze. The boy had been lectured about it so many times, it was impossible for him to pretend ignorance.

After the kids called 911 to report what they believed was a trash fire, deputies and the fire department were dispatched. The boy's father showed up on the pumper. I understand there was a parenting opportunity that involved a little tough love.

That opportunity was probably lost when the embers were raked out and doused. In the center of the smoking pile was a charred lump everyone assumed was a log. When it was hit with direct pressure, the log split open. Under the black surface was pink meat and steaming flesh. That was when they called me.

My phone rang a few minutes shy of two a.m. Late Saturday night—or early Sunday morning—depending on how pedantic you are about that sort of thing. I'm not at all, at least not at that hour. I was in bed, and not yet sleeping because it wasn't my bed.

Every call to my phone rings the same tone except one, the Taney County Sheriff's Department. I knew it was a work call even without the tone. Real life always intrudes whenever I find a bit of peace in my life.

"This is Katrina," I said softly into the phone.

"Who're you whisperin' for?" our jailer asked. He laughed like he actually knew something. It was a thick, rheumy cackle that made me picture the soggy cigar in his jowled face.

I was actually relieved. If he was calling, I might be able to stay in bed. "What do you want, Duck?" His name was Donald Duques, earning him the permanent sobriquet, Donald Duck—always shortened to simply Duck. He laughed again and I became unpleasantly aware of being naked.

"Got a body," he interjected between wet hacks of laughter.

"What?" Given who he was and the old school Ozarks diction, I can be forgiven for thinking he was commenting about my appearance.

I was about to give him some choice thoughts on his manners when he said again, "We got a body. Out on the west side shore of Bull Shoals by Kissee Mills."

Detective Billy Blevins shifted in the sheets behind me. His arm moved against my bare thigh and hip. I was distracted by the warm contact. "What?"

Duck laughed again. "What'd I catch you doin'? Work can't hold your attention?"

"Why are you calling me?"

"I told you—"

"Why you, Duck?"

"Oh," he swallowed the laugh. "Gettin' a little overtime. Workin' weekend overnights on dispatch."

"Then stick to the job at hand, would you? What's the call?"

"Couple 'a kids called in a fire. Calvin called for a detective when the fire department found a body in the brush heap."

"Where?" I stood and broke contact with Billy's arm. My skin immediately regretted the loss.

"That undeveloped bottom land, down the fishing trail that goes off of Hole Road."

"Who's there?"

Duck told me the names of deputies on scene and I started searching for my underthings. They were close by on the floor. Finding them made me think of losing them. I smiled.

"I'll be half an hour," I informed Duck.

"From your place?" He sounded surprised.

"Half an hour," I repeated and broke the connection.

Moonlight through a high window illuminated Billy lying in the sheets. It was a nice sight. I was amazed—and alternately delighted and terrified—by that development in my life. Not as amazed; however, as I was that he'd never woken while I talked on the phone and dressed. Maybe I was projecting. My own sleep was fragile and filled with ghosts. Billy seemed to have the ability to sleep without demons.

He and I had circled each other for years. We were deployed to Iraq at the same time. In the worst moment of my life, Billy appeared for the first time. I don't even know if the memory is real. Everything else about that time is solid and undeniable. I was raped and brutalized by two superior officers. They left me for dead in the blowing brown dust that eddied behind a mud wall. Grain by grain, the dun-colored wind piled a grave on top of me. I pulled myself from the dirt, staggered then crawled to a road. Insurgents found me first. They would have shot me like a rabid dog in a ditch if an Army patrol hadn't shown up. All of that is true. And it's true that a young medic, a corporal, cleaned and stabilized me in the back of a rushing Humvee. There's a little piece of that, the piece I believe but don't know: Billy Blevins was that medic. He's never said and I'm afraid to ask. But I believe.

There were so many reasons why we never should have gotten to this point. I hated giving up any moment of lying naked with him.

Still. . . I'm a cop and the real world was calling.

I kissed Billy and bundled up my clothes. I needed to change. I didn't have anything at his place. Two minutes later, I was outside in my underwear. I held my good clothes and shoes as I opened my truck. You don't dress up for a late night call—in the woods—to investigate a burned body. I tossed the date clothes in the crew seat, then pulled out my old jeans and worst pair of boots. When you've been a rural cop for a while, you're never without disposable clothing. Even though Billy's house was remote and screened by a thick growth of trees, I felt exposed dressing in his drive. I refused to go back in the house. It would be too hard to keep from waking Billy—and that would make me late. I covered quickly.

The night was clear. The day had been so hot that not all of the heat had yet escaped into the bare sky. Before I climbed into the big GMC, I took one more glance at the diamond sky. It always made me think of Bob Dylan.

With the stop for gas and coffee, it took a bit more than thirty minutes to arrive on scene. By then I was wishing I had woken Billy and made him come with me. When I thought about explaining that to the on-duty deputies, I let the wish go out the open truck window.

Deep night in the Ozarks woods was lit up like a Spielberg movie about friendly aliens. Emergency lights and strobes were circling and flashing through a screen of brush and trees. I followed the light show to a rutted mud track between old posts where a gate had once been.

We're a mostly rural county, even on a Saturday night things can be pretty dull after one a.m. Four Sheriff's department cruisers and three fire vehicles were on scene when I parked between scrub oaks. The path was about seventy yards from where the shore line of Bull Shoals Lake was supposed to be. "Supposed to be," because the drought had pushed the shore out another few yards. On higher ground beyond the fence was a housing development adjacent to farm land. Down by the shoreline, it was overgrown and thick with underbrush. The fence row that paralleled the dirt path was clotted with under growth and hedge apple trees. The ground between the lake and the barbed wire fence was private land that had not been redeveloped after the White River was damned. It was freshly cleared, all low weeds burned brown. I could tell the land had been worked before. Around the clearing, there were no original or even second growth trees. All the foliage, oak, and hawthorn—mixed in with hedge apple and coils of grapevine—was no older than I was.

All the activity, the reason I had been called, was centered about a circle, close to the north edge of the clearing.

I was pleased to see that deputies had already put crime scene tape around the burned circle. They illuminated the circle with headlights and spots. I wasn't so pleased to see that one of the volunteer firemen was inside the perimeter.

"Calvin," I shouted at Calvin Walker then pointed to the man within the tape. Calvin is not my biggest fan.

"He's got to make sure the fire is completely dead," he shouted back, "What do you want me to do?"

"I want you to get him out of there unless it's on fire right now," I answered sharply. I wasn't a huge fan of Calvin Walker either.

Calvin went to talk to the fireman. I had another deputy bring me the kids. We had barely gotten started when Calvin shouted again, "Hurricane."

The girl turned from her boyfriend to look me in the face for the first time. "You're her," she said. "Hurricane."

"I'm Detective Katrina Williams."

"But you're the one they call 'Hurricane Katrina'." She had a look of big eyed wonderment. "You kick ass."

"Hurricane!" Calvin shouted with more force.

"You guys stay here," I told the pair, "we have more to go over."

"Check this out," Calvin said as I ducked under the tape. He was standing with the fireman who was leaning on a rake. "This is Cherry," Calvin indicated the fireman. He was an older man, but not as old as he appeared at first. Sometimes life hangs on people in a way that leaves no room for denying the years. His body was lean and hard looking; but in the white wash of headlights and spots, his skin—even that tracked by old blue ink—was thin looking.

"Cherry? Really?" I had to ask.

He gave me a tired look of acceptance, but didn't offer his hand. "Cherry Dando," he said. He examined me with the kind of curiosity that I'd almost gotten used to. "I know you."

"I get that a lot." Shifting my attention back to Calvin I asked, "What have you got?"

"Check it out," Calvin said again pointing into the char on the ground. Everything was black.

"Check what out?"

"Show her," Calvin said to Cherry.

Cherry Dando looked like that was the last thing he wanted to do. He pursed his lips then sucked in his cheeks like he was hoping to find an excuse hidden in his mouth. He didn't. So he reached his rake out and touched the tines down alongside a bit of black shape on burned grass.

I knelt. It wasn't the only shape in the ashes that didn't look like bits of wood. Fishing in my pocket I came up empty. "Either of you have a flashlight?" I asked.

Calvin hit the bone with light. After a second Dando added his. The shape was a scapula, a shoulder bone.

I looked up, then pointed to the larger, black-on-black, shape in the center of the burn circle. Calvin and the fireman turned their lights. The body was intact. It had carbonized on the outside but there were no pieces missing. In the beams of the flashlight it was still steaming.

"There," I said, pointing to the ground under the body. More bones littered the ash. As we swept the burn area with flashlights, we spotted two sets of teeth in lower jaws.

"You think there's any chance this fire could have burned two bodies to the bone and left one intact?" I asked Cherry Dando.

"I look like an expert?"

"Then what are you doing here?"

Dando sucked in his cheeks again. He looked like a man holding something back. "Nope." He sounded more resigned to the answer than confident in it.

"Why?" I pressed.

He sighed. It was the put-upon sound of a kid asked to do a chore with no handy excuse. "See the dark circle?" He outlined the pattern with his flashlight. "It was piled with dry brush. There aren't any big logs at all. Not enough fuel for a long burn. Someone poured gas on a brush pile, set it, and left it."

As soon as he said it, I noticed the scent of gasoline in the air.

"What about around there?" I pointed to the burned area that wasn't as dark.

Dando used his flashlight again to draw out the shape on the ground. It was more of a smudge than a circle. "That's where it caught the grass. If the night was windy, it would'a been a mess—that's for sure."

"Was he alive when it started?" Calvin asked.

"That's for you folks to find out," Dando answered. He turned his head and spit over the tape and didn't turn back.

"Lord, I hope not," Calvin said with genuine feeling in his voice. I was a little less bothered by him.

"Tape up a new perimeter," I said. "Push things out twenty feet that way and this side, all the way out to the truck path. Set up parking over there," I pointed to another clear area on the other side of the road ruts. "I already woke the scene tech as I made the drive. Call him back, tell him to tow the big light rig with him." I turned to Dando. "We'll need you to stick around a while to keep an eye on things. Outside the tape."

He shrugged without looking at me then ducked under the tape.

"Can I keep that?" When he looked I pointed to the rake in Dando's hand.

He stared down at his hand or the tines of the rake—I couldn't tell. He seemed to be giving the request a lot of thought. "I'll need it back."

"I promise."

He put it on the ground and pushed the handle over like he didn't want to get too close to me. Without another word or look, he walked to the firetruck.

I leaned the rake against a scraggly oak, then pulled out my phone to call Chief Benson.

* * * *

An orange-red sun bloomed in the east—giving new life to bleary eyes. Our crime scene was populated with a couple of dozen people by then. The coroner's van was there and waiting with open doors to take in the remains. To one side, Sheriff Benson, Chuck to his friends, was glad-handing with Riley Yates. Riley was one of the sheriff's friends. Almost everyone in the county was. Riley was also a reporter. In that role, he didn't seem so happy with the sheriff. I've heard that conversation before. Being friends didn't mean the sheriff was unprofessional about his job.

With the rising light, I was able to get into my own investigation routine. I retrieved a pencil and pad out of my truck and set to sketching. Photos catch the objective reality of the scene. But I find that, sometimes, the truth of things isn't so objective. It was an old habit that got stronger when I met my husband. Nelson Solomon had been a Marine, and after that a successful artist. When he died, he left me richer in many ways—not the least of which was a better eye for the small parts of a big picture.

I stood by the oak I had leaned the rake against and put the main shapes into the sketch. There was the tape perimeter, three trees, and the push bumper on a cruiser around which the tape was looped. Around the outer edges were tall grasses and weeds. They were all brown and friable from the drought. In the center was a black circle of ash and char. In the middle of that, like a bull's eye in hell, was the burned man's body.

I worked quickly. People were waiting for me to release them to their jobs. Using the side of the soft lead, I made broad shades to fill in the burn circle. With my thumb, I smeared the lines out—smoothing and feathering them from black to grey to almost not there. After that, I used the point and a light touch to draw in the bones.

It wasn't until I had the bones in and compared my sketch to the reality that I noticed what was missing. In the ash were the clear furrows where the rake tines had been pulled. There was something else. Sticks and bits of bark—unconsumed by the fire—were raked out and evenly spread. The bones were scattered widely and—in some cases—covered by ash. They had been given particular attention.

I glanced over and took a look at Fireman Dando—who was standing beside the pumper truck talking with his squad mates. In the rising light, I noticed, for the first time, the close crop of his hair and the corded muscle that I had taken earlier for frail thinness. His thin skin showed the sinew, and the tattoos on his arms highlighted each sharp angle. Even from where I was, it was easy to see the body art was not of the highest quality. It was the kind of old and faded ink you see on retired vets.

To justify my continued staring, I kept sketching the layout of the larger scene. I added Dando at his truck and resolved to hit him with a few pointed questions.

While I drew my notes, a truck barreled up the dirt track. It was an old Dodge, lifted with knobby tires and pipes run out to stacks poking over the top of the cab. The engine snarled. When it passed the fire pumper, but before getting to the spaced out cop cars, the truck slid to a grinding halt. Dust billowed up from the skid and breezed in from the draft. Dangling from the back of the hitch were two huge hex nuts on a chain—truck nuts. Classy.

The driver bounded from the cab before the truck even finished its dieseling death. "You got no right," he shouted. "This is private property. You got no right to be here." He was a big man, wide and strong-looking. His long stride ate up the ground.

Dando bolted forward and tried to slow him down. I saw the two of them exchange quiet, stressed words to no effect. The angry man pushed the fireman aside and kept right on coming.

At the same time the deputies, the sheriff, and I paced in to converge with him.

"Don't think I don't know what's going on," he shouted as soon as he picked the sheriff out.

Sheriff Benson met him with upheld hands and a stoic face. "Settle down now, Johnson."

"Settle down my ass." Johnson shot back instantly. "You're on my property. I want to see a warrant."

Johnson towered above the sheriff. He must have been six-five without the additional inch of heel under his lacer boots. Not just tall; the man was broad. His shoulders, thick with muscle, were as wide as an ax handle was long. He had a faded red beard shot through with grey. It dangled to his chest and was the most striking thing about the impressive man, until I got close enough to see his eyes. They were blue—the color of deep and ancient ice. Johnson looked like Odin stripped from the old, Norse stories. And he was an angry god.

"We don't need a warrant for this," the sheriff said. He was making an effort to sound reasonable. "It's a crime scene."

"Who says?"

"The body someone tried to burn on a brush pile," I said.

"It still don't give you the right—"

"It gives us every right, Mr. Johnson."

"Mr. Johnson?" he looked at Sheriff Benson with an incredulous expression. "Where the hell are you getting cops these days, Chuck?" To me he said, "Keep your dyke mouth closed a minute. I'm talking to the boss."

The sheriff got a look on his face that I always took as license. It wasn't exactly permission for the kind of anger that's defined my career in the department—so much as it was an acceptance of inevitability. He took a small step back—the kind that said whatever happened was not his responsibility. "Hurricane," he said, putting a little extra emphasis on the nickname. "This is Johnson Rath. All around pain in the ass."

"Chuck Benson, all around king of the great society," Johnson spit back.

"I'm a Republican, Johnson. You know that."

"You're a pissant." Johnson pointed a thick finger at the sheriff. "And a traitor." He jabbed the digit into the sheriff's chest. It was what I was waiting for. Any contact with a police officer in the performance of his duty can be construed as assault. The laws are pretty broad and always work in favor of the officer. Johnson's finger made contact just to the heart side of center. The force of it shoved the sheriff back on his heels.

I reached with both hands. With my right, I grabbed Johnson's finger and twisted. I opened my left hand and slapped it, palm up, into his elbow and pushed up.

He was surprised, but strong. His arm bent around, following the force of my hold. His head turned. His cold gaze set on my eyes. From there, it was like a terrible arm wrestling contest. Johnson didn't fight, he simply resisted. The more force I applied, the more he tensed against it. Other than that, he showed no sign that I was bothering him at all.

If I had grabbed his wrist rather than his finger, I'm not sure I could have held him. As it was, the finger was a perfect grip and gave me painful leverage.

Johnson spit without taking his gaze from my eyes. "You sure you want this, little girl?" he asked.

"Talk and insults the best you got?" I asked back. I wasn't feeling as sure as I had a moment before though.

"Think you can hold me? How long?"

"At least until your finger breaks, asshole."

He nodded over his shoulder, almost smiling.

In my hands, I felt him shift and tense. I applied more pressure.

His almost-smile broke into a knowing smirk.

The finger I was holding twisted against my efforts. To keep my hold I had to push harder and force the digit backwards.

Johnson's glacier-blue eyes were locked with mine when I felt the bone break. Nothing changed in his expression. I was startled that it had gone that far. The snap caused me to let go.

He took the opportunity to turn in and bring his other hand high and fisted at my face. I blocked with my upper arm and shoulder, still the knuckles slipped past and caught me above the ear. I went with it, lowering my head and bending at the waist. I came around pulling my telescoping baton. It was too late.

Johnson was already crumbling to his knees as a bright gouge of blood opened on his temple.

The sheriff held his revolver casually by his thigh. The barrel of the brushed nickel .357 was streaked with blood. "Subtlety is wasted on a man like Johnson." He showed me the gun and the blood on it. "Sometimes the old ways are the best." He turned to the deputies standing gape-mouthed. "Cuff him, Calvin. Take him in to cool off a bit."

When they were taking him to a car, the sheriff turned to me and said, "Your temper is going to get you into trouble one day."

"My temper? You're the one who pistol-whipped him."

"I couldn't let him land that haymaker."

"Well, thanks for that. Who is that guy?"

"I can tell you that," Riley Yates said. I hadn't seen him approach.

"Yeah," Sheriff Benson nodded. "Riley can tell you better than I can. And without calling the man a goddamned sack of shit."

The sheriff was a good man, but kind of rough with his language. I always took it as a compliment that he restrained himself for *ladies,* but he let it fly around me. Charles Benson had never made me believe that I was anything less than any other cop in his eyes. It was something I always appreciated.

"What's the story?" I asked Riley. I nodded at the sheriff's back as he went back to his car. He wiped his pistol on his pants leg before he holstered the weapon.

"I'm surprised you haven't heard that one," Riley said. He pointed to the burned circle behind the tape. "Quid pro quo?"

"You know I can't tell you anything more than the sheriff would."

"You owe me a little more."

I hit him with a look. No one likes to be pushed, especially by a friend. Besides, he was right. I owed him. Riley used information I gave him several months back to write a story exposing a group of CIA and private mercenaries who were trafficking arms and women to pay for nation-building by Kurdish separatists. His writing probably made it impossible for the government to retaliate.

"I know I do," I answered. "But. . ."

"Don't sweat it Hurricane. I don't expect anything that you can't share. Maybe you can share a little differently than your boss?"

"Fair enough," I said. "And don't call me Hurricane."

"I think you're way past fighting that."

"Sometimes I wonder if every woman named Katrina has to deal with that hurricane every day."

"It sticks to you because it fits so well."

"Yeah. Thanks." I needed a change of subject. "Tell me about this Johnson thing."

Riley nodded. It looked to be in part agreement, and in part a physical effort to shake loose the memories. "That was a long time ago. It was 1978 or '79."

"Sock hops and soda pop."

"Not *that* long ago. But we still played records with needles, and it was a big deal when gas soared over a buck a gallon."

"Quaint."

"The past always is if you didn't live through it. There was a lot going on. One of those things was the rise of the religious, end-of-the-world, white power, gun nuts, militia guys."

"Like Waco and Ruby Ridge?"

"Nothing like those. Both situations were tragedies that could have been handled with patience and communication. Just because you want to be left alone doesn't mean you're a danger to anyone else. These guys were different—are different."

"These guys?"

"The New American Covenant–The Word and the Sword. That entire mouthful was what they called themselves. They wanted a separate nation right in the middle of this one. One with their own rules, of course."

"Old Testament rules, I'm guessing."

"Old Testament—without the messy Jewish connection. All Aryan and racially pure. They had a big compound across the line in Arkansas. But they liked to come into Missouri to raise money. Robbery. Extortion. Drugs."

"And Johnson Rath was one of them?"

"Johnson was the biggest, baddest, and angriest of them all. He was a founding member of the Ozarks Nightriders. He's still connected to them but has a whole host of new friends. None of them very nice. "

"So what happened between him and the sheriff?"

"Chuck was a brand new sheriff. He'd barely won the election and he lost the next one. He probably wouldn't have even been there if he didn't feel he needed the exposure. It was over in Rockaway Beach. The town still had the resort thing going on, fishing lodges, go carts, arcades. It was Saturday night on a Memorial Day weekend. Hundreds of people filled the streets. Every dock had a band or a juke box going. Nights like that are gone now. Part of the reason was Johnson Rath."

Riley paused. I couldn't tell if he was remembering or wishing.

"Anyway, like I said, Chuck was working the sidewalk crowds, shaking hands, making sure everyone knew his name. Johnson Rath was in the middle of the street where things were thickest. Drinking—probably drunk. He was the kind of man who never had to look for trouble because he brought it with him wherever he went. A kid named Earl Turner walked right into that trouble."

"They had a history?"

Riley shook his head, a firm negative. The thought and memory came after. He looked around like the past would sneak up if he wasn't careful.

"It was a sad and shameful night."

"You were there?"

"It was a big deal. Summer was in the air. A decade was ending. Things seemed bright. It was a good time to celebrate. A lot of us who lived around here were there. A lot of names you would know. Your Uncle Orson was there for part of it. The end."

"What happened?"

"The streets were crowded. People had beer and hard liquor in plastic cups and no one cared. It was like Mardi Gras down in New Orleans— except for one thing. All the faces you saw were white. It was something you didn't think about until you had to."

"Earl Turner?"

Riley nodded, then let his gaze lock with mine. "The one black man in the crowd. He was walking with a white girl when they bumped into Johnson." Riley broke eye contact with me, then turned to stare at the sheriff standing over by his car. Sheriff Benson was cleaning his gun with a rag. He looked like he was whistling. "It was like something out of a movie. Like a silent bomb went off in the middle of the crowd. All at the same time, everyone knew to back away. Johnson stood alone with Turner."

"I imagine Earl had to know he was in trouble. Hate has a way of burning its cues into your head."

"They fought?"

"No. Turner was a skinny, twenty-year-old kid. Johnson was a man with the muscles of a bull. It was ugly and brutal. It wasn't a fight. It was a massacre. There was no stopping Johnson. Not that anyone tried. I saw it from a balcony. I even took a picture that was never put into any paper."

"The sheriff?"

"Sheriff Chuck Benson pushed his way through the bodies. I'm sure he thought that he was coming to break up a drunken fight. What he found was Johnson standing over Turner. The kid was trying to scream. All the wind and pain were locked in his lungs. He was on the asphalt with Johnson's foot on his ribs. His arm was in Johnson's hands. Johnson was twisting it—not like you did with his finger.

"Johnson had the arm twisted out of the shoulder socket. No joint should bend like that. His muscles and tendons had to be stretched past breaking. If Johnson had put any more pressure on the arm, skin would have ripped. That arm was about to come off when Chuck ran in.

"It changed everything for him."

"How?" I looked over at the sheriff. His weapon was clean and put away. He looked to be doing a crossword puzzle.

"Until that moment, Johnson and Chuck were friends."

Chapter 2

"I don't believe it," I blurted. "Sheriff Benson is one of the kindest, most just men I've ever met. How could he be friends with a man like Johnson Rath?"

"Katrina," Riley said kindly, "you, more than anyone, should know—we're not born the people we are. We become them through experience—good, bad, and terrible."

He had me there. It was a lesson I learned every day in therapy, in AA meetings, and just in living. "Hang on a second."

Dealing with the coroner's assistant was a good excuse for stepping away. I needed space and breath. It wasn't that I couldn't imagine the sheriff as different. I simply didn't want to. He, and the example he set, were too important to my daily choices.

I sent the coroner's assistant and two deputies over to recover the body. I reinforced the need to be careful, disturb as little as possible, and to report anything they found. When I headed back to Riley, I noticed that the sheriff was talking on his phone. He didn't look like a happy man.

"What kind of man was the sheriff before he walked into that circle?" I asked Riley as soon as I got close enough. "And what kind was he when it was over?"

"You wouldn't have recognized him. Chuck, like all of us I guess, was a product of his time and place. By that I mean he was a white man who had grown up in a world of prejudice, insulated by the absence of any contradictions."

"He was a racist?"

"Nothing that easy."

"I don't get it. You said they were friends—"

"Friends. Sure. But very different people. Johnson is a man of hate. He wants total agreement out of the world, and he wants it all on his terms. Chuck is a man of tolerance."

"They sound completely different."

"Tolerance doesn't mean much when it's never tested. It's like standing in the middle of the road when there're no cars coming. They could be friends because a homogenous world makes none of those choices. Johnson could prattle on about race and purity. He could rail against blacks and the struggle of the whites. And Chuck could listen without a problem because it didn't matter."

"Until he had to make a choice," I said.

"There was no choice. Chuck was—is—a believer in the law he represents. I doubt he thought about race or friendships when he came on Johnson killing a kid in the street. Chuck waded through the stunned crowd and hit Johnson like the Holy Spirit coming on a Pentecostal preacher."

"Johnson's a monster. How did the sheriff take him?"

"Remember what he said to you a few minutes ago about the old ways being best?"

I nodded, then looked again at Sheriff Benson by the tape perimeter. I didn't see a different man, but maybe a slightly deeper one.

"That was probably as much a dig for Johnson's sake as an explanation. Like I said, things were different back then. A law officer, a county sheriff like Chuck, had a lot more latitude."

"Latitude?"

"Brass latitude."

"He carried brass knuckles on duty?" I sounded incredulous even to myself.

Riley made an exaggerated shrug. "On duty. Off. It didn't matter."

"What happened?"

"Why do you think Johnson wears that big beard? No one's seen the lower part of his face since Chuck took it apart."

"Good for him."

"No—what was good for him was what happened after. He had to take a good hard look at what his friend had done—and what he himself believed in. When the test came, he passed. He wasn't nearly so tolerant after that. At least not to hateful peckerwoods. But he went even further. Chuck got to know Earl Turner as he recovered. Johnson called him a race traitor."

"You said Uncle Orson was there. I'm surprised I've never heard this story."

"It was Orson who showed up and pulled the two apart. He was the one who started first aid and even gave mouth-to-mouth to Earl. I don't think it's a story he would tell about himself."

"How long was Johnson put away for?"

"Six months."

"What?"

"Pled out to simple assault. It set a thorn in Chuck's boot, that's for sure. Johnson shows up and the pair of them go at it every few years."

"Now Johnson owns this land," I said—as much for myself as for Riley.

"Not directly, I'm betting."

"Then how?"

"Through a group. The kind with a message. I doubt that Johnson has changed his feathers."

I stared over at the activity inside the tape perimeter. The body was up on a gurney and the CA was gingerly covering and securing it. The sheriff broke the connection on his phone and immediately dialed another number. He was angry or worried or both.

"I need to get back to the work of investigation," I told Riley. "I'm sorry I don't really have anything to give you."

"No worries," he answered. "I have some new ideas and some research to do. We'll talk again soon."

Riley returned to his car where he leaned over the hood and jotted things into a notebook.

I had more of my own notes and sketches to make. And there was that conversation I wanted to have with Cherry Dando. After what happened with Johnson, that was bumped up on my list. They clearly knew each other.

I decided to return to the burn circle to draw out the scene with the body removed, but first, I wanted to have a talk with the sheriff.

Sheriff Benson was still on the phone, or on the phone again, when I approached. He moved away, not inviting company. I took the hint and went on to my crime scene.

Under the body were more bones. These were grouped—a few ribs, a few vertebrae, longer bones—in clusters. It made me doubly sure that the other bones had been spread out intentionally. The only reason I could imagine was to hide what they were. As I sketched out the locations and shapes, I kept casting my eyes up to where the firemen milled around their truck.

It looked to me like the body or bodies that were rendered to bone were covered over with wood. They were definitely under the unconsumed body. It had either been placed on top of the pile or covered only slightly with brush.

Once things were sketched out, I looked around the unburned part of the clearing. It was obvious where brush had been cut. There were stumps, mostly of red cedar, cropped close to the ground. That's not unusual for the area. Red cedar is actually a kind of juniper. It grows like a weed on any bare ground in Missouri. Whenever you leave a field fallow for any length of time, these trees are what you have to contend with. From the size of the stumps and the standing trees, this ground had been left alone for a few years. Someone was changing that.

In this drought, red cedar cut and piled would take no time to dry into a fire waiting to happen. The bits of evergreen branches that had been dropped and not added to the pile were like dead brown feathers on the ground. I pushed some around with the toe of my boot.

A look at the cut stumps told me something more. The larger ones were smooth topped. They were cut with a chainsaw. Smaller ones had been axed or snipped with loping shears. That made me think there was more than one person working to clear the land. One man with a chainsaw would probably use it on everything he could. The way the work was divided, large and small, suggested something else. It could have been an adult and a younger helper—or an adult and a smaller adult.

I put out my foot to kick aside a small branch. The motion was stopped by something solid. I had hit a rock. In Ozarks fields, rocks grow like a regular crop. Through freeze and frost cycles, bits of an ancient seabed were constantly raised to the light. When my foot passed over the top, I stumbled slightly and came down with my sole flat on the stone.

Flat was the perfect description. The surface under my foot was unnaturally level.

Using my toe, I cleared the tinder-like weeds and grass. What was revealed looked like no stone I had ever encountered in the Ozarks. It was grey and flat without being precisely smooth. It had a texture to it like a statue left in the weather for ages. The stone was split by three big cracks and shot through with streaks of black and white. The whole thing was peppered by green spots of lichen.

I tried to pull it up but failed. The stone was either too heavy or too well stuck. I needed a tool.

The rake I had borrowed from Dando worked perfectly.

The stone wasn't as thick as I imagined. It had simply been imbedded so long it may as well have been part of the ground. When I turned over the first piece, I knew instantly what it was. It wasn't until I had all three pieces that I could read the name: *Freeman Patee*. It was a headstone.

The name was the only information on the incomplete stone. I dug in with the rake, looking for more pieces of granite that might be in the ground. A few minutes later, I hit another stone. This time it wasn't face down, but it was pressed into the ground. Pulling the weeds revealed a cement square about eight inches across. Formed in the surface was the word, *Unknown.*

"Sheriff," I called but didn't shout.

He looked.

"Sheriff," I raised my voice and added urgency.

He waved me off, then pointed to the phone at his ear.

"Sheriff." I shouted. "I need you now."

He hung up as he walked to me.

I didn't say anything as he approached. Kneeling, I held the grass to the side—keeping the stone on display.

He stopped about ten feet away, staring. When he raised his gaze to mine he asked, "Are there more?"

"You know what it is?"

"I know full well. Have you found any more?"

I pointed to the first stone I found. It was pointed skyward now. The mud filling the carved letters of Freeman Patee's name had already begun to dry out.

Sheriff Benson went to it. He watched it for a few moments like it would walk away if he wasn't looking. "Get everyone over here—all the deputies—the firemen too. Send Riley. He'll want to be part of this."

"Part of what?"

"There's going to be more. We need to find them. Tell Riley to bring his camera." He raised his phone again.

"Wait," I said before he could get drawn into another conversation.

The Sheriff didn't say anything, but his look was impatient. I gave him a quick outline of my suspicions and observations about Cherry Dando.

"Then get him out here," the sheriff said. "I'll keep an eye on him. Don't let the CA van go until you have everything you need. I want you to follow it to autopsy."

"Follow it? Why?"

"Because I want to do everything about this righter than right."

"What's that mean? What do you know?"

He didn't answer. When I tried to hold his gaze and keep my questions alive, the sheriff turned away. He punched the phone and talked to Darlene, our daytime dispatcher, with his back to me.

As I went, I heard him tell her to send out everyone not assigned and to call in everyone off-duty. More than that, he told her to ask for volunteers.

I pulled out my own phone and called Billy. He answered on the first ring. "What time did you get called out?" he asked. "I was dead to the world. But in a good way." The flirt in his voice was a nice thing to hear.

Before he could get any deeper into it, I gave him the short version.

"I'm on my way," he said before I'd even finished. "I'll call your uncle. And Clare Bolin too."

That was a good idea. Except for tours in Vietnam, Uncle Orson had lived all of his life in Taney County. Clare Bolin was an old moonshiner and friend of both my uncle and the sheriff. He was also a master distiller and bartender at Moonshines. That made him, technically, my employee. The bar is one of the many assets, or rather complications, my husband left me when he passed away. There was a lot of Ozarks history between those two men, not to mention a general willingness to dig in when asked.

When I got off the phone, Cherry Dando was no longer with the group of firemen. He was standing by Johnson's tall truck with his body half in the driver's side door.

Boredom dropped off the firemen's faces when I told them the sheriff needed them to grab tools and help him search the field. One of them asked where Dando was. He would have called out to him if I hadn't held up my hand. I wanted to see what was going on at Johnson's truck without giving Dando time to think.

First, I caught the coroner's assistant and told him to wait for me. Then, I went back to talk with Dando. He never looked up as I approached. I doubt he could have heard me over the sound of wadding paper and his own cursing.

"What's going on?" I asked.

Dando froze. If it was possible to actually hear a man think I would have heard rusty gears turning and trying to sync up with an excuse.

"Nothing," was the gem he came up with. He followed up with, "What's it to you?" The surly sound was an added bonus.

"Come on out of there," I told him, making sure to sound a little bothered myself.

His arm moved and I heard paper tearing and crumpling.

"Leave things where they are, Mr. Dando."

"Why?" he asked, finally backing out of the truck and looking at me. "You ain't got no right—"

"Sure seems to be a lot of talk of rights here today. All of it wrong."

"What are you talkin' about? I was just going to take Johnson's truck home for him."

"What's with all the paper shuffling?"

"Thing's a mess." He pointed into the cab like he had nothing to hide. "Ol' Johnson isn't much of a housekeeper."

"I bet. You weren't trying to hide anything were you?"

"Just gettin' the burger bags off the seat so I could drive it."

I nodded like I understood, but kept my face immobile. He would know I didn't believe him. I hoped he would feel the need to explain things further.

He didn't. Dando turned his head and spit into the weeds then said, "Well go ahead and look for yourself. I can't stop you."

"How do you know Mr. Rath?"

"What? Johnson?"

"Yes," I agreed. "How do you know Johnson?"

"You ain't asked how I know you," Dando fished.

"I don't care. I want to know how you know Johnson."

"We got chummy in the brig. Subic Bay."

"You're not from around here."

"Naw. I'm a Texarkana boy."

"Which side?"

"Shoot. You gotta ask? I'm a Razorback, born and bred. But I'm still the wildest and lovinest hunk 'a manhood in either state." He grinned like he was posing for his close-up.

"That work with the ladies where you come from?"

"Oh, now honey—you would be surprised the ladies it works with right around here."

"That's a lot more of what I don't care about. How'd you end up here?"

He rubbed his jaw then spit again. It seemed to be a kind of a habit with him. His eyes, were a flattish brown. Like a bad hair dye job—they were all one color. Even without contrasts, they were bright and focused. "I came up here 'cause Johnson invited me. I get around some though—goin' here and there the way a free man will. I come back though, cause of one of them ladies."

"Tell me about the bones."

He was surprised about the change in direction. "Bones?"

"Over there," I looked over at the burn circle in the taped perimeter.

"What about them?" His eyes narrowed and his voice sounded cagey.

I got the impression that Cherry Dando was no stranger to police interrogation. That didn't mean he had any mastery of the process. "You moved them."

He spit again. "It was a fire. How was I supposed to know what was what?"

"You tell me."

"I ain't telling you anything. I know my rights."

"How is it that you guys all know your rights, but you all spend so much time in jail?"

"I'm not talking."

"No problem," I said waving him away from the door. "I'll pull your sheet. I'm betting you left a trail all the way back to Texarkana."

"They said you was a hard-ass bitch."

"People say a lot of things."

"Maybe so. But I'm thinkin' they were right."

"Maybe so," I echoed. "But I'm thinking you're neck-deep in something you're going to want out of soon."

"What are you talking about?"

"You've already been caught tampering with a crime scene. What say we add interfering with an investigation to that?"

"You can't."

"Oh I can, Mr. Dando. And when I reach under the seats of this truck, maybe run my fingers between the seats and back. . . Think I'll find a little more to talk with you about?"

"Whatever you find has nothing to do with me."

"Then why were you trying to hide things?"

"As far as I know, there's nothing to hide." Dando sounded smug.

"How long till all these nothings lead back to that body?"

"What?" He was startled by the thought. "You can't."

"Can't what?"

"I was on duty last night. Ask anyone. I was at the stationhouse when this call came in."

"You don't have to be here to be a part of things. A worldly man like you knows that, don't you, Mr. Dando?"

"I'll tell you what I know." Cherry spit again. That time he didn't turn his head far enough or put enough force behind it. The weak drizzle fell on his boot. He didn't pay it any attention. "I know you're picking on me because you don't know anything. I didn't have anything to do with killin' that *boy* and you can't show I did."

Two things caught me by the ear. Dando said "boy." And he said it in a way that raised my red hair up like an angry radar.

"Boy?" I asked.

Dando looked at me but didn't answer.

"Why'd you say *boy*?"

He shrugged and turned his head to spit again.

"Stop it," I ordered. "Keep your nasty habit to yourself and answer the question."

"I don't have to answer anything."

"Those nothings keep turning around to point at you, Cherry."

"It looks like a boy," he said petulantly. "All right?"

"He."

"What?"

"You're talking about a human being. Say—he."

Dando spit again. That time he didn't bother to turn his head.

To keep from getting his drippings on my boot, I lifted my foot. I resisted the urge to whip it into his kneecap. Instead, I grabbed him by the shoulder and flung him around to press up against the truck cab.

"Hey, you can't—"

"Are you sure?" I asked him. "Because I seem to be doing it." I pulled out my cuffs.

"You got no cause."

"Questioning," I said bluntly. "You're lucky I can't arrest someone simply for being an asshole. You would never get out of jail." I turned him back around with his hands secured behind his back.

"You got some hard lessons to learn, little miss—"

He couldn't finish his sentence after I hit him in the solar plexus. It's hard to talk without air. I led him gasping back to where the cruisers were parked and left him in the back of one.

Under and between the seats of Johnson's truck were stacks of paper. Most were photocopied racist posters. They looked like Hitler Youth kindergarten art projects. Some of the papers—the ones wadded and shoved into the deepest corners of the upholstery—were recruiting flyers for the W&S. I puzzled that out to be short for Word and Sword. The combination of so many American flags and the phrase "White Power" left me feeling both charged and sick.

I read every word then flipped it front to back looking for an address. Nothing. Meetings must be word of mouth only. No surprise there.

A set of keys dangled from the truck ignition, along with a metal coin that had lightning bolt SS markings—rather than stars—in the blue field of an American flag. The flip side bore inscriptions in German surrounding the words *Race Patriot*.

I took the keys and locked the truck—taking a couple of the flyers with me. As I walked across the cleared field back to the sheriff, I kept my eyes down looking for other grave markers. I also made a quick call to get Johnson Rath's truck towed to our impound lot.

Firemen and deputies had uncovered five more markers in the cleared part of the field. Four of those were concrete squares imprinted, UNKNOWN.

The last was concrete as well. It was a homemade circle—decorated with imbedded marbles and toy soldiers. The scrawled inscription said, *Baby Boy Roger.*

The sheriff was several yards beyond these discoveries, kicking through the grass and working his phone. For the first time, I took a good look around at the cleared area. It wasn't a circle. It meandered out from the wide center, claiming ragged parts of the overgrowth. Beyond the edges, it crooked and twisted like a drunkard's walk home. The cuts made secret rooms in the foliage in which were hidden more piles of brush.

I followed Sheriff Benson clutching the flyers in my hand, little flags of color that he ignored. He killed the connection on his phone just as I reached him. It wasn't done on my behalf. Even though I called his name he didn't turn. His gaze was fixed ahead.

I put a hand on his shoulder. It slumped under the touch as though conquered. I followed his gaze and saw three open graves.

Chapter 3

The graves were not in a neat line like you expect to find. They were all roughly facing east—but spread at random levels like crooked teeth.

"You know what's going on here?" I asked the sheriff.

"I have ideas," he answered. His voice was as wasted as his posture. "None of them good."

"I found these." I held out the flyers.

"Johnson?"

"In his truck."

"You searched his truck?"

"Yes. I—"

"Hang on." Sheriff Benson squared his shoulders and took a hard breath before he looked me in the eyes. His expression told me this was one of his *Come to Jesus* moments. "Under what circumstances did you search the truck of Johnson Rath?"

I understood without asking. He was making everything that happened today official, and careful.

"In the course of investigating, I went to question Cherry Dando as a person of interest, believing he had information about or personal knowledge of the current crime scene. Mr. Dando was found attempting to hide or destroy materials in the vehicle driven by Johnson Rath. Mr. Johnson, already in custody for interfering and assault on an officer was already a subject of investigation. The vehicle was opened by Mr. Dando. His activity and Mr. Rath's gave probable cause to search the vehicle without a warrant."

"Think you can unspool that again?" he asked me. "In your report. Logged today."

"I can. I'll take care of it as soon as I get back from escorting the body for autopsy."

"Good. I want to be careful about *all* of this."

"Do you want to tell me what's going on?"

He shook his head then took off his summer straw hat to wipe his sweating brow with the bandana pulled from his pocket. "We'll have a long talk about it soon. Right now, you work without my. . ." The sheriff thought about the word he needed. He put the hat back on and seemed to settle. "Prejudices," he finally said.

"You mean these guys?" I held up a flyer.

"Just follow the evidence. See if we end up in the same place."

After that we talked a little more. Neither of us had gone any closer to the gaping graves. I told him about my discussion with Cherry and the word, *Boy*, that he had worked over so hard. I also informed him about having called Billy and his idea to call in my uncle and Clarence Bolin as volunteers.

"Billy's a good man," the sheriff said.

"So you you're always telling me."

Several months ago, Sheriff Benson had been ready to retire. He told me in no uncertain terms that I would not make a good sheriff, but Billy Blevins would. That was about the time the mercenaries and government agencies were working the smuggling operation with the Kurds. Billy had gotten a pretty severe beating. He was still on light duty. It wasn't a good time for the sheriff to retire. It wasn't a good time in general.

"You should marry that boy."

All the men of a certain vintage in my life want me married, but this suggestion seemed to come out of nowhere. "Why are you saying that now?" I asked. I added, "And he's not a boy."

He resettled the hat on his head. "Billy is the kind of man people will think of as a boy when he's my age. Everyone likes him. They trust him."

"And they call him Billy."

"Yep. They always will."

"Why bring it up now?"

"Look at that." He pointed to the graves. "People were buried here and forgotten. Then someone came and did this shit. If a person disrespects death, they don't respect life. I'll be gone one day, sooner than later."

"Sheriff—"

He put up a hand to stop me. "It's not sadness or being morose that makes me say it. It's time. And my hope for the people in my life is that they go on. Secure and happy."

"It's a nice thought."

"Maybe. But nice thoughts don't make the world better. Hard action does. That's what we're going to do here."

"I understand."

"Let's get back." Sheriff Benson turned and walked back toward the burn circle. "You need to get that body to autopsy and I need to make a lot more calls."

When we came around the cut into the larger clearing, I was struck by how large the area was. If the whole thing was a graveyard, we could be talking about hundreds of plots. I was about to ask Sheriff Benson what his thoughts were, when a shout took my attention.

My Uncle Orson stood at the open back door of the cruiser I had left Cherry Dando in. Orson was yelling and reaching into the car, while Clare Bolin worked to hold him back.

I started running across the rugged field. There was no point in calling out. It wouldn't do any good, I knew, and I needed my breath and concentration to navigate the holes and stumps.

Orson pulled Dando from the car and threw him to the ground. Clare imposed himself between them—giving Dando the second he needed to roll, then wiggle—still cuffed—under the car. My uncle kicked a foot out and hit the sheet metal. From the sound of it, Dando was lucky it didn't connect with him.

As I got closer I could hear Dando laughing. It was a taunting hoot that didn't sound at all afraid.

I heard Orson too, but I didn't understand the words. His shouting had escalated almost to the point of screaming rage. I made eye contact with Clare, and he looked glad to see me coming.

I put up both hands as I reached him, pushing into Uncle Orson. "Stop it," I shouted and shoved.

"Stay away," he screamed, but not at me. He reached over my shoulder to shake a fist at Dando still hiding and laughing. "Stay the hell away or I'll gut you—"

I slapped a hand over Orson's mouth. "Stop it," I said again. "Stop. Calm down and tell me what's going on."

Dando laughed harder, "Hell yeah. Tell the princess what's going on." He seemed to think that was even funnier than my uncle's rage.

"Shut up," I ordered without looking at him. To reinforce the point, I kicked back with the heel of my boot against the car. To Orson I said, "You can't do this."

"You have no idea what I'm ready to do to this son-of-a-bitch."

"And I don't care. I don't want the story. I don't need to know why. Not yet. But I can't have you hurting my prisoner."

"Then I'll make it quick and painless."

Clare, who had been pulling my uncle as I pushed, let him go and walked away.

"Where are you going?" I called.

"To call on a higher authority," he answered and disappeared.

In addition to being a moonshiner, a former teacher, and a closet Democrat, Clarence Bolin was an ordained Assemblies of God minister. Honestly I didn't think that was the kind of help we needed at that moment.

Uncle Orson sidled around me and pointed his finger like a bayonet at Dando. "You should have stayed away. Next time you disappear you won't come back."

"Knock it off, Orson." Sheriff Benson commanded. His voice wasn't raised, but it wasn't something to be ignored either. He was the higher power to which Clare had referred.

Orson stopped to look at the sheriff. It was only a pause. I felt the tension of his muscles still under my hands.

"I've got this," I told the sheriff. I didn't want this to get any worse than it already was.

"Are you going to cuff your own uncle?" he asked. "You going to arrest family?"

I took my hands away and set my gaze right into Uncle Orson's scowling face. "If I have to."

The anger drained and Orson said, "Yeah. She would."

"Maybe so," Sheriff Benson said. "But she won't slap the sense into you that I'm ready to. Clare told me the situation."

"Anybody mind telling me?" I asked.

"Oh, hell yeah. Let's all share old home stories." Dando chimed in.

The sheriff crouched down and looked at the skinny man hiding under the car. "You come on out of there and keep your ugly mouth shut. One word—only one word that pisses me off—and I'll hand you over to Orson and walk away. I'll let you know right now, you're dancin' on my last nerve."

Cherry Dando squirmed out from under the car without a sound.

Sheriff Benson stood and looked at me. "You need to get that body to autopsy."

"But—"

"I'll handle this."

Dando was grinning at me with secret joy. The sheriff was looking with expectation. Clare and my uncle were looking off into the distance with pointed avoidance. I went.

As I followed the coroner's van along the rutted trail I pulled alongside Billy's car. He had steered into the weeds to give us room to pass.

"Where are you going?" he asked through his open window. He smiled in the kind of way a woman wants a man to smile after they spent the night together. It was a nice moment—that ended when he raised a straw to his lips. Billy Blevins had a soda problem. The problem being, he was always drinking soda from one of those giant, convenience store, refill cups.

"You need to knock that off," I said. "You're going to get fat."

He raised the insulated container. "I switched to diet."

"Yeah, chemicals. Much better."

"A man's got to have a vice."

"I didn't know that was a rule."

"Guy code. What's going on?"

I pointed over at the coroner's van as it pulled carefully onto the rutted path. "I'm following the CA to drop the body off for autopsy." I watched the vehicle's slow progress on the dirt track. There was no chance of losing it anytime soon.

"Why?"

"Honestly, I don't know. The sheriff is being weird and cagy about this one."

"I think I know part of the reason. Your uncle and Clare mentioned something."

"What?"

"Missouri was a slave state. And after that it wasn't much better for free blacks."

"They said this is a black cemetery?"

"From what they said, cemetery might be putting it kindly. Part cemetery and part dumping ground."

"That fits," I said, thinking of the UNKNOWN markers and the haphazard layout. It made me wonder how many graves were there with no marking at all. "I have to go."

"Will I see you tonight?"

"I'm thinking we'll both be working tonight until too late for what you have in mind."

He smiled with the straw in his mouth. The expression had just the right combination of lust and humor. "It's never too late."

"Keep telling yourself that, Romeo." I pressed the gas and caught up with the van.

We're a big county with lots of rural space and giant tracts of National Forest lands. The county is served by an elected coroner who is really a bureaucrat. We send autopsies out of county to a private contractor. From where we started, it was shy of thirty miles, but the drive would take closer to an hour. County blacktop laid over the twists and turns of old game trails gave me time to think.

Morning had burned away. Summer was dying a brown death without giving up the grudge it seemed to have against the Ozarks. It would have been a good time to roll the windows and let the A/C cool me down. It was an even better time to keep the glass down and let the wind have its way with my skin.

I thought better in the freedom of roads and open windows. There was a lot to think about. As much as I wanted to bask in thoughts of the night spent with Billy, my mind kept pulling to other concerns. Racists. Grave robbing. Possibly murder. Those were all mismatched pieces of a puzzle. The biggest problem with that was my ignorance of the picture I was trying to put together. That didn't bother me half as much as knowing that the people I needed seemed to be keeping the big picture from me on purpose.

After a few winding miles, I put all of that aside to think about one question that I couldn't get out of my mind. Why would avowed racists own a piece of land that held a black cemetery?

I pulled my phone and called the County Recorder's office.

"Are you asking about the same plot of land the sheriff called about?" the secretary asked in response to my question about the cleared land.

"Yes." I was relieved. I didn't have a plat map or the legal description of the land. I thought we would go through a lot of back and forth only for her to tell me the parcel could not be found over the phone.

"The sale was closed a month ago," she told me. "The buyer was the W&S Foundation."

Surprising—but not a surprise. It was exactly what I expected, and—I imagine—what the sheriff expected when he made his call.

After that, I kept working the phone. A lot of investigation is routine. It's information gathering. I gave one of the station deputies a list of people to pull CDR's on. Call detail records, or local usage data, are the records of local traffic on a specific phone number. They provide phone numbers connected, who initiated, and call durations. Since there is no information about the content of the call, there is no requirement for a court order. Another part of the routine was pulling the jackets on Johnson Rath and

Cherry Dando. I also asked for any available information on The New American Covenant–The Word and The Sword. I suspected that there would be federal, as well as state and local, files on them.

At the intersection of highways 65 and 160, we had a choice. Both would take us to the same place, but 65 was four lanes and straight. 160 was slower going, but more fun to drive. The CA made the reasonable choice and turned right onto 65. I hated him for it. There is something about back roads to me. Travel should be active. The wide, gentle ribbons of concrete get you there quicker—but there is no joy in the trip.

There is something to be said about boredom as well, I guess. We glided down to the Bear Creek overpass and I noticed a truck. It was stopped and waiting at an intersection well ahead of us. On the twists of the other highway, I doubt I would have paid any attention to it. On 160, it was impossible to miss. The truck was an old Chevy. Some kind of 1950's custom pickup with shining black paint and deep tinted windows. In this part of the country, it wasn't unusual. The fact that it was sitting there—seemingly waiting for nonexistent traffic—was.

As we passed the truck, I shifted my gaze to the rearview mirror. The black truck pulled out behind us.

We were keeping a steady sixty-five miles-per-hour pace. The old truck must have hit the gas pretty hard. It caught up to me in no time and drafted my rear end too close.

I lifted my foot off the big GMC's pedal and coasted. It put more distance between me and the van and forced the Chevy back. In the mirror, I could see the driver was a woman—but no details. For a couple of miles she seemed content to follow. That changed with a sudden, swerving lane change. At the same time, she accelerated up to where the bumper of her truck was riding just back of my cab. She held there, keeping pace, as I sped up and slowed down.

I was about to get a little reckless, and enjoying the thought, when I saw three big motorcycles ahead of the van. From where I was I couldn't read the bikers' colors or rocker patches. I didn't need to. I'd run up against the Ozark Nightriders before. They were a local club that messed around in meth and pills. A couple of years back, I had put some of them away and hurt a few pretty bad.

The question was, were the Nightriders there for me or the van?

The question was answered pretty quickly—when one of the bikers peeled off and dropped alongside the CA's van. At the same time, the Chevy gunned it and tried to cut me off. The woman driving was timid and not up to the task. She got ahead of me. When she cut in though, she pulled back at the last instant—fearful of making contact. For my part, I didn't waiver. My truck was a GMC 2500HD. It had the edge in power, weight, and handling. I had the edge in experience and willingness.

After she pulled out of the cut off, the woman sped up and tried to get in front to block me. I didn't let her. I stomped the gas and raced right up to the bumper of the van. We drove like that for a bit, with the Chevy edging over every so often to try to shake me loose. Each time she got close I held my ground and she pulled back.

There was no telling if she got tired of the impasse or the Nightriders did. It didn't matter. The woman dropped back. The biker riding at the van's window slowed, falling back into her position. When he was at my bumper, he released his throttle and pulled a pistol from inside his jacket.

Before he could get a bead on me, I slammed my brakes. The bikes, van, and black truck rocketed forward as my speed was given away. When I opened up enough space, the Chevy took to the center line and let herself fall back from the convoy.

She had a lot more confidence in front of me. When I caught up, she kept me from passing by blocking each time I went for a side. The more time I took trying to pass, the more distance the bikers and the van were getting ahead. I had no idea what they planned on doing when I was out of the way, but I wasn't going to let it happen.

Again I hit my brakes and fell back. Just as quickly, I slammed the gas pedal to the floor.

The GMC must have looked huge and angry to the woman in the Chevy as it ran up on her. She accelerated. The old truck had a modern, custom engine. It was able to stay ahead of me, but only barely. It didn't matter. Her job was to cut me out of the convoy and we were coming up quick. She took the desperate route and stood on her brakes.

The skid turned the Chevy sideways in the double lanes and I had nowhere to go. I could either stop—or T-bone the hot rod. I stopped in a tire-smoking skid.

Even before my truck was completely stilled, the Chevy was peeling out and running again. I did the same. In a few seconds, I was back on her ass and she was weaving to keep me from passing. She didn't understand I was finished playing. For a few moments, I held my speed and path without trying to get by. She got tired of the side to side pattern and settled down right in front of me. Just where I wanted her.

The van and bikers were probably a mile ahead of us by then. I saw them climbing the top of the next hill as we were diving into the valley. Our speed was about sixty when I surged. She saw me coming and went

into overdrive as well. I'm sure she was waiting for me to go right or left
and ready to react in either direction. I'm just as sure that she wasn't ready
for me coming straight on again. I didn't barrel up on the Chevy. I caught
up and eased in. When there were only a few feet between us, I pushed
right and gave the GMC more speed. It's called a *PIT Maneuver*: precision
immobilization technique. By ramming her bumper in the right, it pushed
her front to the left. She corrected by jerking the wheel to the right and
losing control. I fell back as she fishtailed and spun out. We were both lucky
she didn't hit a rail or roll the truck. The bump and go thing works better
at city speeds. On the highway, it's pretty dicey and definitely dangerous.
I wasn't worried about her safety at that point, but if she cracked up hard
I would have been obligated to stop.

As it was, I waited for her to settle—facing the wrong way in the
middle of the road—then I raced ahead. The van was out of sight, and I
didn't want to give them any time to take a turn that I couldn't see. The
GMC powered forward—eating road with hard rubber teeth. The roar of
the tires and the engine worked in my mind and, for a moment, I was in
the back of a racing Humvee on a broken Iraqi road.

People like me, survivors of trauma, have triggers. Sounds, tastes, smells,
words—anything can make a connection in our brains to the moments
we most want to avoid. As recently as the beginning of the summer, the
memory induced by the low hum of tires on asphalt would have shut me
down. That was before I stopped fighting therapy. That was before I stopped
feeling guilty and fighting the feelings I had for Billy.

Absently, I reached and touched the scar around my eye. It was a habit,
self-soothing and not nearly as important as it had been for a long time.
The touch let me relax and think through the feeling. I realized I had let up
off the gas. With new resolve, I pressed it to the floor again. At the same
time, I picked up the radio and called in for any Highway Patrol assistance.

No one was close. They would have had to be right behind me to do
any good. When I came over the next hill, the van was in sight and going
slow. The bikers were forcing it toward an unmarked dirt cut off.

That was when I lit up the emergency lights behind the grill and hit the
siren. Coming off the hill I was going about eighty-five and accelerated
going down. I gave a warning because I didn't plan on stopping.

The Nightriders must have seen me coming and got the message. Before
they could make their turn, the three of them swung back onto the highway
and twisted everything they could out of their throttles.

They had a long head start and the big V-twin bikes were fast. So was I. By the time my truck screamed past the coroner's van I was going over a hundred.

At that speed, traffic—which had been light headed north—got dense. I caught the bikes but couldn't really do anything other than scare them a little. So I scared them a lot by pulling up close behind their exposed tires. When cars came up in our path, the bikers were able to weave in and out. I had to let the sirens clear my path.

I called in a BOLO, a be-on-the-look-out, for the bikes and the custom Chevy, then pulled aside to let the van catch up.

We spent a few minutes on the shoulder. The CA was rattled so we talked and let the adrenaline drain. He seemed to be a good kid—and gun-waving bikers were not a usual part of his job. A highway patrol cruiser pulled up behind the van. I recognized the officer and we spent a little more time briefing each other.

The custom Chevy was gone. So were the bikers. It was no great surprise. There were any number of unmarked drives and trails that intersected the highway. They could have gone into any of them. To be cautious, I asked the patrolman to provide additional escort as we continued on to the pathologist. He called it in and we got on our way.

The rest of the trip was uneventful. The body was taken into the facility. When the CA and the patrolman had gone, I idled the GMC and called the sheriff. After I gave him a short synopsis of the trip, I asked how he knew something would happen.

"I didn't know," he said. "But Johnson Rath and his militia buddies have a history of using intimidation and tampering to cover their tracks. Most of them have military backgrounds too."

"If you don't need me there, I think I'd like to stick around up here." I told him. "At least for the night. I have my appointment in the morning anyway."

"I'm glad to hear you're not fighting the bit on that so much these days."

"You're the sheriff. If you say I have to go to therapy to keep my job, I go to therapy."

"There's showing up, and there is learning from the process." He waited but I didn't say anything. "I can see the difference in you lately."

"Thanks." It was hard to say, but I meant it.

"Be careful."

Despite their brazen action on the highway, I thought there was little chance that the bikers would try anything at the pathology facility in the bright light of day. I left the parking lot and made a stop at the police station. They needed to know what had happened. I asked that they keep an eye on the pathologist's building. After that, I made a circle of town. Nixa, Missouri was my hometown. Every time I visited, it seemed to have drifted further from me and grown a little more.

After a quick circuit, I went to my father's empty house. His funeral had been early this past spring. Like Billy, he was caught up in the government's conspiracy to break its own laws. My father, a US Army veteran, was killed in the turmoil. If anyone asks, I say I'm not bitter. That's part of what therapy is for.

At the house, I parked and sat for a long time—putting off the moment I walked through the door. It wasn't the first time I had been back, but returning no longer felt like a homecoming. It was more like a visit to a cemetery. Home had become a place for talking to ghosts. The house itself was a headstone inscribed with memories and memorials. It struck me that, as bad as I was feeling about it, I was lucky to have the house and my father's genuine grave to visit. The people who were buried in the field we found that morning were cut off from memory and mourning. UNKNOWN seems like a curse of loss, rather than any kind of remembrance.

Even with the windows down, the truck was hotter than a sane woman would put up with. I got out and stretched under the shade of a maple. There was no breeze to be had. I climbed the porch steps and waited at the door with my key poised. Something, procrastination, made me turn around. Brick houses stood in long parallel lines—surrounding them was brown foliage. The grass was dead—except for one house that poured away gallons of water each night to preserve a lawn that served as a home for gnomes. Everything else was a dun-colored waste. Leaves curled and browned, rather than turning for the fall.

A surge of gritty wind kicked up. It rasped over me, rough as spite, and I was back in Iraq. The officers who had raped and cut the tracks of their hate into my skin left me for dead behind a mud wall. Creeping wind spit the dust of ages over me—as though the whole world was ashamed of my naked, bleeding body. The red of my life poured onto the dirt, becoming just another shade of brown in a wasted world.

PTSD flashbacks are more than memory. They have the substance of reality. They are real moments and experiences simply shifted in time. I was slowly learning not to live in those moments when they came.

I gripped the porch rail and forced my lungs to work. Breathing is my first step. It is active, focused, and deliberate. I had to think about the process. Doing so helped to calm my raging mind. Any bit of calm in the current of trauma is a lifeline. I grabbed it and concentrated. I thought about my heart and worked to slow the pounding. I imagined the muscles in my hands, and one by one, loosened my fingers from the wrought iron.

When I opened my eyes again, a black shine loomed large in the roiling brown. It took a moment to understand it, but the glare of glossy paint resolved into a pickup truck shape. The custom Chevy was parked across the street.

I hadn't heard it approach. Was it possible that it had been there all along?

The truck was situated in such a way that I could see the woman behind the wheel. She was slim to the point of being boney. Her hair was short, but it caught the light—reflecting something between copper and rust.

She watched me.

I watched her.

My legs were immobile. My breath was not yet completely under my control. If the woman in the truck wanted to hurt me, she had the perfect chance.

"What do you want?" My voice was so weak I doubt it carried to the maple—let alone past the limit of the yard and across the street.

My answer was a firing of the engine. It was a loud, rumbling growl that communicated nothing I could understand.

The woman in the truck made the engine race and then let it fall back to idle.

"What the hell do you want?" I asked. My mind was split. Part of it struggled with the past and part with the present. Neither part was strong enough on its own. I was the fulcrum over which two worlds teetered. I had the feeling that no part of me needed the part that was standing on the porch, shaking with the effort of remaining upright.

"Get out of here," I said—not exactly sure which world I was speaking to. Only the truck answered. The woman pressed the gas again.

Another blast of hot wind and flying grime prickled my skin. I managed to let go of the past and grab the present. I pulled my hand from the railing and put it to the grip of the pistol on my hip. I lifted a foot high enough to take a step toward the end of the porch. It was the freedom of my voice that gave me the most strength. I shouted. I bellowed out my anger. "Bitch. I'm coming now."

Ordinarily, I would never use that slur against another woman. It seems like an epithet aimed at femaleness. There is enough of that in the world. Men are a different story. I've used it against a particular kind of man many times.

Despite my choice of invective, the woman probably reacted more to my movement than my words. The truck spun its tires and ran as soon as I took my first—and only—step.

I let her go. There wasn't much I could do. I was in no condition to run or to climb into the GMC chase after her. In the house, I called the locals and told them what happened—or at least I told them most of what happened.

After that, I went around pulling all the curtains and darkened the house until it had the feel of an upholstered tomb. When everything was dark and quiet, I sat without moving for two hours. For the first time in my life, I was glad to have an appointment with my therapist on Monday.

Chapter 4

I rose out of the darkened house into a blaze of heat and light. The sun was the kind of searing yellow that made shadows on my closed eyelids. It pulsed like a spike hammered into my optic nerve, as I stood back on the front porch and waited for everything to adjust. It didn't happen quickly. The desire to return to darkness and cloistering silence made me feel like a vampire.

There was a time when I would have given in and gone. There was a time—before—that I would have gotten drunk instead.

Suck it up, buttercup.

I pulled my phone and called Billy.

"How's it going?" he asked.

"Don't ask," I answered right back. "This thing is as much a mess as I am."

He listened as I detailed the drive and the told him about the black truck.

"Go see Roy Finley," he said.

It made me feel like an idiot. I should have thought about that myself. Roy Finley was a guy I had gone to school with. I had introduced Billy to him at a Branson car show. I'm not usually a car show kind of girl, but Billy was booked there. He and his guitar—moonlight singing old 1970s country rock. He plays and sings the kind of soft oldies that half the world makes fun of, and the other half has forgotten. He does it so well, though, I would go and listen when I could.

Billy and Roy hit it off right away—talking about hot rods and old cars they admired. Billy admitted he was saving up for an El Camino. Roy had promised to do the body work, and they had fallen right into talking ideas for the nonexistent car. I had no idea what an El Camino was, until that day.

If anyone around would know anything about the Chevy, it would be Roy. Chances were good that he had a hand in the custom work.

"I think I want rally stripes," Billy said.

"What?"

"On the El Camino," he explained. "I want either a cherry red or orange soda paint job with white rally stripes."

"You know I don't care."

"Yes. I do know that. It doesn't mean you won't listen."

"Why would I do that?"

"Because you like to hear my voice."

"Pretty sure of yourself aren't you?"

"No." Even through the phone, I could see him shake his head and take a drink through a straw. "I'm sure of you."

"What are you so sure of?"

"I'm sure you need a little peace in your life. And I'm sure you don't mind me going on about a car or a song that you've never heard because you know I want that peace for you."

"I had a couple of bad hours," I admitted.

"I heard it in your voice."

"I thought I was getting better."

"You are."

"I don't feel like it right now. I didn't feel it when I couldn't move or even shout at the woman in the truck."

"What are you afraid of?"

"Everything I remember—"

"That's not it."

"How can you say that?"

"You've been through that. It's behind you. What are you afraid of that's in front of you?"

"I couldn't move."

"I don't think it's about movement, is it?" he asked. His voice reminded me of the words I'd been told in the back of a racing Humvee. The medic, the one I believed was Billy Blevins, looked at me with big eyes after he cut the clothing from me. He looked like he'd never seen a naked woman. I'm sure he'd never seen one as cut and ragged as I was. The fear in his face was smoothed out by his calm voice and his words. 'You're going to be all right.'

"I couldn't act." I finally said. "What kind of a cop can I be if I let that happen at the wrong time?"

"Has that ever happened to you?"

I thought about it. "It's come close."

"But no cigar."

I laughed. "You're an idiot."

"You're a woman with options," he told me earnestly. "More than almost anyone. You don't have to make your whole life about the worst moments."

Billy always gave good advice.

We talked for a while, and I felt better for it. We would have stayed on the line even longer—except I got another call. Sheriff Benson.

"I need you to do something up there," the sheriff said as soon as we connected. "Two somethings."

"What do you need?" My fear and tension were gone. Billy had soothed me and the idea of work had steeled me. I released the worry for the time being.

"Goddamnit," he moaned into the phone. The sheriff was the best man you would ever know, but everyone sweats under stress. He just happens to sweat vulgarities. "This is shit I don't want to dump on you but. . ."

"But?"

"But I'm going to."

"Is it about the autopsy?"

"It's about the kid being autopsied."

"You know who he is?"

"Know. Believe. Hell I'm fucking sure, Hurricane." I hadn't heard so much pain in his voice since his wife passed away. Whatever was bothering him was personal. I didn't want to press so I waited for him to tell me. "His name is Tyrell Turner. He's the grandson of Earl Turner—the man Riley told you about."

"The one Johnson Rath almost killed."

"It was more than almost. He was a heartbeat away from murder in the eyes of the law. Even closer than that—if you think about what was done to Earl's life. It was taken away just as surely as if he had been laid in the ground."

"What do you want me to do?"

"Go into Springfield tomorrow and meet Earl Turner. Talk with him. Get a statement."

"That's all?"

"That should be enough. It won't be easy. There's a lot of anger. A lot of hurt. But you're right."

"About what?"

"There *is* more. I want you to meet with Devon Birch."

I understood immediately why the sheriff didn't want to tell me that part. Devon Birch is DEA. He comes with a lot more baggage than federal credentials. He's a black man working the lily-white Ozarks. Every day, he deals with pot growers on federal lands, hillbilly meth peddlers, and the creeping intrusions of Mexican cartels. As if that wasn't enough for anyone, he has to do his job within an armed and angry population that has a long frontier tradition. His attitude reflects his circumstance.

He wasn't the only one with baggage though. That was why the sheriff was being gentle in making his request. I had a long history of not getting along with the feds—for a lot of good reasons.

"What do you want me to see him about?"

"There may be crossover. Johnson is tied up with the AB and those bikers. He wants to rebuild his whole white separatist, end-of-the-world, welcome-home-Jesus compound. That takes money."

"Drug money." It made sense. The initials AB were short for Aryan Brotherhood. They are a white prison gang, made up of avowed racists and known killers, who funded operations mostly through drug trafficking. Mostly. Their membership has been tied to every kind of criminal enterprise imaginable.

"You told him to expect me?" I asked.

"I haven't talked to him about it."

After that we had a few choice words—that amounted to me refusing and him cursing. In the end, I would do my job—and we both knew it. I returned to the house and threw open the windows to spite the darkness.

A shower and change of clothes later, and I felt almost human.

* * * *

Roy Finley was under an old Mustang when I found him. His shop was between his house and the private junkyard of car parts he kept on two acres just outside of town.

"Hurricane," he said from under the car before I had said a word.

"How did you know it was me?"

"No six-foot man I know has feet that small."

"Thanks," I said. "I think."

"Where's Billy?"

"What do you think, we're attached at the hip or something?"

"Or something." He said it with a smirk. Before I could say anything, he added, "But that's none of my business, is it?"

"You've got that right."

Roy rolled out from under the car then wiped his hands on a rag—which only seemed to make his hands grimier. Extending his greasy right he said, "Help me up. I've got something to show you."

"I don't want to touch that." I pointed at his hand.

"When did you get so prissy?" He got to his feet without help and returned to working his hands in the rag.

"I'm not prissy. I'm clean and want to stay that way."

"Come on." He canted his head toward the back of the cavernous shop and started walking.

"I'm not here to see your latest paint job," I told him. "I have some questions you can help me out on."

"Questions? You mean like cop stuff?"

"Yes. Exactly like cop stuff."

"Cool. I've never done that before. But you'll want to see this first."

"See what? And why? You know I don't care about your boy toys."

"You'll care about this one." He stopped beside a tarp-draped car. The only thing I could tell about it was that it had four tires and one of them was flat.

"I'm working, Roy. We can do this another time."

He went to the back and pulled the canvas drape. It caught on the front bumper and he said, "Give me a hand."

"Really?"

"Prissy."

"I'm not prissy," I protested as I released the snag. "I'm just not interested."

The tarp slid away and the car was revealed like a snake shedding its skin—if the snake's new skin looked like a faded old car with rust spots.

Roy spread his hands and announced, "El Camino."

That's when I got it. The car was one of those 1970's Chevrolets that was half car and half pickup truck. It was exactly what Billy had been talking about.

"What do you think?" Roy asked.

"It looks like junk."

"You're such a girl."

"This isn't a gender thing. That car looks like recycling waiting to happen."

"That's because you're not looking past the obvious."

"There's something past the obvious here?"

"There's so much here." Roy's enthusiasm was almost religious. "It has the original numbers matching 454. The frame is in great shape. That rust you see is all surface. This thing's been in a barn for thirty years."

"It should have stayed there."

"Billy will love it."

"Is that why you have it? You want to sell it to Billy?"

"I can sell this tomorrow for a good profit. But Billy is the guy for this car."

"Why?"

Roy gave me a long look. His grin melted down. Enthusiasm became a kind of disappointed understanding. "I'm sorry," he said—and he sounded like he meant it.

"What for?"

"I kind of jumped to a conclusion."

"What conclusion is that?"

"I thought you and Deputy Blevins were a thing."

"You didn't know? It's Detective Blevins now." I laughed. It might have sounded a little defensive. "What kind of thing?"

"I thought you guys were together. You know, romantically."

Honestly, it had been something that I worked hard to keep quiet. I had my own issues and it was hard to build a relationship on the job. Still, the suggestion that there was nothing between us offended me slightly. "What makes you so sure there isn't?" I tried injecting the question with more humor than confession.

"I figure anyone close to Billy would know how much this means to him. He's been saving all his pay for years to have the kind of car his father had." Roy dragged the canvas back over the car. "Hell, I only met him the one time and I know about it."

It was something I've been accused of before. Billy himself showed me that I get wrapped up in my own issues and become blind to the people around me. Selfish is the word he didn't use.

"Were you going to make him a good deal on the car?" I asked Roy as he tugged the corners of the drape into place.

"Sure. He can't afford a top of the line restoration. For the twelve grand he has, I'll sell him a car that runs and is road safe. He'll do more as he has the money. I told him he can come help and do some of the work himself."

"That's very kind of you."

Roy shrugged dismissively. "Money won't ever be your pall bearer." He wiped his dirty hands against themselves like he expected a miracle of cleanliness. "So what did you want to know from me?"

I told him about the black custom Chevy pickup truck.

"What year was it?"

"How would you tell?"

"What was distinctive about it?"

"It was an old 1950s truck. It was black."

"Look, '50s trucks are popular. There are a lot of them running around out there. You need to give me more."

"Like what?"

Roy shook his head like he was tired. I know he was thinking how much easier the conversation would be with a man. "Paint," he said. "Black, but what kind of finish? Was it smooth and shiny or flat?"

"Glossy. Like it was brand new."

"Did you see the wheels?"

"What about them?"

"Were they mag or chrome?"

"Chrome with hubcaps I think. They were smooth and shiny."

"Moons." He said. "Dual pipes or single?"

"I don't know." I was getting a little annoyed. It really would have been an easier conversation if a man, or at least an interested woman, had seen the truck.

"How did the truck sound?"

"Like a hot rod, loud and rumbly."

"Did you see the tail lights?"

"They were red circles in the fenders."

"In? They were in the fenders and not stuck on the side of the truck bed?"

"They were inset, just red circles in holes in the fenders."

"French."

"How am I supposed to know?"

"That's not a question. When you build a tunnel in the metal and put the light at the bottom of it, we call it *Frenching.*"

"Why?"

"I don't know." He laughed. "We just do. Did you see the back window?"

"Sure."

"Was it one big one, or a center one with smaller ones at the sides?"

"It had three. There was the center one and smaller side windows that curved around the cab."

"You have a 1956 Chevy, five window pickup, with *Frenched* tail lights, and baby moons."

"You got all that from what I said?"

"I've got more than that. I can tell you who owns it."

"Who and how?"

"How is easy. I *Frenched* the lights and did the paint. I know the engine guy, the suspension guy, and the upholstery guy too. We were all surprised by the job. There just aren't that many black guys that come to us for custom work on an old truck."

I had a long sinking feeling—like an avalanche of melting snow in my stomach. "His name?"

"Earl Turner. Guy with a gamey arm and a chip on his shoulder. But he loves that truck."

* * * *

I sat in my truck, under a ratty smoke tree, at the back edge of the pathology building. It wasn't likely that the bikers would try anything there. I wasn't going to take any chances though. They had already shown a willingness to do the unexpected. With the radio playing low on the oldies station, I settled in to watch.

The worst part of solitude is the ghosts' visitations. There are so many of them. In my mind is the ever-present shadow of the young woman I was *before*. She is another ghost.

As if it anticipated the haunting, light seeped from the world. Night, weighty with humidity and heat, nestled in. The fall of the sun was long and slow. It burned down from red to orange. By the time it slipped under the horizon, it looked like embers of a dying fire. It left the heat behind when it went. All of it, the sinking of the sun and the rise of night, seemed to happen between instants of my thoughts.

I'm a recovering alcoholic, a recovering trauma victim, a recovering widow; shades of grief, all of them. I'm not doing nearly as much recovering as it sounds. On the radio, Bruce Springsteen sang about Thunder Road in a voice filled with longing and regret. That pretty much sums up life, I thought.

Air, hot, harsh, and rough, slipped through the open windows. It was a specter knocking at a door that was already half open. Trauma is like that. It breaks all the locks in your mind so they never set well again.

I was afraid. I always was when I knew the past was coming to visit. It wasn't the past I expected. It wasn't fearful.

The wind settled into a constant caress and it cooled. I turned to the right to face the breeze, and Nelson Solomon was sitting in my passenger seat. It wasn't the first time I'd seen my dead husband. Usually he came in my dreams, sleeping and decomposing in the bed next to me. That time he was whole and intact. He smiled.

I cried.

There was no helping it. He was the first man I loved—and I had only a year with him. He died at home, but he was killed in Iraq. He was on one of the teams that assaulted chemical weapons storehouses. His wounds were invisible and slow-acting.

"I miss you." I spoke in a whisper when I could manage the words. "I miss you so much."

Nelson smiled.

More than anything, I wanted to touch him. But I didn't want to break whatever spell allowed him to be there. I looked and sat as still as I could.

Over Nelson's shoulder, the window began to rise. He hadn't moved to touch the button. My hands were gripping the wheel with white knuckles. The ghost of my dead husband turned and raised a finger to the glass. In life, after he had been a Marine, he was an artist. In death too, I thought, because his finger moved and left behind light on the darkness.

The light he painted became bright ripples in black water. Over that he painted a boat. It was bright white with a bit of red rising up above the water line.

Before he died, Nelson painted us as boats in the lake. It was my favorite work of his. The original still sat on his easel in my home.

Ghost Nelson finished the boat. It looked lonely, empty, and adrift in dark water. Then he added another at the far edge. It had a dangling rope. I knew without words that it was him, drifting away and out of the frame.

The image drove me to despair. I cried, a gut churning weeping, with fat tears rolling off my cheeks. But I didn't reach for him.

Nelson looked at me. He smiled again. It was an expression of care without sadness. There was no pity. His mouth opened and I thought he was going to speak. Instead, he turned again and began to paint.

He worked on the other edge of the glass. That time he added another boat. It was emerging from shadow and moving toward my boat. On the bow of that second boat was a coiled rope.

It was a beautiful image of broken light on rippled water, three boats drifting, one retreating and one advancing; all of it was in sunshine so mottled and expressive it was heartbreaking.

Without my having seen him turn, Nelson was looking at me again. "You're going to be all right." Then he was gone—leaving behind the distant roar of hard Humvee tires on broken asphalt—and the sense that someone was working on my behalf.

For what seemed like hours, I stared at the painting on my window. I might have stared forever if the reflections in the water didn't get brighter and ripple away into the real darkness. A pair of headlights swept across the glass. Suddenly, I could hear the radio again. Bruce was still singing. I heard the rumble of the loud pipes too. The headlights belonged to the black truck. Before the real world flooded my senses again, I noticed one tiny aspect of the other reality remained: my passenger side window was up.

Out past the glass, the black Chevy idled. The high beams fixed on me, staring eyes—old, yellow, and menacing. I opened my door and stepped out pulling my service weapon as I did. As soon as my foot touched the ground, the truck backed away. At the edge of the parking lot, the driver spun the wheel—whipping the truck to the side. The engine revved and the tires spun as the Chevy ran back to the road. It only went so far when it stopped.

It was waiting for me. I didn't take the bait.

We stood like that for a few minutes, tempting and threatening each other. From behind me rose another thundering sound. Motorcycles. I kept my automatic in my hand as I pulled my phone with the other and called the local cops. Before they arrived, four bikes rolled into the lot and circled.

It was a relief. In my life, violence often is. It was the reason I had an appointment the next day with a therapist. That was tomorrow. At that moment, I was in the perfect mood to shoot someone or to extend the telescoping baton I carried and break a knee.

I shut the truck door and stepped out into the beams of jittering headlights. No one took my bait either. The bikers shouted and twisted their throttles—filling the parking lot with noise and fumes. Bravado evaporated and they ran when strobing lights approached. When I looked, the black truck was gone too. I wasn't sure if I was glad or not.

The Nixa police put a car in the lot so I didn't have to stay any longer. Driving back to my father's place, I put in a call to Roy. After that I called Billy. We talked until I fell asleep on the couch.

Chapter 5

I woke with the sun reborn and already heating the Ozarks. I had the feeling that I'd missed something important about the day behind me. It was one of those nagging feelings, an itch in the center of my brain. Usually a feeling like that would resolve itself when I concentrated on another task. Sometimes the mind works a problem best when you're not paying attention. That time, the problem came to the front door and solved itself.

Uncle Orson banged on the aluminum storm door, rattling it in the frame. He never used the bell. The moment I saw his face, I knew exactly what had been nagging at me. Orson had pulled Cherry Dando out of the car and started a fight with the handcuffed man. I never asked why.

"We need to talk." He pushed past me and went straight to the kitchen. "Is there coffee?"

"Good morning to you, too."

Uncle Orson checked the percolator on the stove. It was older than I was. My father had never transitioned to a coffee maker. Good thing, too. The old pot made the best coffee. "It's almost there," he pronounced.

"What happened yesterday?"

He pulled two cups down from the cupboard. "That's what I wanted to talk about."

"So. Talk."

"Yeah. That's the thing."

"What thing?"

"The talk. What I wanted to talk about was that I didn't want to have to talk about yesterday."

"Wait—what?"

"You heard me." He touched the sides of the coffee pot to gage its readiness to boil.

"You know, when the pot starts to perk, you can see it in the glass top."

"Do you want me to make some grits?"

"Did you think it would be that easy?"

He held up the canister of grits and shook it at me as if it was the greatest temptation in the world.

"Uncle Orson," I warned.

"I hoped it would be."

"It's not. Nothing's that easy."

"Grits are easy."

"Okay. You can make some grits, but you have to talk too."

"I'm not sure I can do both at the same time."

"I'm not sure either. You can give it a shot."

He rattled pots in the cabinet until he found the right one. "Is there any butter?"

I checked the refrigerator as Orson filled the pot with water. "There's one stick."

"It'll have to do." He turned the burner on high then sat the water on to boil.

"How much are you thinking of cooking?"

"All of them."

"It's a full box."

"I'm a hungry man."

"Why are we talking about grits?"

"I like grits," he said without missing a beat. "They are one of my favorite things in the world."

"You know what I mean."

The pot was percolating. Orson poured two cups and left them black. "I knew you would ask about what happened." He pushed a mug over to me. "He's a son-of- a-bitch."

"Dando?"

Uncle Orson lifted his scalding cup to his lips. He blew once and sipped. It was the way a lot of combat veterans drank their coffee. They learned in the field to suck it down when they got the chance. Hot was just another hardship. He nodded in answer as soon as the coffee left his lips. "A bastard son-of-a-bitch."

"So you don't like him?"

"Like's got nothing to do with it."

"Then what?"

"That's what I don't want to talk about."

"If you don't talk to me, we can make it official and talk to the sheriff."

"He knows." Orson turned to the pot that was ready to boil and opened the seal on the canister of grits.

"So you came all this way to talk to me because you knew I would want to talk about it. But the only thing you really want to say is you don't want to talk about it."

He nodded and added salt to the water.

"And. *And*—everyone already knows what it's about but me."

"I told you what it was about."

"What?"

"I told you he's a son-of-a-bitch." He stirred the boiling water as he added grits right from the canister.

"You know I'm going to find out."

"I'm asking you not to."

"That won't cut it. If it wasn't about me, and if it wasn't important, you wouldn't be making a big deal out of it."

"I'm not making a big deal. I'm making grits." He cut the stick of butter in half and dropped it in the pot. "These would be better if we had some bacon grease."

"Who's Cherry Dando to you? And don't say a son-of-a-bitch."

"He was around here a long time ago. He shows up every so often and is always dragging trouble along—like a dog with a burning branch tied to his tail."

"What kind of trouble?"

Uncle Orson stirred the thickening pot of grits and turned down the flame. Other than that, he didn't say anything.

"No answer?" I asked him, knowing it sounded like an accusation. When he didn't respond that time I said. "You're hiding something. The only question is, does it protect you or me?"

He turned to look at me that time. The sadness in his eyes said it all.

"So it's me. What makes you think I need protecting?"

"What makes you think you don't?"

"I don't want to have this conversation."

"See how it works?"

"It's not the same, and you know it. You don't want to talk about—" I waved my hands in the air at invisible thoughts. "Who knows what? I don't want to talk about how you think I'm some delicate flower you have to protect."

"Delicate?" Orson looked genuinely surprised. "Have you met yourself, young lady? You're the strongest, most righteous person I've ever encountered. And I fought George Foreman in '71. Kicked his ass."

"That George Foreman was a white kid—and you had fifty pounds on him. I've seen pictures."

"Are you calling me a liar?"

"Yes."

"Grits are ready." I handed over a couple of bowls. He scooped out heaping spoons full. When the bowls were filled, he dropped in more butter to melt over the top. "All I'm trying to say is that you're the toughest person in my life, man or woman. But the past weighs more than the proverbial camel's straw. Memories and secrets—yesterdays—they're all bricks. They are thick, stone loads that bear down until they crush you. And it's not that they smash you flat, the weight crushes you down and shapes you until you become just another piece of rock in a wall."

"That doesn't sound like something you can protect anyone from."

"I can keep this one brick off your back. I can keep the load from growing quite as quickly." He stirred his grits with a fork—mixing the yellow melt of butter into the creamy mass. "I'm asking you to let me keep a secret."

"Whose?"

"Your father's. Yours. The family's. A past that should be forgotten, but can't be. That's pretty much the nature of living with family sometimes. All those yesterdays staring at you—the same old eyes—each new generation." He took a bite of his breakfast. "It needs more salt." Then, after another sampling bite, "And more butter."

We talked more. Uncle Orson evaded more. I got nothing from him except a headache and new bit of anger that sat in my chest like a splinter of hard wood.

At one point, I gave up and went to shower. While I waited for the hot water to wind through old pipes, I called Devon Birch of the DEA. We agreed to meet later that morning.

When I was out of the shower and dressed, I tried, one more time, with Uncle Orson. He seemed sad again at first—then became mad. I let it go for the time being. I told him that I had to get going to my meeting with Birch. It was half true. It would be my second stop of the morning. My first stop would be with Earl Turner.

I never called Turner. The visit would be a drop-in. Sheriff Benson asked me to talk with Earl Turner; to take an official statement, but that was before I learned about the truck. If I made an appointment, there

would be more time to think about what to say. I wanted his thoughts to
be a little fresher.

Turner lived in the north side of Springfield. His home was a beautiful
cottage made out of field stone. Everything about it was perfect. The lawn
was lush and green. Flowers were blooming. I was surprised that the
windows were open and lace curtains were billowing out. There didn't
seem to be an air conditioner. Out back there was a detached garage. To
the right of the bi-fold door was an old fashioned gas pump. More than
old fashioned, the pump was an antique with a big glass globe on top that
showed the gas for your car.

"What're you doing here?"

I stood in the drive, looking around for the owner of the voice.

"I asked you, what're you doing here?" A sharp-faced black man glared
distrustfully at me from a small window. He was visible only when he
leaned close to the screen.

"Are you Earl Turner?"

"Who's askin'?"

"I'm Detective Katrina Williams, Taney County Sheriff's Department."

"Lemme see a badge." His face came close to the screen then faded back.

I pulled my credentials and held them up toward the window.

"Get closer," the invisible face demanded.

I stepped in and pressed my ID and badge right up to the screen.
"Can you see that?"

"I'm not blind."

I pulled back and tucked the ID case away.

"Benson send you?"

"Sheriff Benson asked me to speak with you, yes." I was already annoyed
by his attitude and at trying to talk through a screen. "May I come in?"

"I'll come out."

It took a minute. Earl Turner appeared from the back of the house and
waved me down the drive. He disappeared again as I walked. At the end
of the drive, I was stunned to find a whole other building at the back of
his property. It was an entire gas station from another age. There was a
steep, peaked little building with two garage bays on the side. An island
with two pumps was in front. The entire place was gleaming with bright,
white paint and gloss, red trim. Standing over it all was a big, red, white,
and blue diamond-shaped sign that read, *DX*.

When I stopped gaping, I found Earl seated under a big Catalpa tree. He
gestured to one of the three other Adirondack chairs in the shade. "Come
on," he said, waving again. "You wanted to talk, come do it."

I decided to get right into it. "Tell me about your grandson," I said as I sat.
"What do you want to know?"

"Anything you have to say. The sheriff has some suspicions—"

"I know what he thinks. And I'm thinkin' he's right. Those old boys killed Tyrell."

"Why are you so sure?"

He fixed me in a look that could have been pity—if it wasn't coming at me like the point of a nail.

"You're that big ass deputy from down there."

"Don't call me that, Mr. Turner." I waited for an apology. Then I waited for any kind of reaction before I said, "It's Detective. I'll treat you with respect and I ask the same."

"You ain't takin' notes."

"You haven't said anything I need notes for."

"You know ahead of time what I'm going to say?"

"I beg your pardon?"

"Chuck said a deputy would come to take a statement from me."

"Yes."

"A *statement.* Isn't that official and permanent?"

"Are you afraid I'm going to forget something?"

"Hell, girl. I'm afraid you're going to make stuff up. I'm afraid that when it comes to the word, any word, of a white cop against the word of an old black man, the only word that matters is 'black.'" He sucked his teeth and added, "You dig that?"

"You think I'm here to work against you?"

"I think things are the way they are."

I took a long, slow breath. "Mr. Turner, this isn't an official statement about anything. When we get to that point, notes will be taken. I promise." For a second, I thought he was going to say something. He didn't, but the look on his face told me Earl was keeping an account of everything I said. Nothing was passed without being weighed and tallied. "How old is Tyrell?"

The gap between my question and his answer was pretty deep. Earl finally said, "Nineteen."

"Where are his parents?"

"His mother is dead." The statement left little room for a father.

"He lives with you?"

"He did."

"You seem pretty sure he's been killed. Why?"

"Experience."

"Yours or his?"

Earl grinned. It wasn't a happy look. "Guess."

"I understand you have reason to distrust. . ." I pointed at myself. "The system. Maybe white people in general. I'm no one to judge. I have my own issues. But you don't know me as an individual. I'm asking you to give me a chance."

"You don't know *me*, missy. You think you do."

"That's not true—"

"Yeah? Tell me somethin'. And answer without thinkin' it through, or making it right in your head."

It was my turn to stare at him. I nodded.

"Just spit it out when you have an answer," he demanded again.

I looked but gave nothing more.

"Where's the boy's father?"

"I don't know," I answered without pause.

"What do you think?"

I opened my mouth to speak, then shut it.

"Yeah," Turner agreed. "It's an easy thought ain't it?"

"I apologize."

"Don't say you're sorry. Say your thought."

I stared for a long time and he kept his gaze welded to mine. I broke first and looked away before I said, "I assumed you had no idea who the father was."

"Black boy. No daddy. That's a conclusion it don't take much jumpin' for someone like you to get to."

"Then tell me. Where is his father?"

"Shit." Turner spit the word. "Who knows? But you're thinkin', it's about black men and bastards. Everyone thinks it. Even a lot of black folks. We judge each other just like the white world is judging us. Black boy without a father. Hell we made clichés out of ourselves with that one." Earl stopped his rant and looked straight at me again. "Did Chuck tell you anything about him?"

"Nothing, except he was your grandson."

Turner held up his good arm and put it on display for me. "What makes me black and you white?"

"You mean skin color?"

Earl nodded knowingly. His face took on a lawyer's look, the kind that said he's caught you in a trap with your own words. "If it was just about skin color Tyrell Turner would be white. Sure he had a tan, but the boy was closer to your skin than mine."

If an old car had pulled up to Earl Turner's personal gas station and a bow tied attendant had come out to pump the ethyl—I could not have been more surprised. "You're saying his father is a white man."

"Assumptions," Earl pronounced. "Ain't they a bitch?"

"You think it's news to me that being a poor father knows no race? I'm a cop. I've seen it all. I know the worst of us resides in the deep red of our hearts—where skin makes no difference."

"Oh you think it's that easy? You imagine my daughter had a fling with some white boy? Or maybe you think she was in love with some college boy who promised her roses and picket fences. Is that it? You think it was young love gone bad?"

I didn't have any answer for his questions or for the simmering anger that threatened to boil. I kept my mouth closed and listened.

"It was rape."

The word hit me like being punched in the gut with a fist made out of ice.

"See? That's the thing. A man who wouldn't waste his spit on a black girl won't think nothin' about taking her body like he picks an apple out of a neighbor's field. It's easy. Like breathin'. In your mind you make a person into an animal. Then you can do anything."

"Mr. Turner, I'm so sorry." It was all I could do to get the words past the burning sand that clogged my chest.

"Her name was Elaine. Twenty years ago she was workin' at one of those tourist places down at the lake. She didn't come home one Friday night. She was found where they dumped her on the side of the road. Crying. Beat up. Bloody."

My heart was in a wrench and being twisted. Even under the shade, my skin burned; all of it, not just what was uncovered.

"She was a beautiful girl. That one thing used her up though. I asked her—I begged her to talk about it."

A bead of sweat rolled from out of my hairline, down the side of my face and neck. I felt every inch of its travel. When it streamed under my collar, I suddenly remembered myself naked—exposed.

"The marks they left on her no words could wipe away. It was all I had." Earl Turner looked at me with depths of pain in his eyes that saw no bottom. Not from his side or from mine. "Elaine had Tyrell. She lived for fifteen more years before she. . . I don't think she ever left that ditch."

The tiny rivulet hit the thick track of scar that curled under my left breast. I jumped to my feet.

"You goin' somewhere, girl?"

I know I said, "I have to. . ." And I remember saying something more. I don't know what it was—or if it had any real meaning to anyone. I don't remember much of anything until the moment I walked into my therapist's office.

Chapter 6

Dr. Regina Kurtz was the kind of woman I could never be. She was poised and stylish in heels and pearls. Each time I saw her, I had to convince myself that she was not judging me for my boots and jeans. Her effortless femininity put me on defense. Usually. Right now, I needed the company of a woman.

My arrival, early and agitated to the point of sobbing, caused a flurry of activity that the doctor handled with quick assurance. I was ushered into her session room while plans for other patients were shifted. When we were alone, I didn't wait for her to ask what had happened. I spilled like a British Petroleum oil well. It all rushed out in what felt like a single gasp of air—the night with Billy and the euphoria, the truck and bikers, my gradual slide into depression and the flashback to Iraq. All of the feelings and incidents were like tremors before the quake that was Earl Turner's description of his daughter's rape. There was a resonance to it, a sympathetic vibration that worked in my life.

I didn't finish so much as end. My words dissolved to meaningless sounds, and I cried again.

"You did the right thing," Dr. Kurtz told me. She matched her voice to the room, making it soft. Even her words seemed chosen for the light, indirect and soothing. "I'm glad you made it here."

"Nothing feels like the right thing."

"You got out of a trigger situation. You sought help." She let the thought hang for a moment. "Do you realize how big a step that is for you?"

"I'm crying." I took a tissue, wiped at my running nose, and dabbed at my eyes. "Hell—I'm blubbering like a child, out of control and useless. It doesn't seem like a step at all. If it is, it's backward."

She let me cry some more. I almost thought she had fallen asleep when she asked me, "Who got hurt?"

"No one got hurt. I—what do you mean?" I wiped my face with the wrong tissue, then rubbed at that with the back of my hand. "What's that supposed to mean? It wasn't about anyone getting hurt. I fell apart. I ran."

"And that's a bad thing?"

"I'm a cop. I can't crack up and I can't lose control."

"Is it so important to be a detective?"

"What do you mean? To me, or in general?"

"You're evading."

As soon as she said it, I pictured myself that morning—talking with my Uncle Orson. "Not evading, just. . ."

"Evading," she finished for me. "Avoiding. Running."

"It's not the same kind of running."

"Running is running. Especially the kind that doesn't take you anywhere."

"What do you want me to say?"

"Answer the question."

I didn't. I sat and looked at her shoes. They were black, with a moderate heel and a little strap around the ankle that closed with a gold buckle. I looked at my feet. There was no comparison. I was wearing western boots with a soft point at the toe and a two-inch riding heel. They were shined, but not girly at all.

"You have options," she prodded.

"Everyone says that to me these days."

"You don't agree?"

"I don't care."

"That brings us right back around doesn't it? Why is it so important to be a detective?"

Sometimes I hated that woman more than anything else in my life. "That's not what I'm here to talk about."

"What are you here to talk about?" She had one leg crossed over the other. The foot off the floor twitched.

"I like your shoes," I said without any idea where the words had come from.

"You do?" Dr. Kurtz was surprised. She leaned forward and twisted her ankle to look at the strappy shoe.

"Is it so amazing?"

"Not at all."

"I never wear pretty shoes. I wear dresses mostly to funerals." Words came from my mouth unbidden and without thought. Instead of relieving the tension, I felt they dammed my feelings, choked me—both figuratively and literally. Dr. Kurtz watched me. She waited for the next words—as if one of them would be a secret key. I didn't feel like unlocking. "Do you think how we dress shows who we are?"

"I think how we dress is who we project."

"Who we want to be?"

She shrugged and half-way smiled. "Who we need to be."

"Who do you need to be?" As soon as I asked, my face burned with a blush. "I'm sorry," I said. "I shouldn't have asked that."

"How come? Don't you think it's natural to wonder about the person who listens to all your secrets?"

"Boundaries." I turned away and looked at the generic art on the wall.

"Another thing that is important to you." Her voice was knowing. I pictured the nodding that went with it.

"You sound like you're driving at something."

"You sound like you're driving in wide circles around something."

"This isn't getting us anywhere."

"Did you know. . .I've always envied you your boots."

I looked at her. "That's hard to believe."

"Because you buy into the projection of my clothing. I think part of the problem is that you buy into the projection of your own clothing so much that you've forgotten there are other things to wear. Other parts of you to dress up."

"You're going to have to explain that to me."

"Really?" She uncrossed her legs and put both feet side by side on the floor. "Do you think I dress like this at home?"

"I've never thought about it."

"This is my doctor uniform. A skirt, wool or silk depending on the season, light make-up." She turned her ankles to show off the shoes. "Daytime heels. I keep my nails polished and my hair done. Why do you think that it is?"

"I always thought you were kind of prissy."

Dr. Kurtz laughed. It wasn't a put-on thing. It pealed like a dropped tambourine and she suddenly seemed human. "That's the most honest thing you've ever said to me." She laughed again and pointed to herself. "Look at me. What would happen if you dressed like me on your job?"

"My job would be a lot harder. No one would take me seriously."

"I agree." She leaned back into her chair and re-crossed her legs.

For the first time I noticed that she had no notepad or pen. It made me think of Earl Turner asking me about making a record, and his mistrust.

"And if I sat here in jeans and boots looking grim and tough, do you think I could do my job?" The smile was still on her face. The laughter was gone. "No. Who would open up to me?"

"I get it," I admitted. "Projecting. But I'm still missing the bigger point. What's it mean to my life?"

"What's the difference between you and me?"

"There's not enough time left in the day to write that list."

"The difference, the real difference, is that when I go home, I change clothes. I bet you didn't know I have horses." I didn't and it must have shown on my face because Dr. Kurtz started laughing again. "I go home and tie up my hair. I put on boots and the oldest, softest jeans I have—and I'm not fussy about how clean they are. Then I take care of my animals. I talk to them too."

"Why are you telling me this?"

"Because I think you're really close to taking off your work armor. I think you need to put on a pretty dress and dance with a smile on your face. And—that is terrifying you."

"You think I'm afraid of putting on a dress?"

"I think you're afraid of letting yourself be happy. I think you believe someone will take it away again. That's a conflict because you're so close to losing that giant stick up your behind."

"Between the two of us, doctor, you're the one who's crazy." She laughed and I stopped her. "It's not funny. I came running in here. I was in tears. A man told me a story about his daughter being assaulted and raped, and I lost control. How can I do my job like that?"

"Katrina." When I didn't look at her, Dr. Kurtz said, "Hurricane." I looked. "Why are you here?"

"I just said—"

"Not this moment. Forget that. Why did you start coming to me?"

"You know why."

"It was a condition of keeping your job."

I nodded.

"Because of the violence you brought to the job."

I didn't nod. I didn't look away either.

"Not just the job."

She waited. I waited. It was impossible to tell if the silence was building a bridge or tearing one down.

Finally she said, "What happened today is going to happen to you. You know that. Maybe what you don't know is how to react when the old ways are gone."

I shook my head. Then I shook it harder.

"How would you have reacted two years ago?" The pause she left after the question didn't leave a lot of room for me to answer. "You would have gotten drunk. Someone probably would have gotten hurt. Am I right?"

There was no answer in my head, only numb confusion.

"For the first time in years, you reacted to a trigger by allowing a crack in your shell. It wasn't self-destructive and wasn't violent. You cried and sought help. Are you going to sit there and tell me that's not a reach for happiness?"

I didn't buy it. The entire idea that falling apart could be an attempt to be happy, and that happy was something I was afraid of, seemed too easy. And anything easy is something to be wary of.

We talked it out for a long time. When I—again—pointed out the foolishness of believing that I had a fear of being happy, Dr. Kurtz said, "You're not afraid of being happy, Katrina. You're afraid of losing happiness again. There's a big difference. And it's a perfectly reasonable fear."

I left the session feeling hollow and wasted. The sun was still burning the town. In places where tar had been used to fill cracks in the parking lot, my boots stuck. Each step pulled up a gummy string of blackness. It was easy to imagine that, if I stood still, I would be glued down forever. There was some kind of ancient Greek myth in there somewhere. I wasn't the one to find it.

I had missed my appointment with Devon Birch. Not that I cared. It was good to keep the feds a little off balance. Otherwise, they were always willing to believe they owned you.

I started the truck and opened the windows while the A/C got to cranking. I'm a windows-down person—except when the thermometer is sitting at ninety-six. Honestly, despite the heat and the feeling I'd made a fool of myself, I felt better. Dr. Kurtz had given me one thing that had nested in my mind. That bit about wearing an identity. She was right. Since I had come home from the Army, I had worn a badge, manly boots, and unflattering jeans as armor against the world. It was a take-me-seriously façade that transitioned easily into a fear-me look.

I needed to make some changes in my life.

"Sheriff called me about. . ." Earl sat heavily on an uncomfortable looking couch. He grunted as he settled and pulled his left arm up to rest in his lap. "You know, I guess. It was dental records. They were sent over first thing in the morning. There's no doubtin' it. Tyrell had two fillings right next to each other. His only two. I guess that's what they look at."

"I'm sorry." I said gently. I meant it.

"It's a hell of a thing." Earl stared straight ahead. He wasn't really talking to me. "One bad day can ripple out like a big stone in a small pond—until it fills every nook and hole with waves. It's like certain kinds of wrong never go away. They smooth over. But they are always there—waiting for any kind of disturbance—to set the waves back in motion."

"You're thinking about that day you were assaulted by Johnson Rath."

"I'm thinking about Tyrell." He let the correction sit there without making more of it, an unembellished fact. Then he added, "And I'm thinking of Elaine."

"You think something started the day Johnson attacked you."

"Ended, you mean."

"Ended?"

"Any chance to live right. That moment took lifetimes of security away."

I waited, but he didn't seem to want to say more. "I'm sorry," I told Earl again. "We can talk another time."

Before I could turn to leave he said, "You know."

"Know what?"

"You know."

"I don't. . ." I couldn't finish. Earl Turner looked at me. His eyes bore a strange light. It was the backward looking gaze of memory, but it fixed me in the then-and-there.

"You understand." He stated it simply. "I saw it when I told you about Elaine. There was no missin' it when you got up to run from her story. You been hurt in that way that changes a person. I could see it. I watched the waves rippling around you."

"Mr. Turner. . ."

"Hate." The word was as heavy and solid as a cinder block. He dropped it like he was dropping muddy boots on the dinner table. It was to make a point. I just didn't know what the point was.

"Earl—"

"There's only one thing that will take more away from the people who get touched by it."

"I don't understand, Mr. Turner."

"Money."

Chapter 7

The truck cab cooled and I put the windows up. I turned on the oldies station and eased out of the parking lot. I had visions of hot tar being thrown by the tires against the body. An old song by ELO played, and I drove for the highway—aiming for home.

I missed. ELO bled into Elton John who became Fleetwood Mac— without me even noticing the transitions. I sang along and drove. The next thing I knew, I was pulling up in front of Earl Turner's home again.

That time he met me on the porch with a sad look and asked, "Back again?"

"We still need to talk." I tried to sound like nothing had happened. I'm pretty sure I failed.

"I got a call from your boss."

"Yes?"

"I didn't tell him what happened."

"There's nothing to tell."

"Sure there ain't."

"Tell me again about your daughter."

Earl looked me over and shook his head. "Nah," he said slowly. "I don't think I want to do that."

"Why's that?"

His face twitched between expressions. It was like the old car radios, before the world went digital. Back then you could put the knob between two stations and get bits of one, then the other. He seemed to be tuned between something cruel and something kind. He gave up trying to decide and turned to the door. "Come on in."

The house was dark, even with the open windows. Air was stirred by a ceiling fan. It wasn't nearly as hot as the outside. That didn't make it cool.

When you're investigating a murder and someone starts talking about money, it changes everything. I can't say I understood better, but I sure was listening closer. "What money?"

"You know what Judas got?"

"Thirty pieces of silver."

"Uh-huh. Silver."

"I don't understand what you're trying to say. What about silver?"

"It wasn't an accident."

"You're losing me, Mr. Turner."

With his good hand he pointed at his limp arm. "This wasn't an accident. Everyone thought it was. It looked like that big bastard jumped me because he saw me walking next to that white girl. It was his excuse. Not that he needed much of one."

It's a funny thing about the job. No matter how screwed up my life is— and it gets pretty messy a lot of the time—when I start learning the things I set out to uncover, the badge takes hold. Tyrell Turner was murdered. Discovering it was about anything more than race was a revelation. My own pain kept falling further away as Earl told me his story.

"It wasn't the first time I'd been confronted by that redneck. A few months before, my daddy had passed. After that, Johnson showed up wanting to buy the low land. Course, it wasn't always low. It had been hill land, a level spot and a gully, when my daddy's granddaddy had bought it. Back then, it was a big thing for a black man to own land in these hills—even if the land was just rocks and bad soil. He worked it. And I guess it worked him too. The way land has of workin' the life out of a man."

Earl stopped talking and stared. He gave the impression that he was seeing memories of things that happened a long time before he was born. I was about to prompt him when he asked me, "You ever hear of the Spanish Mine?"

"It's a legend."

"That's what people say. Now. You ever hear of a Yocum dollar?"

I shook my head.

"That's how great-granddaddy paid for his land. In Yocum silver dollars. They say he had a barrel full of them. They said he found the old mine and coins Yocum had made out of the Spanish silver."

"Those are just old stories. They can't be true."

"True's a thing isn't it? True enough to throw that big rock right into the pond. True enough to make ripples through generations. First, they said great-granddaddy had silver. Then it had to be that all the black folk were keepin' a secret hoard of silver. There wasn't a lot of blacks then.

This part of the country was even less friendly to 'em than most places. But the ones there, around that patch of land, they was doing okay.

"The talk was about the silver and the sneaky *niggers.* Seemed it was thought, *not right,* that black folks had more than their white neighbors. It never could be that they worked harder and longer and wasted less. White people started killing the blacks and working to run 'em off. The Nightriders came. *Bald Knobbers,* they called them, 'cause they had meetings on the clear cut tops of hills.

Blacks who stayed mostly died. Not even in death were they welcome. Great-granddaddy, then granddaddy, gave up plots to family who had no place to rest. All our folks, the Turners and Patees, got buried there. Then they had to bury friends with no place to lie. People kept coming and my family kept burying them.

When my daddy's daddy passed, what prosperity there was for our folks was no longer shinin' so bright. For the white people tellin' the stories, that could only mean that he was buried with his treasure. The land was left to go to seed and the ghosts to go to eternity. No one worked it after my daddy was born.

"That land stayed in my family until Johnson Rath twisted my arm into a lifeless burden. Not only could I not work, I couldn't pay the bills I had. Ol' Johnson thought he was sitting in the catbird seat. I didn't sell. I let it go to taxes in 1983 just to spite him. By then, the lake had made that old spit of dirt into valuable property. Johnson couldn't beat the prices developers were willing to pay. And you can't twist a corporation's arm. So the land was going to become just another flat space to put up cracker box homes. That was the thinkin'—'till it flooded. What was hill land had become bottom land—and everybody was fine with that, so long as no black folks were on it and doing well."

"That's an amazing story."

Earl looked at me as if I had suddenly appeared in his dim living room. "The truth always is."

"I don't understand something, though."

"Only one something? You're doing better than me."

"You said developers were going to build houses on your old land."

"It's no lie."

"How could they? I mean if it was a cemetery?"

"You sound just like the boy. Tyrell asked questions like that. Like he expected the world to make sense and the rules was the rules."

"There are laws—"

Earl laughed. It was a forced cackle, rusty and without mirth. "Laws. Laws work for the pocket book. Don't you see it? *Cemetery* is one of those legal words. That land was just a place where dead people was buried. White folks had cemeteries. Wouldn't a made any difference though. You know how all these big lakes in Missouri and Arkansas were made?"

"They're all man-made. Dams and reservoirs."

"That's right." He nodded like I had gotten a difficult problem correct. "And do you think there were no people and no graves in any of that land they covered with water?"

"They moved everyone. Whole towns. Cemeteries were relocated."

"Cemeteries."

"That's what I said."

Earl nodded again. I couldn't tell if he was agreeing or finding his own difficult answers. "Cemeteries," he said again. "Not graves."

"What's the difference?"

"Laws. It's one of those legal things. They moved the markers. They left the bodies buried. All you need for a cemetery is paper that says it's so. The flip side of that coin is true."

"If it's not a legally-defined cemetery, no one is getting prosecuted for grave robbery."

Earl's cackle sounded like a rusty hinge in the wind. He held up a finger as he laughed then touched the tip of his nose.

* * * *

My windows were down when I finally hit the highway headed home. To my right, the sun was at nadir. A razor edge of red rippled in heat waves. Sunset was a slow motion explosion of light, casting itself on the underside of high clouds. Above them, purple graduated to black: night peeking through a curtain.

Some people say they do their best thinking in the shower. Uncle Orson said there was no problem so big he couldn't solve it with a fishing rod in his hand. For me, it was driving. My mind would split and one part would joyously take hills and curves in hand—the other would work behind a curtain, invisible to my driving mind, and make connections.

The parts coming together for me were all about Earl and Tyrell Turner. I believed everything the older man told me about the past and the turbulent history of his family. When he talked about the present, I was less convinced.

After we talked about the graveyard, I asked about Tyrell. Earl claimed not to know why he was in Taney County—or why he would have been on the old property. When I asked him where his truck was, he claimed it was in the garage. I asked to see it. He asked if I had a warrant. As I drove, I tried to keep my focus off the mental back room. Still, I could almost feel puzzle pieces being picked up and tried against each other. At least I would be home and in my own bed soon.

Once again, I fooled myself about my destination. At least, that time, I was aware of the lie and able to join in on the conspiracy. When the little puzzle room in the back of my head wanted more pieces to play with, I turned off the highway. A half-hour later, I was parked again in the field where Tyrell Turner had been burned.

There was a difference. It was nothing physical. Aside from additional ribbons of barrier tape, the landscape was the same. The difference was exactly like those between photographs of the scene and my drawings. It was all in what I saw. The patch of ground had gained a history, the weight of lives was upon it.

My quiet musings were interrupted by the sound of approaching engines. They were distant, but not for long. In moments, the darkness was filled by the bobbling glare of headlights on rough roads. Loud pipes spit staccato burps as throttles were twisted and released. It was a show—put on for my benefit.

The bikes sidled in, making slow circles.

I reached to make sure my weapon was in the holster and unobstructed. Satisfied that it was, I kept my hand on the grip, ready.

The circle flowed until it eddied into a ragged crescent with all the lights facing me. Engines died. Not in unison.

One of the lights settled sideways as its rider put it onto the stand and got off. I took a step back and pulled at my service weapon. It wasn't a full draw. The pistol was still—technically—within the confines of the holster. It was as ready as it could be without being aimed.

"There ain't no need for that shooter," the shadowy shape said. He stepped forward and resolved into a man. There were still no features. I saw only dark arms and legs and a mane of wild hair behind the glare of headlights. He was one of those men who had been big and kept getting bigger with fast food and hard living. He had thick arms and a round gut.

"Says the man hiding behind five other men with the light in my face." I relaxed slightly but kept my hand on the weapon. If they were here to hurt me, they probably would not have started out by talking.

"You're sure a feisty one, Hurricane."

"Feisty? You've been reading too many cowboy romance books. I'm not feisty. I'm no filly. And if you call me darlin' or sweetheart, I'll shoot you on principal."

"No one's here for gunplay."

"You know me?"

"Who doesn't?" The shadowed man pointed to the gun at my hip. "What you got back there? Nine mil? That's a bitch gun if there ever was one."

"You know what the best gun is?" I reseated my 9mm pistol then took my hand from the grip. I made sure my movements were clear and obvious. The shadow man was definitely dangerous but he was there to talk.

"What's—"

"Anyone that lets you do the job." People don't like being cut off; it puts them off balance. There was no benefit in having this guy too comfortable. "And I guarantee I can do more with nine millimeters than you could manage with a cannon."

He grunted a laugh. It was put on and derisive. For a guy like that, it's the difference between being in charge and acting in charge. "We didn't come to talk about guns."

"You brought it up. You have something else to say, spit it out. You're starting to bore me."

"Is that why they call you Hurricane? Because you won't shut up?"

"I don't know. Why do the women call you a disappointment?"

The other men leaning on their bikes laughed.

The shadow man stepped up alongside the handlebars of his motorcycle. The change brought him up to the edge of the bright arc. Details were still missing. What I could see were his arms. They were bare and coming from under a cut—the denim jacket a lot of bikers wear with the arms and collar sliced off. In this case, I was pretty sure there was an Ozarks Nightriders patch on the back. From what I could see, his arms were thick, muscled, and tattooed. "Knock it off," he ordered. The laughing men fell silent. To me he said, "Okay. You got balls and a smart mouth. You're not afraid. So can we talk?"

"What's your name?"

"Anonymous."

"Then what's there to talk about?"

"We didn't do it."

That got my attention. "Tell me exactly what you didn't do."

"We didn't kill that black kid."

"Who's we?"

"Forget it." The shadow man stepped back like he was going to remount the bike.

"Who did?" I made it a question but made my voice loud and bold, like a command.

He paused. "We don't know."

"But you want me to believe you didn't."

"It's the truth."

"Truth doesn't need to hide behind blinding lights."

"What world do you live in?"

He had me there. Who could deny that neither the truth nor innocence were perfect defenses within the legal system? "Okay. I'm listening."

"I already said it."

"Look. You want to tell me the truth, that's fine. But I need more than, 'We didn't do it.'

"Off the record?"

"I'm not a reporter. I'm a cop. Everything is on the record. If you want to get ahead of this, that's what you want. Show me you want to help. Show me something with a little teeth."

"Don't tell her anything," one of the other shadows said.

"Let's get out of here," added another.

"Go then," I said. "You're wasting a chance."

"Story of my life." The big shadow in the center turned and remounted his bike.

"You know there's no silver out here." It was a swing in the dark, but maybe it connected.

The man remained straddling his bike but didn't bring it upright or start the engine. "What do you know about it?"

"I know it's a story that's nothing more than a legend."

"That's not really our deal," he said, "but I'll pass it on."

"Tell me why at least."

"Why what?"

"You said you didn't kill Tyrell Turner." I felt a twinge of guilt dangling the name like bait, but I needed something.

"I said *we* didn't kill him."

"We? You mean the Nightriders?"

"I didn't say that."

"Okay. Not *the* Nightriders. Are you saying *a* Nightrider killed him?"

"I'm not saying anything more. Figure things out for yourself."

"He was only twenty years old."

"That's old enough, isn't it?"

"Why did he die?"

"He got in somebody's way, I guess. You be careful you don't do the same." The big shadow stood and jerked the bike off the stand then started it with a high rev roar. The other bikes followed, and soon the air was screaming with their sound and billowing with their exhaust. Short of shooting someone, I couldn't do anything but watch as they circled out and disappeared the way they came.

Chapter 8

Surprisingly, my sleep was that of the dead. There were no dreams of other times or violence. No ghosts visited me. Instead it was filled by, or perhaps empty with, the void. There was peace in the infinite absence. There was also a sense of something impending. It was as if my mind knew that awareness of emptiness was in fact denial of it. If the darkness was not empty. . .

Morning came early and hot. I greeted it with decision. Rather than thoughtlessly pulling on the usual formless clothing to hide behind, I carefully dressed in a suit. It was nothing special. It looked good—even if I was saying so. When everything was in place, I checked myself in the mirror. I looked like a woman.

Downstairs, I stopped on my way out to talk to Nelson. The corner near the fireplace was his work space. The floor was still covered by a drop—on which sat his easel with my favorite painting. It was of our boats—separate, but drifting together. We, that is the boats that were us, rode the same water in different light. Impermanence, but forever with meaning.

The painting had been damaged by someone trying to do the same to me. It almost worked. I had it conserved and repaired. After that, I got into the habit of saying something to the image each morning. That morning I said, "Thank you," and went out the door.

My first stop was at the Taneycomo Café—where I was not a stranger. A dozen pairs of eyes shifted my direction when the bell over the door tinkled. The usual response would have been silent nods of greeting, a few raised hands, and—always—one or two calls of Hurricane. There were no happy greetings. Every gaze that turned my way seemed to signal a kind of betrayal. Their cop was a woman, wearing women's clothing.

It was a mixed blessing. Their reevaluation was clear. I wasn't sure the judgement was positive.

Someone in the back, one of the regulars at the big table, called out, "Hurricane blew in."

It seemed as if a spell broke all at once. The waitress told me how good I looked. One of the octogenarians gave a quavering wolf whistle. Another in the little old man crowd said, "Arrest me."

I exhaled for the first time since walking in. All seemed right with the world. I sat at a table, honestly basking in the attention.

Duck walked in. Our jailer was a regular at the early breakfast too. We often crossed paths as I was avoiding sleep and he was avoiding his return to work.

"Hurricane?"

"Don't call me that," I told him. "You can sit down."

"Don't mind if I do." He ordered the artery clogging special, then turned to me. He didn't say anything.

"What? No smart comment? No contribution to your sexual harassment file?"

"Yeah. . . I mean, no. Wait. What?"

"Brilliant conversation, Duck."

"Yeah. Sorry it's just. . ."

"Just?"

"Everyone has a surprise or two in them I guess. I'm sorry. You look nice."

"Don't tell me you're turning into a gentleman in your old age, Duck."

"You're not the only one who's more than a nickname," he said before he grinned broadly.

"I'll drink to that," I said raising my coffee cup. I took a sip then told Duck, "I'm glad I ran into you this morning."

"We run into each other all the time."

"I wanted to ask you about the guys we sent over Sunday."

"You mean old Johnson Rath and Cherry Dando. What about 'em?" He laughed hard and jolly then added, "I tell you, Dando was madder than a scalded cat about your uncle getting hold of him. I don't blame Orson for the attempted ass kicking—or Dando for hiding. That's a comeuppance that's long overdue."

"So you know what all that noise was about?"

"Well hell yeah. I was surprised you didn't—"

I literally saw a thought blooming in Duck's eyes.

"You don't know?" he asked. All of his good mood and laughter seemed to drain with the color from his face.

"Know what?"

"That's not for me to say."

"Duck? What's going on? What are people trying to keep from me?"

His breakfast started arriving, three plates full of eggs and bacon, pancakes, and a side of grits with toast. Duck stared down at the feast then he looked up at me. I couldn't say if the regret in his face was because I was keeping him from eating or for something else.

"Hurricane..." he said not yet even reaching for his utensils. "Katrina..." Definitely about me.

"You reach a certain age..." He took a breath shifting his thoughts. "You live—you live long enough—you come to realize that the past is full of promises we never even knew we made. You see? There are things we know that maybe we wish we didn't."

"Like?"

"Like things that hurt when you hand them over to the owners of the present."

"I never took you for the poetic type, Duck."

"I'm not. But I know the place of an old man isn't to give away secrets that aren't his."

"How bad can it be?" I asked as gently as I could. "If it was so long ago."

"Some things never get to be long ago. You should know that. Some things are always new wounds."

A darkness passed over Duck's eyes. I realized that he was thinking of other things, and not everything was about me. I took a last sip of coffee. It had cooled. When I sat the mug down, I did so carefully. Despite the noise of the café, I was afraid of breaking his reverie. That happened when I scooted back my chair to leave him in peace.

"Did you know I used to ride with those guys?" he asked. "It was different back then. We liked to ride and that was all that mattered. I was a founding member of the Nightriders. Bet you didn't know. We were riders, not bikers. There was no politics no drugs. I bet you didn't know."

"I didn't."

"Most of us served in Nam. Most of us had buddies who were black. Hell, all of us had been with Vietnamese women. The color of your skin wasn't such a big deal out there. Back home... Then there were the guys like Johnson Rath. He was hateful from birth. When he came back from his two hitches in the Navy, he carried a whole new bundle on his shoulders. Maybe it was a different kind of hate. Maybe it was just a new level. For him, skin was everything. And he had a plan—a plan that wasn't about riding. It was about race and war. Militias and guns cost money. So it got to be about that too."

"So what was it that made you leave? The racism or the war?"

He shook his head. The movement was slight and seemed difficult, as if his thoughts had turned to heavy stone. "I didn't leave. They put me out like a flea-ridden dog. My own friends. Buddies I had known for years. I'm a race traitor. Bet you didn't know that either. Bet you couldn't imagine."

Duck put a fat finger to his eyes. He was hiding them more than wiping them. I stood to leave. He was a man who needed a bit of privacy.

Before I could excuse myself, he said—from behind still covered eyes—"Cherry Dando is a bastard. We were friends once. Don't hold that against me."

I didn't know what to say. That didn't matter, it turned out. I said, "I promise," by reflex and because I felt sorry for him.

Duck took his fingers from his face and grabbed up his silverware without looking at me. "The paperwork should be in from the bondsman. I'll be opening the door for Dando and Johnson after I finish up my breakfast."

He should have been clearer with his suggestion. I went straight over to the jail intending to have a talk with both Johnson Rath and Cherry Dando. The overnight jailer wouldn't give me access. The sheriff had left explicit orders that I could not interrogate or even chat with either man. When Duck showed up, still brushing at his face with a wadded napkin, he said he only intended that I could see them outside, away from his responsibility or control.

So I went outside to wait, and watch, from my truck. In less than a minute, Earl Turner's black truck pulled slowly to a curb. If a vehicle could move suspiciously, this one was managing it. The Chevy stopped, but didn't park. I could see the woman inside craning her neck to see the jail's entrance. After a moment, she eased the truck forward for a better view, but kept the engine idling. If we were sitting in front of a bank rather than a jail, I would have thought she was positioning for a quick getaway.

When I was sure her attention was on the jail, I stepped out of my truck—carefully opening and closing the door to create as little noise or eye-catching motion as possible. The fact that I was not wearing boots helped. My sensible shoes made no sound as I closed the distance between our two trucks. It occurred to me that everything I was wearing served as an aid to stealth. Anyone familiar with me would never expect me to sneak up on them wearing a medium-blue, silk blend suit.

I was able to stalk right up to the passenger side of the black Chevy without the woman inside ever taking her eyes off the jail door. I stopped and watched her through the open window. She was angular and hard. There was a shape that remained behind the edges. Her body made me think of a beauty queen who had been whittled down to heartwood. She wore a ball cap with her hair tucked up under it. I could only see her face in profile. It was like an antique cameo carved from shell. Perfect lines drew my gaze and I wondered what color her eyes were. The longer I looked, the more I became aware that the sense of beauty was coming from a face that should have graced the black and white movies from the thirties—old Hollywood.

She stared across the lot, watching the jail door. Her movements were quick but controlled, confident. But something had her nervous. She glanced forward a couple of times—without looking far enough to her right to catch me. I had the sudden thought that she may not be watching for Dando and Rath. She could be keeping an eye out for me.

I opened my mouth to speak. It was a failed effort. There were no words poised on my tongue. When I first walked up, I could have announced myself. It would have been the easiest thing in the world to pin her with a command—easy until I got a good look at her. I was becoming certain that I knew her in some way.

The jail door opened—breaking the connections my mind was trying to make. Johnson came through first. He was pointing a finger at Cherry Dando and making a hard point. I could hear his voice but not the words. It was a snarl of sound without definition. The meaning was clear though. Johnson Rath was angry and near violence.

Dando didn't exactly stand up to the bigger man. He didn't back down either. He walked a step behind Johnson, keeping his hands open and spread. The further they got from the jail door, the more he fell behind. "It wasn't my fault," he said in answer to Johnson's growling. "And you need to understand—"

"I don't need to understand shit." Johnson barked the statement out loud and clear as he spun on his heel.

Dando jumped back. It wasn't quick or far enough to evade the grabbing hands that came at him. "Don't you do it!" His voice was tinged with panic.

I bolted around the front of the Chevy at the same time the woman in the cab pushed through the door.

Johnson raised his hand. It was balled into an incomplete fist, with his splinted index finger awkwardly pointed at the sky. Even like that, his arm was like a loaded cannon aimed right at Cherry Dando's head. "Whose fault is it now?" Johnson bellowed. With his left hand gripping the front of

Dando's shirt, he shook the smaller man as easily as a dog shakes a rabbit. He yelled again, but the words were buried in the rage.

I cleared the front of the truck, pulling my weapon. Before I could issue a command, the woman from the truck raised a pistol. The revolver was much too big for her. Her hands shook with the weight and the adrenaline. Even at thirty feet, there was little chance she could hit what she wanted. It didn't matter. If she fired, there was a chance rounds from that big .357 could go through a wall and kill someone on the other side.

I shifted my trajectory as she shouted at the fighting. I don't think they ever heard her. Running hard, I put my left hand out and my right shoulder down. At the same time, I grabbed her hands, forced them up, and I hit her sideways. The revolver came away and she sprawled.

With her disarmed, I was able to give my attention to the men. Cherry Dando was bloody. His head was lolling as Johnson shook him and cocked his fist for another hit. He struck not with his knuckles, but with the back of the hand. Then he raised it again, pummeling down like a hammer, protecting the broken finger.

Even limp and gushing blood from a broken nose Dando was still grinning. He saw me coming.

"Let him go," I shouted at Johnson. "Let him go and step away."

I know he heard. There was a catch in the motion of Johnson's next punch. His head canted slightly in my direction. It was enough for me to read it as both an insult and a dare. He was telling me he had no concern for me.

I didn't wait for another impact to Dando's face and I didn't shout either. Honestly, I thought about shooting him—but I wanted to make a real point. Rushing in, I went behind him. With a long stride I planted my leading left foot and kicked with my right. I missed the steel toes in my boots.

The kick landed hard in the crook behind Johnson's right knee. It gave way instantly—bucking forward like a dead fish. As he fell, I caught the look of surprise on the big man's face. It was like a gift. I got greedy for more. He hit, flat on his back, woofing out his air. My foot was already back in the air. Before he could catch the escaped breath or make any kind motion to evade me, I brought my heel down on the front of the same knee I'd kicked.

His scream was surprisingly high and satisfying. I pointed my weapon at his chest then, just for good measure, and asked him, "Are you going to cry now, princess?"

Fighting to find breath, Johnson said, "Huk—hue."

I knew what he meant. Keeping my aim, I reached for my cuffs. That was when I noticed that I was still holding the woman's revolver in my left hand. Without taking my eyes off the man on the ground, I turned the .357 around one-handed and gripped the cylinder pin. One quick jerk and the weapon opened—spilling cartridges. When the last one hit, I dropped the revolver and kicked it away.

"Katrina?" It was the woman asking. There was shock in her voice—as if she was asking my name and not believing what she already knew.

I looked, but she seemed fine. Then I turned to Dando. "Are you okay?" I asked, knowing it was a stupid question. He grinned, showing bloody teeth, but not at me. His smile was for the woman.

"Katrina?" she asked again. That time the question in my name had more of an edge to it. An expectation.

It was Dando who answered—in more ways than one. "Carmen," he called. "Let it be and come help me."

"Carmen?" That time I was the one using a name as a question. "He called you Carmen."

The woman nodded and smiled at me. More expectation. Finally she said, "It's me. It's Mama."

Cherry Dando pulled himself up onto an elbow and laughed that awful cackle. It turned wet. He spit out a wad of clotted blood, then said, "I told you. Hee yeah, I told you. I knew you. It's old home week again."

"Stop it, Cherry," the woman who claimed to be my mother said. Her voice had a gentle, suffering quality that I had never heard.

"I don't believe you," I said. In my own ears it sounded wishful.

Johnson Rath, still lying on the parking lot clutching his knee, started laughing. "Stupid bitch."

I kicked him in the ribs.

He grunted. Hard. I relished the sound—until a siren sounded from behind me. Right after the sound came the lights. I glanced back. It was Sheriff Benson. Right behind his SUV came a black sedan with government plates. DEA Agent Devon Birch stared indictments at me as he parked.

Before either of them got out of their vehicles, two deputies came out of the jail door with weapons drawn. "Johnson Rath, you're under arrest for assault, failure to comply, resisting arrest, and anything else I can come up with."

"Good luck with that," he said. "My ticket's here."

To the nearest deputy, I said, "Cuff that one," indicating Johnson. To the other I called, "Request an ambulance for Mr. Dando."

Dando cackled again. And again it turned phlegmy causing him to hack out a wad of blood. "I don't need no ambulance. And I won't be preferring any charges."

"Your nose looks broken."

"There goes my cover-girl career." He lifted a hand to the woman. "Help me up."

Instead of reaching for him she put a hand out toward me. "Katrina."

I was getting sick of hearing my name come from her mouth. I ignored her gesture, turning away and holstering my weapon. Sheriff Benson and Agent Birch were approaching in lock step.

"Dammit Katrina," the sheriff said.

"Good job." Birch added. There wasn't any joking in his sarcasm.

I ignored Birch. "Is it true?" I asked the sheriff.

He leaned his head to look beyond my shoulder. I was pretty sure he was watching Carmen assist Dando to his feet.

Sheriff Benson nodded. It looked like it pained him to do so. "Yep."

"What are we talking about?" Birch asked.

"This is how I find out?" My gaze stayed fixed on the sheriff.

"I thought it would be best if Orson talked things over with you."

"Orson was hoping it would all go away. That she would go away."

"We all were. Given a little time she would have."

"Well we're all out of damned time now aren't we?" I turned to head back for a confrontation with the woman who had left me outside Uncle Orson's dock when I was six.

"Katrina, wait." Sheriff Benson's voice was soft and regretful.

"Stop right there, Detective." Birch's voice was firm.

I turned to face him.

"We have a lot to talk about."

"Talk with the sheriff."

"I'll talk with you—if I have to put you in cuffs to do it."

"Who the hell—"

"Hurricane." That time the sheriff was loud and certain. It was a boss's voice, not a friend's. Then he smiled. Everything about him relaxed. "You look nice," he complimented gently. "It's good to see."

If there is one person I can count on to douse my burning fuse, it's the sheriff. And honestly I appreciated it—both being told I looked nice and being pulled back from another round of rage. Even I can spend only so much time angry.

"We need to talk," he told me. "And we need to do it before you go talk to your mother again."

"What's she done?" I looked over my shoulder, then over at Earl Turner's Chevy. "Never mind. I can start building a list on my own. Give me a second."

Rather than going to talk to Carmen and Cherry, I crossed at an angle over to the black truck. The door was still open. I reached in and pulled the keys from the ignition. Then I came back to where the sheriff and Birch were watching me.

"The truck belongs to Earl Turner." I held up the keys. "He wouldn't let me verify it was missing. I'm thinking Tyrell took it without permission. I'm also thinking he was driving it the night he was killed."

Sheriff Benson looked over at Dando and Carmen. They were staring back. They didn't look happy. "How'd they get it?"

"That's a question I need to be over there asking." I answered. "That truck is the one that tried to block me on the highway when I was following Tyrell's body."

"Duncan," Sheriff Benson called over to the second deputy. "Take Mrs. Dando into custody."

"Dando?" My exclamation was loud enough both Carmen and Dando looked my direction. He cackled that choking rooster laugh again. "She married that ass?"

* * * *

Sheriff Benson put his summer straw hat on his desk, crown-down, then dropped into his chair. Agent Birch stood ramrod straight. You can always tell ex-Marines. He gestured at one of the chairs for me to sit before he would be seated. It's the clothes I told myself.

"Sit down, both of you," the sheriff said—kicking back in his creaky chair. If he was alone with me or a handful of other detectives and deputies, he would have put his boots up on the desk. With a fed in attendance, Sheriff Benson was on his best behavior. "Now what we got here is a grade-A cluster-fuck." Best behavior is relative, I reminded myself.

"What are you talking about?" I asked.

"It's your pig in the poke," he said to Birch. "You tell her."

"Tell me what?"

"Well I'm not going to tell you to keep your hands off a federal investigation. We all know how well that works." Birch spoke to me, but he looked at the sheriff.

"Someone has to clean up the messes you make." I looked right at Birch.

"Stop it." Sheriff Benson jumped in. "Just stop." He looked at both of us. Then he said to Birch, "Give us the story."

"Johnson Rath is a federal witness and confidential informant," Agent Birch said.

"I don't believe it." My reaction was probably as much to his bald statement as much to the information.

"Believe it or not, that's the situation and all that matters."

"You think that's all that matters?"

"Hurricane," the sheriff cautioned.

I didn't listen. "What about the dead kid? Does he matter?"

"Conduct your investigation, but you share everything with me. And you have no contact with Rath unless I'm in on it."

"No."

"*Hurricane*," the sheriff said again, coloring the word with meaning. "Katrina."

"None of this is a request, Detective." Birch was looking at me then, hard and square. He kept his voice level but he was close enough that I could see the slight flaring of his nostrils.

"You keep a pretty tight rein on yourself," I told him. "But you don't have one on me."

"If you want to keep your job. . ."

My laugh surprised him. "There are so many ways that's not a threat that I can't even explain it."

His mouth twitched and I noticed the gray hairs in his mustache. "Maybe jail time is a threat."

"For what?"

"For meddling in a federal investigation—one in which you have a family interest."

"That's not—"

"Not what? Not true? Or not fair—because you're going to say you didn't know she was your mommy?"

I stood. I was about a half-second away from reaching out to rip that hair off his lip when the sheriff jumped to his feet. His hat fell to the floor, landing brim down, spilling out all the luck.

"No one—and I goddamned mean no one—is going to make another threat, accusation, smart comment, or even so much as a fucking harsh word." The sound of the sheriff's words matched the fire in his eyes. "We're going to be quick. We're going to be professional. And we're going find that boy's killer." He turned and pointed a gnarled finger at Birch. "Make no mistake. At this time—in this case—that boy is the priority of this department." Then he pointed the finger at me. "You—sit down. Keep it civil or I'll be the one making changes to your career path. You're not indispensable around here. Get me?"

"I've got you, Sheriff."

"Whatever." Birch was mocking me.

It was the sheriff who answered. "Shut up." He held the other man's gaze until Agent Birch looked away. "Now tell it. And do so with respect." He retrieved his hat and slapped it on the desk.

Birch took a deep breath, then put up his hands. I thought he was going to say something stupid. He said, "You're right." Turning to me he added, "I'm sorry."

That pissed me off almost as much as anything else. I wanted to stay mad at him. I wanted to hate him and make it his fault. It would be hard to do if he suddenly started acting like a human being.

"This whole thing has me on edge and I'm ready to take it out on anyone."

"I know the feeling," I said.

"Johnson Rath was asked by some other Aryan brothers to reform his militia slash old-time religion. This time around, none of the players are even pretending that The New American Covenant–The Word and The Sword is about anything but moving meth and making money for the cause—the cause being lining the pockets of some very bad assholes."

"It's not a racist organization?" I asked.

"Oh hell yeah. It's as racist as the Klan at a Saturday night cross burning. They talk hate. They spread hate. And they do it all under the banners of freedom of speech and freedom of religion. But it's all a coat of paint over the drug dealing."

"I guess it's a big network or you wouldn't be so worked up."

"The AB got their start moving junk in prisons. That's a big network all by itself. But they've been spreading out, taking on the white trash, trailer park market."

"Why here?"

"Really?" He twitched his mustache and looked a little like he had a bad taste in his mouth. "You have to ask?"

"This is my home, Agent Birch."

"Maybe so, but half the local economy is built on the hillbilly mystique."

"You can't argue with that," the sheriff chimed in.

"What's the real reason?" I asked.

"Highways." Birch sounded exhausted saying it. "I-44 runs north of here up to St. Louis. From there you can go east or west. South of here, you have I-40. That covers the whole south. The cheap product comes out of Mexico and hits the highways. The other reason is that the Ozarks have been open territory for a long time. The Ozarks sit right between the Mexicans and the Dixie Mafia. The AB has a long standing alliance with La eMe and—well the Dixie boys are kind of kindred spirits."

"Okay," I said, thinking it through. "Maybe you have something on your shoulders we don't. But why Johnson Rath?"

"And how?" the sheriff asked.

"Rath is a true believer. He wants the race war and expects the apocalypse to come any time. In his thinking, it will cleanse the world of people like me. And he can't wait for it to happen."

"It doesn't sound like the basis of a good working relationship."

He smiled, shaking his head. I think for the first time both of us relaxed. "It doesn't. But it's the only one I have." To the sheriff, he said, "And to answer your question, he thinks he's a lot smarter than he is."

"Shit." Sheriff Benson leaned farther back in his chair. "I could have told you that."

"Sure. But who knew he was dumb enough to come to us?"

"He volunteered to be a CI?" I asked.

"Rath did a dime upstate in Crossroads. Hard time with the AB opened his eyes. Money is the only religion they bow to. He saw them dealing with, and to, people of all kinds of colors. All the master race BS about purity and God's destiny tarnished pretty quickly—at least as far as the brotherhood went. Rath still thinks he's something special. That's why he took their money and came to us. He believes he's smart enough to work both sides and come out all polished, silver armor again."

Chapter 9

I came to realize that Sheriff Benson liked and trusted Agent Devon Birch. The sheriff is not a complicated man. He's honest, he's often vulgar—but never misogynistic, and he understands nuance in social situations. When he kicked back a little more in his big leather chair and put his feet up on the desk, it was like he was with family.

Personally, I have a history with the feds that isn't so easily overlooked. I was reserving judgement. "So God's gift to the white race thinks he can use Aryan Brotherhood money to fund his new Caucasian utopia on the banks of Bull Shoals—and betray them to you."

Birch nodded like he knew what was coming.

"Why wouldn't he murder Tyrell Turner if the kid got in his way?" I finished.

The nod transitioned to a head shake. "I don't think any kind of violence is out of reach for Johnson. My issue is with the timing."

"What timing?"

"You don't know when the boy was murdered. Given the condition of the body, we may never know. But we know for certain that the fire to eliminate evidence was set early Sunday morning."

"Okay."

"Johnson Rath was with me from midnight until three that morning. He was in Springfield, at the federal building, briefing me."

"Nothing is ever easy."

"Sure it is," Sheriff Benson said. His hat was hanging off the toe of his boot. "We just never notice the easy things."

"You have a hat rack, you know." I pointed over my shoulder at the pole in the corner. "There's no telling what's on your feet."

"Fertilizer is good for the hair. Keeps it from getting too thin."
Birch chuckled.

I said, "I don't know what you're laughing about. You could use a little fertilizer up top."

"Maybe," he smoothed back his tight crop. "But cowboy hats and cow flop aren't my style."

"You have a style?"

"Speaking of style. . ." Sheriff Benson didn't finish the question, but I knew the target he was aiming at.

"I'm just trying something different. Is that okay with you?"

"It's fine with me. He bobbed the hat on his toe. "It's about time, I say."

I couldn't let that pass, and the conversation kept going for a while. Birch turned out not to have as thick a chip on his shoulder as I had thought. He was smart, and friendly, and—I came to realize—forbearing. The two men were allowing me to avoid asking the questions they knew I had to. There was a kindness to the talk that carried me to a natural pause. With a deep, long breath I asked, "What about my mother and Cherry Dando?"

Birch looked at the hat hanging off the sheriff's boot. The sheriff looked at me. His gaze was something that asked more of me than the bald question I had put out there. I knew what he wanted. Reaction. Hope or hate. I didn't have either to give. Calling Carmen my mother, especially in the same breath as the name Cherry Dando left me hollowed. She had abandoned me. The hole she left grew up with me until the barren space was impossible to fill with honesty. Every feeling that sneaked in seemed like a lie.

It was my friend and boss who broke the silence that followed. "Which one of us are you asking?"

It wasn't a casual question. The sheriff understood that—pointed at him—the query was filled with history and family. Asked of Devon Birch, agent of the DEA, it was a question of law, suspicion, evidence, and motive.

I hesitated. Then, just for the smallest slice of time, I felt the same roil of fear, confusion, and loss that I experienced watching my mother drive away from me in a car loaded with all the things of her life. All the things but me. I understood then that I was wrong about the hole she left in me. There was one thing that fit it perfectly and honestly. Anger.

My gaze remained on the sheriff for a beat before I turned to Birch. "Are they on your radar?"

"They have been." His answer came quick and ready. "Cherry Dando has a long association with Johnson Rath. He was involved with the Ozark Nightriders in the eighties. He's more of an opportunist than a racist.

According to Johnson, it was Dando's idea to buy that piece of land. They've been arguing about it since."

"Arguing?" The sheriff asked.

"It's not very good land for building churches, or compounds, or much of anything. It's prone to flooding any time the lake rises."

"Did they know about the graves that are there?" I asked.

Birch looked at me and paused a second before saying, "I think they all knew."

"Meaning that Dando knew. And that Carmen knew."

"Your mother seems to have known. Johnson says Cherry and Carmen are looking for something."

"Silver."

"Silver?" Birch sounded confused. "You mean like silver, silver? A mine?"

I explained about my conversations with Earl Turner, and the story behind the land that Johnson Rath had purchased with AB money.

"You're saying they believe those old stories about Yocum silver dollars and are willing to grave rob to get it?" The sheriff didn't even try to keep the disgust out of his voice.

"Wait," Birch held up a hand. "What's a Yocum silver dollar?"

"That's an Ozarks story. Most of it's legend." The sheriff held up two fingers an inch apart. "About this much is true." He spread his hands as if he was showing off a trophy fish. "About this much is wishful thinking."

Birch looked lost.

"There was a family up in Stone County. Some of the first white settlers. They made their own coins for trading." Sheriff Benson explained. "No one knows exactly where the silver came from, but there are still people who believe it came from a lost silver mine started by the Spanish Conquistadors. If it's out there, it's covered by Table Rock Lake now. That doesn't keep people from looking."

"There really were Yocum dollars?" Birch asked.

"I've never seen one," the sheriff answered. "But I've known many people who claimed they have."

"What's it got to do with Tyrell's murder?" I asked. "And how do we stop them from building a racist, militia compound on that graveyard?"

Sheriff Benson reached for his hat and plucked it from his toe before putting his feet on the floor. "It's not going to be as easy as I thought. I called the county historical society and the state Historic Preservation Office."

"And?" I prodded.

He fiddled with his hat. "These things take time."

I thought about that and nodded. "Maybe."

"Maybe what?"

"People keep telling me I'm a woman with options. I just realized that there's another way of looking at it."

"What's that?"

"I'm a woman with resources."

I excused myself and went right to the phone on my desk.

As soon as I lifted the handset, I heard a footstep behind me. The sound set me on edge. Every nerve in my body tingled. When the next sound came, the liquid slosh of ice and soda in a thermal soda cup, the anxiety collapsed. When I turned, it was with a smile I couldn't control. Not that I tried.

"Detective Blevins," I said. "You don't have anything better to do than sneak up on me?"

Billy grinned. The straw remained locked in even white teeth until he said, "Nope." He looked with a brown-eyed gaze. "Nothing better to do. Nothing I'd rather do."

"Careful." I inched closer. "People will talk."

"People talk." He shrugged and set the big cup on my desk. "People always talk. And they are already talking."

"You're not bothered by what they say?"

"What do they say?"

"I don't know. I guess I'm asking."

"What makes you think I would know?" He came a little more toward me. Everything between us was in diminishing measurements. I liked the physical proximity. I was still a little fearful of the other kind. "Because you're everyone's friend."

Billy started to shake his head.

"No." I stopped him. "You know it's true. Everyone loves you. No one calls a grown man Billy unless they like him. Especially a sheriff's detective."

"I've always been Billy."

"That's because you're the favorite brother for the whole county. I'm the Hurricane, who blew in and shook things up. Riley Yates told me, more than once, that I was a loose cannon."

"And he told you that the sheriff's department needed one of those to keep people on their toes."

I had a lot to say about that. And I was opening my mouth to do it when Billy stepped even closer. My breath caught. The words disappeared from my throat. His chest pressed against mine. He knew what he was doing. The smile on his face made no secret of the meaning behind his encroachment.

"I need to make a call." It was a foolish and feeble excuse. I wondered for an instant why I'd said it. Then I wondered why I thought I needed an excuse. "I asked your uncle to call Whilomina," Billy said. "He did it this morning."

Congresswoman Whilomina Tindall was the resource I had been thinking of. She and my father had a relationship. They were going to be married before he was killed. "What did she say?"

Billy smiled again.

His expression made me painfully aware of his body pressed to mine. I wished I wasn't so tall. It's a silly thing—a small thing—sometimes I read the kind of novels about women who find romance where—and when—it is least expected. In those books, the main character is always shorter than her lover. She tilts up her head, or even gets up on her toes, to kiss her man.

I was only a shade less than six feet tall. I wasn't wearing boots, so I was shorter than Billy—not by much, but enough that my gaze was turned upward at that moment.

"She said she would help. The graves would get federal protection—at least for a while."

"How?" That was a mind question, not a heart question. My heart was thinking of other things entirely.

"She didn't say. Only that it would be taken care of."

"Okay."

"Let's get out of here."

That was a surprise. I eased back to ask, "Where?"

Billy followed me keeping his chest against mine. "Some place special."

"I have a lot to do."

"There's always a lot to do."

"But. . ."

Billy interrupted me—but not with words. He put his face against mine, cheek to cheek. His nose touched my ear. Warm breath crawled down, under my collar. "You look wonderful," he whispered. "But I think you look pretty amazing in the worst jeans. Or bare skin."

I swear to God, I blushed. I didn't pull away because I didn't want him to see my eyes turned to the floor in shame. It was wonderful that he would say that, but I had so many scars.

"Stop it," he said quiet but firm.

"What?"

"Stop thinking. Stop worrying." He took me by the hand and pulled me along. For the first time in my life, I let a man simply take me along without questioning or fighting.

* * * *

Billy stopped his truck and killed the engine. I'd had no expectations when we started driving. It was a good thing—where we ended up would have been impossible to anticipate.

I climbed down and stepped from the gravel road into manicured grass. Ahead of me were ordered rows of marble headstones. In the distance—it was impossible not to look—was the grave of my husband, Nelson Solomon.

"Why are we here?"

"For a picnic," Billy answered. He grabbed a paper bag and a cooler from the bed of his truck.

"A picnic?"

"And talk. And..."

"And?"

"And I'm going to kiss you." Billy walked past me and canted his head in the direction of a huge spreading oak—no more than thirty feet from Nelson's grave. "Come on."

I followed. Slowly.

Talking over his shoulder to me as he walked for the shade of the tree, Billy told me, "And I'm going to do it like I mean it. Like I don't care what people see or think."

"Here?"

He stopped and turned to face me. "I won't have any secrets from your dead husband." Billy turned and walked again. "Apparently, he won't have any from me either."

"What's that mean?" I asked. Billy was already at the tree and setting his bag down. I hurried to catch up and asked again, "What do you mean, he won't have secrets from you?"

"Sit." Billy emptied the bags, set out a blanket, and laid a box of fried chicken on top. He added a tub of potato salad and a tin of rolls. Opening up the cooler, he held out a carafe. "Iced tea. No soda." He sat.

I turned to look at Nelson's grave. It was facing me as if the carved name and dates were eyes with questions.

"I don't understand this."

"Sit down and I'll share it all."

I kept looking at the headstone.

"He won't mind. I promise."

That made me laugh—and laughing broke some kind of lock that I didn't even know was holding my heart. "I know he won't." When I turned away from the grave to look at Billy I was smiling. I felt good. Better than I thought was right—but I wasn't fighting it anymore. "How do you know?"

Again, Billy gestured to the ground for me to sit. As I did, he pulled a card from his back pocket. "That lawyer friend of yours, Daggett. He brought this to me." What he held up was a postcard of one of Nelson's paintings. It was one of the many licensing issues that was left to me when my husband died.

"Why?" It was impossible to keep the suspicious edge out of the question.

"This." He turned the back side of the card to me and handed it over.

The card was dated less than two weeks before Nelson's death, written in his handwriting. Under the date was a note:

Billy Blevins,
When the time comes—
Care for her, with my blessing.
I think she needs us both.
Nelson Solomon.

When I looked up from the card, my eyes were swimming with tears. Billy was chewing a chicken leg. "How can you eat?" I asked him.

He winked, then swallowed his bite before smiling at me. It was pretty much a perfect smile. And I had the feeling he thought so too.

"What?" I couldn't help it. With my eyes still wet with tears, I smiled back.

"The way I see it, there was only one thing keeping you from falling for me."

"Falling?"

He leaned across the blanket. "Head. Over. Heels."

"You sound pretty sure of yourself for a man named Billy."

He shook his head letting the smile die. "No. But I'm sure of you."

We didn't eat much of that picnic. We did talk a little more and we flirted a lot more. It was a wonderful and weirdly normal time. He kissed me. I kissed him. And everything seemed good in that little corner of the world. In the end Billy cleaned up while I went to Nelson's grave.

"Thank you," I said, refusing to feel foolish about it.

When I reached the truck it was repacked and Billy was leaning on the bed with his back to me. "There's something else," he said without turning to look at me.

"About Nelson?"

Billy shook his head slowly. He still kept his elbows on the truck and his face directed away from me. "About me." He spread his hands open. "Us. Maybe. I guess. If you want it to be."

"Billy," I spoke as carefully as if my teeth were broken glass my tongue needed to tip-toe over. "You're not asking me to. . ."

He laughed again, sounding like a man having a lot of fun. "Nope. Not that. Not here."

I was relieved that it wasn't a proposal. I was also a little put off that he seemed to think it was so funny. "Just say it then."

"A bit ago you talked about how people call me Billy and how I'm everyone's friend." He turned to face me then, but kept leaning on the truck. It made me wonder if he needed something to prop him up.

"I remember."

"You're not really the 'friends' kind of woman." It was a simple statement, without judgement. We'd had the conversation before. "I'm not saying you're not friendly—only that you don't put yourself out there or invite anyone in."

"That's a way to say it." I leaned on the truck too. "I've heard selfish, standoffish, closed off, and my favorite, ice bitch."

"I don't want to make anything harder on you."

"How?"

"The sheriff talked to me again about retiring. About me running for the job."

"Oh." I pushed off the hot metal of the truck bed and stepped back into the grass looking at the green under my feet. The cemetery was one of the few places not burning up in the drought. "That's your choice." I kept looking at the green, moving the thick grass with my toe. "And I'll be your biggest supporter."

"Don't do that."

"What?"

"Don't dismiss it—and don't accept it thoughtlessly. Don't act like you don't know what I'm saying."

"Well, what are you saying?"

"I'm saying my choices affect you. At least I want them to, and you know I do. I want an honest reaction and an honest opinion."

"I don't know how to react." That felt like a lie in my mouth. Reactions come no matter how you think they should. The truth was that I stifled my impulse to say nothing—or to pretend. Honesty was the wrong thing. I knew that. Still. . . I looked up to meet his eyes. "The sheriff asked me what I thought about it when he first considered retiring."

"And?"

"Things are changing around here." I held back, hoping he would take the hint and let me off the hook.

"I don't know what that means. What things?"

"Everything. The county. The people."

"You don't think I can be sheriff?"

At that moment I could have changed everything. I could have explained. I could have said what he needed to hear. Instead I saw a hair and I split it. "I think you would win the election in a walk."

"But?"

There it was. He was asking for the real truth, and I had the feeling of a bluff being called. "Being sheriff—this place—this time—is kind of a hard ass job."

"You don't think I'm a hard enough man."

"I'm not sure you're willing to do some of the hard things." I knew what I was saying and doing—and I did it anyway. There must be a word for the kind of fool I am. Maybe I just need a fight sometimes.

I didn't get it.

He nodded and stopped leaning to walk around to the driver's side door. The engine was running and the truck in gear before I was in my seat. Despite the heat, it was a chilly ride.

* * * *

Most people would be dismayed to see how much of a cop's life is spent at a desk. After the highs and lows of the last couple of days, I was sitting at mine—staring at the pile of work. Staring wasn't getting any of it done.

I was burrowing into my own mind and obsessing about all the ways I was my own worst enemy. Dr. Kurtz said such thoughts were probably healthy, at least in my case, because of my tendency to lash out and blame others for the choices they made. I didn't buy it. The people I lashed out at were not the cream of society, and I don't feel very conflicted—thinking of them as deserving the trouble I bring into their life.

This was different.

Since the Sunday morning discovery of Tyrell Turner's body, I had been in a turmoil of blame and anger and fear that left me circling the drain for most of Monday. It was Tuesday afternoon, and I was all but paralyzed by self-doubt and guilt.

The doubt was no stranger, but guilt. . .

What did I have to feel guilty about?

It was a self-serving and defensive question. I felt terrible about what I had said to Billy. Feeling and thinking led me to a worrying fear that, in retrospect, should have been obvious. The latest cycle of anger and tears may have begun Sunday morning at the murder scene, but its roots were planted the night before—when I slipped into Billy's bed and dared to think my life was normal. I'd thought also that love without rage and resentment was possible.

I had married Nelson after only days of knowing him. It was like love in a panic. And no matter how much I told myself that it didn't matter, he and I each knew his life expectancy boosted us over walls we might otherwise have never dared climb.

The dictum, Know Thyself, is wise and terrifying advice. I did everything I could to ignore it. Literally, I shook the thoughts from my tired brain. When that didn't help, I looked back at the pile on my desk. There's another dictum, this one my own—hard work is good forgetting.

I started with phone calls. Paperwork was too easy to skate over. Besides, the stack of case logs and incident reports was daunting. That's the thing about a cop's life—it's all written down and filed away. It helps to keep things on the up—and it's always necessary in court—but it's terrifyingly dull.

My first call was to our impound lot—to make sure that Turner's truck was secured. Then I contacted our evidence tech and confirmed the old Chevy was on his list. That was the easy stuff. The hard things felt like two ends of the same, tangled string. Earl Turner and Johnson Rath. Along the twisting path were hard little knots—Tyrell, his mother Elaine, Cherry Dando, and the Ozarks Nightriders.

I'm not deluded enough not to realize that I was ignoring my own mother. I was painfully aware that I had kept her behind a mental gate since discovering she was part of the mess. Being aware of the problems in my life has never been the issue.

I called Earl Turner. We needed to have a harder talk about the truck. He was hiding something about it, or Tyrell, or both. No answer. No voice mail. Just a ringing phone. I moved on.

Part of the paperwork sitting on my desk were the CDRs that I had requested. I started with Tyrell's phone. Right at the top of the page was the first surprise. It was still active. Earl Turner had called his grandson at least once an hour—sometimes more often—that Saturday and into Sunday morning.

A quick check on Earl's record told me that he'd stopped trying after he received a call from the sheriff. Another cross check told me that Tyrell had been in frequent contact with Dando for the past couple of weeks. That, combined with the bone raking and his history with an avowed, violent, racist like Johnson Rath, put Dando at the top of the list. Suspicion doesn't equal conviction though. There would be a lot of work to do.

Since I started with Turner, I decided to stick with the theme. It was the last thing I wanted to read, but I needed to see the case work on Elaine Turner's assault. The report was too old to be on our computer system. Our department had no digital case logging until 2001. I spent an hour digging into old file cabinets before I gave up. The report was missing or never existed.

It was time to move from files to people. I decided to dig into the middle of the string. I called a woman I knew who thought it would be exciting and glamorous to be a part of the biker life. Twenty years later, she was still unable to completely untangle her life from the Nightriders. She led me to some new names—most were familiar, some new. First, I followed up with the ones I knew.

It's an awkward call anytime a cop reaches out to someone she's arrested. It's worse when the contact is a walking soup of testosterone and ignorance—who makes up your average one-percenter. At least the modern world was working in my favor. These days, even bikers had cell phones. A few years ago, you had to physically track them to whichever flop they called home.

Between the personal insults and obscenities, a pattern began to show itself. The motorcycle club was an organization in flux. Before, it was always local boys content to deal local. A couple of years ago, they tried expanding into meth production and we had come down pretty hard on them. The group that rose back up was a mix of the hardcore old schoolers and the new blood. What they all had in common were ties to the AB.

There was no point in cold calling bikers who didn't know me and whom I had nothing on. I dug into the new names electronically. In twenty minutes I had jackets on half a dozen guys and found a nugget. There was a *known associates* notation on one of the new guys that sounded too familiar. The name was Roland Duques. I didn't even know that Duck had a son.

Secrets. Hidden guilt. Relationships. Sometimes thoughts are like tumblers in a lock—they fall into that empty space your mind leaves for connections. It's always a revelation and a surprise to find your mind works unsupervised. Earl and Tyrell were carrying the burden of family secrets, Elaine, and her suicide. Duck was hiding, or at least trying to ignore, his son's involvement with the Nightriders and possible involvement in Tyrell's killing. I was hiding behind my desk hoping my mother, and the secrets she carried, would simply disappear with the hot winds of summer.

That little bit of knowing myself left me feeling like something between criminal and victim. Stuck in the middle with no solid balance. So I jumped. I called Uncle Orson. When he answered I said, "We need to talk." That's all. I disconnected before he could say anything. I chose to hear acceptance in his lack of a return call.

Two minutes later I was logged out and on my way to the residence of Roland Duques.

* * * *

Duck's son, Roland, lived in a rented single-wide—in the kind of trailer park that gave and demanded little. Lawns were ragged and untended. Children loitered, more than played, among dead cars and rusting propane tanks. The road was a meandering loop of dirt and gravel. I followed it almost all the way around before I parked—straddling beer bottles and fast food trash.

I'm almost ashamed to say that I felt a little better about the mess of my life when I got out of my truck.

The aluminum storm door rattled louder than my bare-knuckle knock.

Someone inside yelled, "Yeah."

I knocked again.

"What do you need, an invitation?" The same voice called. "Just come in."

The entry door opened with a push. The reek of old beer and weed crawled out to die on the burned lawn. Inside, the trailer was dark. All the windows were covered with foil. From around the fake wood paneling hallway the voice said, "Hang on. I'll be right out."

I heard the toilet flush.

Roland Duques stepped out still buckling his pants. "You're not. . ." He seemed confused.

"Not who?"

"Hey. You can't be in here." Roland fumbled getting his belt buckle with the beer company logo closed.

"And yet here I am." I didn't want to sound like the kind of cop everyone hates, but I couldn't stop myself.

"You have no right."

"Are you sure about that?"

"My dad's a cop. I know what you can get away with."

"Is that so? Did Duck tell you we're like vampires?"

"You know my dad? Wait. What? What are you talking about? Is that a joke? How are you like vampires?"

"Never invite us in."

Roland thought about it for a second. The connections worked behind his eyes and played on his lips. He smiled. "I get it."

"I need to talk with you, Roland"

All the guile fell off his face as it firmed into a stone mask. "Nope."

"Were you there the other night?"

"The other—" His mask cracked slightly. "I don't. . . I don't know what you're talking about."

"When you and your buddies confronted me at a crime scene to tell me the Nightriders didn't kill Tyrell Turner."

It looked as though relief and confusion were having a wrestling match on his face. The confusion, I thought, must come from the fact that he wasn't at my parlay with the Nightriders. It begged the question, what was he relieved about?

"I'm not dumb enough to talk to you." He tried to re-mask his face.

"You're dumb enough to tie yourself to criminal organizations."

He glared. Roland didn't like to be called dumb. "You don't know what you're talking about."

"Worst of all, you're dumb and unhygienic."

"I'm not dumb." He didn't like that at all. "And what do you mean, unhygienic?"

I pointed at his fingers, which he was anxiously flexing. "You didn't wash your hands."

He opened his hands then pulled them up to his chest, rubbing them together as if concerned about being caught in a social mistake. "Screw you." There wasn't much fire in the invective.

"Don't worry about it, Roland. Some things can't be washed off. Maybe there's something else you feel on your hands."

"What're you talking about?" That didn't sound like an honest reaction. His question was careful. Not dumb at all. "You talk a lot, but you don't make much sense."

"I'm talking about what other people put on your hands. Blood. Guilt. That's the real dirt. Choices you let other people make for you don't wash away."

"And that's what *I'm* talking about. Talk. Talk, talk, talk. It's all noise. You got something to say, say it straight."

"Are you trying to say you're dumb?"

"Stop saying that. I'm not dumb."

"That tag on your cut says you are." I looked right at the *Prospect* tab sewn over the pocket of his sleeveless jacket. "Prospect. That says you have to do what you're told by the full members, doesn't it? Anything you're told."

He stared at me. His eyes were set and hard, but his mouth worked slightly. He was looking for words that were hiding behind his teeth.

"What have you done to earn your way in?" I put the question out there without expecting an answer. No matter what he'd done, it would be nothing to be proud of or brag about to a cop.

"You don't want to know," Roland told me. He sounded as though he was the one who didn't want to know.

His regret was so sincere my heart tripped. For an instant I thought he was going to unburden himself of something. But life, and my job, is never that easy.

A loud motorcycle rumbled up the bad road and there was no doubt where it was headed.

"That's Charlie," Roland announced with obvious relief. "That's who I was waiting for."

"Is he going to pick you up at the door like a gentleman, or sit outside and honk?"

"What? I don't get you, lady."

"Don't hurt yourself trying to figure it out."

"Why did you come here?"

Outside, the sound of un-baffled pipes rose then dropped dead silent.

"Your master's voice," I said.

"You don't know."

"I know a lot more than you think."

"Are you getting blown by the Hurricane, Ro?" The question was followed by an explosion of laughter without mirth. Charlie Lipscomb stood in the trailer door and lit a cheap cigar.

He was part of the Nightriders old guard. I'd dealt with him before for a lot of reasons. But he'd changed since the last time I'd seen him. His long, wild hair was grayer. His beard was tied up in three little bands that pulled it to a point. One other big difference—his bloated, round gut. Different, but familiar. His vest had a new tab on it as well. Over his heart was a white patch with red stitching. It said *Sgt. at Arms*.

"She was asking me questions," Roland blurted. "I didn't say anything."

"Nope." I agreed. "He's a good soldier. He follows rules and does what he's told. Living the free life of a biker."

"What do you know about freedom, cop?" Charlie puffed out a cloud of blue smoke, then folded his thick arms over the swelling of his belly. "We live for freedom and ride where we want. There's nothing more important in our world. And there's no freedom behind a badge for little piggies." He laughed again—still without humor. The sound was more like score taking than expressing any pleasure.

"Guys like you spend half your life behind bars, and always talk about freedom. You need to get a dictionary sometime."

"That's what she does," Roland chimed in. "Always saying we're dumb."

"It wouldn't bother you, if you didn't believe it," I told him.

"Whatever," Charlie said without laughing. He rolled the low budget cigar around his mouth—dropping ashes into his beard.

"Where were you last night, Charlie?"

"Riding."

"Just riding? Where?"

"Riding with friends." He puffed more smoke. It occurred to me that he was blowing smoke in more ways than one. "We went all the way to Joplin for some barbeque. Didn't get back until early morning."

"Convenient."

"We got places to be. Lock up on your way out." He went out the door with Roland following quickly behind.

I didn't touch the door.

Chapter 10

The feeling I had walking in my own front door was one of isolation. Originally, it had been Nelson's door. I still lived among his art, his house, his furniture. It was all beautiful, but a beautiful wall was still something to be climbed over if a woman is to become. . .

What?

And why did I feel it was so important for me to think of these things now? Stupid questions.

The house was one of those prefabricated log homes that Nelson had placed on a sandstone cliff, looking over a finger of Table Rock Lake. Extending over the fifty foot drop, the glass front of the house looked like the prow of a ship—another voyage going nowhere.

I regretted having stopped drinking—a thought that demanded honesty. I stared out of the windows at the burning world and admitted, *I want to drink.*

Times like that I had support. Uncle Orson understood. He would help. Clare Bolin understood. He would be there for me. The sheriff. Even Billy. He's seen me at my lowest—and protected me from myself more than once. Men. All the people in my life that I counted on were men. By any accounting, I had a troubling relationship with the other gender.

That was another thought that made me crave a drink. It was a lie. I knew it even before the idea was fully formed. I didn't want a drink. I wanted to be drunk.

Someone knocked at the door. It was Billy coming to talk—I was sure of it. He was a good man for talk, and I was glad. Still, I took the time to kick off the sensible shoes and drop my gun and badge.

I opened the door. It wasn't Billy. Carmen Dando, my mother, stood there with a hopeful semi-smile on her face. It was a familiar look. I'd seen it in the mirror a million times.

"What do you want?" I didn't have any smile at all.

"Don't I deserve better than that?"

"Do you?"

"I'm your mother."

"*Are* you?"

Carmen opened her mouth to speak, but nothing came. Her hands fluttered about—nervous birds looking for a perch. She touched a strand of hair and pushed it away from her face. That was familiar too. Although, after Iraq, I touched the scar that ran out from under my eyebrow.

Before she could find her words, I added, "And I don't think you want to start any conversation about deserving."

"Katrina. . ."

I waited.

Her hands fluttered more. "It's been such a long time," she finally said.

"Yes, it has."

"You're not going to give an inch are you?" There was a low fire under the question.

"Where were you?"

Carmen looked as though I had slapped her. When she recovered, she said simply, "Life."

"Yours or mine?"

"I don't want to fight with you."

"Then you should go."

"Do we have to do this here? Like this? Standing on your doorstep. Inside and outside? Can't we be on the same side of the door? Katrina?"

I pulled the door closer to myself, narrowing the gap. "Too many doors between us, Carmen."

"You used to call me—"

"Don't."

She didn't look surprised or hurt. Something in her eyes shifted—the color or the cast—something that didn't have an exact definition, changed. It was pale smoke in a soft breeze. After that, Carmen's face opened into an evangelical smile. Her expression dressed up—becoming the kind that knocked on your door early Saturday morning to tell you everything you believe is wrong, but there's good news. "This is a moment," she said explaining. "Let's not waste it on the past."

"Is my past such a waste to you?" The question was as rough as a grindstone in my throat.

"You know that's not what I'm trying to say."

"Don't try to tell me what I know."

Her lips kept smiling without showing teeth. Her eyes had that glaze of curling smoke. She saw something I couldn't. "It happened," Carmen said. "Things. . . Happen. In a life. . . A long, living time. But you're looking at it from the child's end of the line. Try looking from mine."

"You're not making a bit of sense."

"Moments," she said again. "Everything is a moment. This one, the next one, and the one before. When you're young, you look at the tiny segments and think you see everything. When you look from this end, you see the whole thing was one moment. Time and the errors you make smear into one thing."

"Is that your way of asking for forgiveness or of telling me my life was a momentary mistake made in yours?"

"I'm saying we only have this moment. This time. It shapes everything before it and after. Think about now. Not then. Not later."

"I don't think about you at all. Too many silent moments have gone by."

"You were such a sweet young girl. You've become a hard woman."

"You have no idea."

"Katrina. . . I want to be a part of your life. I want you in mine—"

"Tell me this—did you come back for me or for something else and I'm just—" I waved my hands in front of me, then recognized the gesture. I put them to my side and said, "A moment's worth of unfinished business?"

Over her shoulder, from around the corner of the house, a face with two dark eyes peeked out. Cherry Dando.

"Get out of here." I aimed the command at the both of them.

He ducked back. She tried to speak.

I backed into the house and returned with my baton.

Carmen didn't move until I pushed the door wide and let the metal weapon drop to full extension. She walked backward along the path to the driveway. Dando was standing beside an old beater of a car.

"Did you ask her?" He called when we came around the corner. As soon as he saw the baton in my hand he came forward with his palms showing. "We're sorry," he insisted. "It was a bad idea. My idea. No reason to be taking anything out on your mother."

"I haven't had a mother since I was six years old." I stopped advancing when I said it.

Carmen continued retreating to Dando. "We needed help," he explained. "That's all. You know. To do things the right way. There's a fortune in silver in that ground. There's no reason for it to just sit and do no good to no one."

"That's why you came?" I asked Carmen.

For the first time I saw shame painted across her face. Then it was gone. "No."

"Get out of here."

"Now hold on," Dando implored.

I never looked away from Carmen. "You didn't come when my heart was broken. You never showed when my body was ravaged. You were absent for my father's murder. When I drank to oblivion. When I fought for my sanity and my life. Those are the moment you talked about. My moments. All moments you missed."

"Katrina—"

"You came for money."

"No—"

"Is that why you left? You loaded up the car and dropped me off at Uncle Orson's dock. Do you remember that? You didn't even walk me in."

"I'm sorry."

"What was waiting for you? What payday was so important you that had to leave me standing in a parking lot?"

"Freedom. I had to get free."

"From what?"

"Everything."

"You're still free," I said.

"What about my truck?" Dando yelled the question from behind the fender of the old car. "I want it back."

"That's Earl Turner's truck." I answered. "It's one more thing you and me have to talk about. Why don't you be at my office tomorrow morning?" I looked back at Carmen. "We can talk there."

"I got nothing to say to you," he called over.

"I have plenty to say to you." I was still looking at my mother. "Don't make me come looking."

Then I turned and returned to my house—locking the door behind me.

* * * *

Showered and dressed in jeans with a jacket and my service weapon tucked into the small of my back, I showed up at Uncle Orson's boat dock just as the sun was burning the horizon. The sky was red-dark—and getting darker—like blood cooking black on hot concrete. The night sounds were rising from the lake and shore. Cicadas, frogs, an owl from across the water, and the flop of a fish all printed the evening with living presence.

Uncle Orson had purchased the dock after retiring from the Marines. It was old when he got it—and it still looked like a mistake in time. As I stood in the parking lot at the end of the gangway, the lights came on. They were clear bulbs strung from one end of the dock to the other. In their light, colors popped with an otherworldly glow. The electric yellow burn of twisted filaments birthed tiny stars in the black lake water.

I was standing in the exact spot my mother had left me when I was six. My father was out of town on one of his consulting jobs. Carmen had loaded up the car with her belongings and brought me to the dock. She was gone and out of sight before I went to find my uncle.

Watching it again in memory, I understood it no better than I had as a girl.

"I saw you out there," Uncle Orson said as I came in the door. "I put some brats on the grill."

"I'm not hungry."

"But you want to talk."

"Not anymore."

He slid aside the top of an ancient chugging cooler and pulled out a pair of sodas. "Orange or grape?"

"I don't care."

"Orange it is." He popped the top off in the machine's opener and handed it over.

The bottle was crusted with pellets of ice and almost painfully cold. I took a long drink that left me gasping.

"You sounded pretty firm about wanting to talk," he said, after I'd caught my breath.

"Sometimes even I figure things out for myself."

"What things are that?"

"You were trying to protect me. That was obvious. Who from and why I needed protecting wasn't. Until I talked to her."

"I'm sorry."

"We never talked about it. Dad. You. I don't think I heard her name more than a half-dozen times between when she left and when I went to college."

"Well. . ." Orson opened his grape soda and took a quick swallow. "Carmen kind of kicked your dad's ass. In the way only a younger, pretty woman, can."

"I wouldn't know."

"How much younger than you is Billy Blevins?"

"That's not the same. And it's not the subject at hand." I tilted the bottle high up and took another deep pull, but I kept my gaze fixed on my uncle.

"No. I guess it's not." He waited for me to lower the bottle from my lips before he continued. "She didn't just run off that day. She ran off with him. Cherry Dando. It wasn't bad enough that he was Navy. He was a dishonorable discharge. You know how much pride your father took in his service."

I nodded, staring into the half-empty bottle in my hands. My mind was filled with the pain of missing my father and the secret wish that the soda was whiskey.

"Proud of yours too," Uncle Orson added.

"I know."

"Drink your soda. It helps. Part of craving is the habit."

My wish wasn't as secret as I thought. I should have known better. Orson has his own issues with drinking. As far as I know he's never tried to stop, but he informally counsels other vets. He understands a lot.

"So. . . They ran off—and have been gone all this time?"

He shook his head, put the grape soda to his mouth, and walked at the same time. Pushing through the screen door to the lake side of the shack he said, "Time to turn the brats. I had the butcher make them special. Jalapeno, cheddar, and jack with cilantro and lime zest."

"I don't know if that sounds horrifying or delicious." I followed behind him.

"Don't listen to the recipe. Smell what's cookin'."

Outside, the scent of the cooking meat and spices made my mouth water. Suddenly I was hungry. I suspected that Orson knew the effect the sausages would have. But I wouldn't be deterred. "They didn't disappear?"

He picked up tongs and turned the brats with a lot more concentration than the task required. "No. They didn't."

"And?"

"For years I'm pretty sure your father knew exactly where they were. He was angry and hurt."

"And a trained intelligence officer."

"His Phoenix Program training stayed with him all his life. To his credit, he only kept track so far as I know." One of the sausage casings leaked grease causing a flare of flame in the grill. In that light, I saw a sadness on Orson's face. "I'm not sure I could have maintained such restraint. But your father was always stronger than I was."

His expression was deeper than sadness. Like me, he occasionally saw things that were there only in the past. I saw sand and swirling dust.

I relived the betrayal of my superior officers and watched myself bleed into the featureless brown of Iraq. Uncle Orson went to another place, and another time. He'd told me before about the flash of fire when a Zippo catches the dry thatch of village hooches. From him, I knew the terror of a nighttime ambush in the jungle, and the rippling waves of helicopter wash in elephant grass.

"Uncle Orson." I pulled at him only with my voice. "Orson."

"Some of us are different after. . . All of us really."

"I know."

"But your father held it all back and lived a good life." Orson moved the brats around absently. "I suspect that he had rage in him. I imagine also that the tabs he kept on them was part of it. But he never did what I might have. And I know that was because of you."

I nodded and put my hand on his arm.

"I miss him," he said.

"Me too."

Uncle Orson keeps a houseboat tied to the dock. It's a perfect little home for a hermit—or for a sheriff's detective who didn't want to go home late at night. There was a time it served as my floating apartment—whenever I was too drunk to drive. I'm ashamed to say, there were times I was in that condition—but still took to the roads. That night, with only amazing brats and another soda weighing me down, the bunk seemed smaller.

My dreams were a jumble, more sensation than image. Anger. That's often the centerpiece of my sleeping world. I could feel it the way an epileptic feels an aura of impending seizure. It snaked under my skin and curled around my heart—then it whispered something new.

There were no words. The soft voice carried only feeling. It was as if I was the innocent in the garden and the fruit was held out to me. All I had to do was take it. It was not the serpent's voice. I sensed no menace. The voice that urged me on was kind. But I was rejecting the kindness. I rejected the offer retreating again into the comfort of anger.

When I woke, cold water was already sending tendrils of vapor into the heat of a rising sun. The dream voices faded, leaving me adrift in wakefulness. Whatever they wanted to tell me was lost.

Awakening, I was certain I had sorted out my conflict. Smug, under clean sheets and years of distance, I congratulated myself at understanding. What I had to do was not personal. Cherry Dando had killed Tyrell Turner. I was convinced. If Carmen wasn't involved, she knew.

There would be consequences.

I cleaned up and dressed. Once again I put on jeans. It was choice and necessity. There was nothing else on the boat. Grabbing coffee from the dock shack, I set out to begin my day with a rare sense of purpose. Either I would find the evidence I needed—or I would get a confession.

* * * *

I skipped the breakfast stop at the Taneycomo Café, afraid of running into Duck. That was sure to be an uncomfortable conversation—and I wanted to put it off as long as I could. I should have had a good breakfast—because Donald Duques was sitting in my office when I arrived.

"Duck," I said.

"Hurricane," he responded.

Already there was gambler's tension between us. We both had cards to play, but neither one liked the game.

Duck started. "You could have given me a head's up. Professional courtesy."

"I would have if you had told me your son was a Nightrider right off."

"You know I couldn't say anything."

"You know you should have. I would have asked you to bring him in."

"Roland wouldn't have come."

"You should have tried." I said it hard. I set my mouth and eyes like they were in cement and stared at him. "You should have done something—because he looks involved. If not in murder in the cover up."

"How bad is it?"

"It's worse than you think."

"You have evidence?"

"You know I can't tell you that."

"What can you say?"

"I can say he needs to get in front. This thing is bigger and messier. . ." I thought about what I could and should say to Duck. He was, if not a friend, a colleague. And a father. "Look. No matter what he feels about you—or what he thinks about cops in general—you need to make him see that there are two sides. No matter what, we'll treat him fair. *But.*" I looked harder and leaned in to make my point. "You need to convince him that he doesn't have friends on the other side."

"You mean the club."

"I mean the low man carries the weight, Duck. You know how it works."

"Who?" His question was urgent and hopeful.

"I can't tell you anything that's part or product of my investigation."

"Fair enough. Maybe I can tell you something."

"I'm listening."

"Ro told me why they were trying to keep that boy's body from going to the medical examiner."

I didn't say anything. The poor value of the hand Duck had been dealt showed in his eyes and the slump of his body. He needed to put them on the table. He simply didn't know how without failing his son. "DNA." He laid the phrase out like a last chance gambler folding.

"What about it?"

"That's all I know. That's all he said. It has something to do with DNA."

"Whose?"

"He didn't say."

"He's not telling you much, Duck."

"He's afraid. I can tell that. They've got him into something that he can't get out of. I tried to tell him—I tried to tell him a lot of things."

I didn't know what to say to that—or to the hurt in his eyes. Luckily I didn't have to. Footsteps scraped the tiles and stopped. Someone passed my door then came back. Earl Turner was there holding a cell phone in his hand.

It was a strange triangle. Duck looked at the man and turned pale. Earl Turner saw him. He tried to ignore Duck, and looked at me. For my part, I was caught looking from one to the other.

"I want my truck." Earl was the first to break the silence.

"It's in your garage," I told him.

"You know it ain't true."

I looked at Duck—who was staring at Earl. He made no movement. I'm not sure he was even breathing. "Duck?"

"Duck?" Earl startled slightly.

"Are you alright, Duck?"

He turned to face me. I could see his eyes angled over at Turner though. "Yeah," Duck answered. "You gave me a lot to think about."

"They call you Duck?" Turner asked.

Duck nodded and touched his head. It was an awkward movement, and I couldn't tell if he was hiding his face or touching the brim of an imaginary hat. "Yes, sir. And I'm headed back to work."

Turner backed up to let Duck through the door then stayed in the hall watching the other man go.

"Mr. Turner?"

When he looked back at me, gears were turning behind his old-copper eyes. He started to say something but stopped.

"Earl?"

Sometimes you can see someone rewriting their thoughts. Cops see it all the time in suspects. They try to edit every word. Usually it's so obvious you can't help but catch them in the lies. With victims and witnesses it's different. Everyone lies. Everyone holds things back. Often, it's just an honest attempt not to make things worse. Even more often, it's about not letting yourself look like an idiot. In his head, Earl Turner was running back a tape and thinking through what was on it. "I want my truck." The anger had become evasion.

He wanted his truck. I believed that. I didn't believe that was why he'd come here. "What's going on?" I hoped the generic question would allow him to lead himself to the truth.

"It means a lot to me."

"I know. It's a beautiful truck."

That thawed his chill slightly. Turner allowed himself a small smile. "It took a lot of work. One day it was going to be Tyrell's." Saying the name put the hurt back into his face.

"Why didn't you tell me it was gone when I asked?"

"Tyrell had it."

"I believe so."

"He took it without askin'. I didn't want anyone thinking he stole it. He's a good boy. He's the best kid a man could ask to raise."

I took note of the slip into present tense and the fatigued slump of his body. The fact of his loss had become real for Earl Turner.

I pointed to a chair in front of my desk. "Why don't you have a seat?"

He did. Then he turned to look out the open door. I though he was going to open up. I was wrong. Earl stared then fiddled with the phone in his hands.

"You have a cell phone?" I asked trying to prod him into talking.

He looked at the device in his hands as if he was seeing it there for the first time. "It's not mine. It was Elaine's. I keep it going for emergencies." His attention and voice faded again.

I waited hoping he would come to the decision to talk to me. I noticed that his hands no longer fidgeted with the phone. Instead, he had it pressed into a tight grip that paled the thick brown skin at his knuckles. When waiting reached the point of wishful thinking, I got bolder. "You didn't come here about your truck."

"No?" He didn't look at me.

"No. You have something else on your mind."

"I have a lot on my mind."

"Yes, you do. But you have something specific to share with me."

"I may not have learned every lesson life sent my way. But I have learned one thing."

"What's that?"

"No one is as smart as they think they are."

Chapter 11

Neither Cherry Dando nor my mother showed up at my office that morning. Not that I'd really expected them to. It didn't matter. They wouldn't be hard to find. I wasn't in the kind of hurry I had been earlier in the morning. I still believed that Dando probably killed Tyrell Turner and burned the body—because somehow the kid had interfered with the grave robbing. But belief is just that. I didn't have real evidence.

After Earl Turner left my office, I had additional worries. The tangled string was messier and longer than I thought. Earl was hiding more than he said. I wasn't sure if Duck was hiding anything: but the men who visited me that morning were reacting to pressures I couldn't see. The problem with that was my inability to judge their understanding of the forces that moved them. Were they planning or reacting? Desperation was a powerful motivator. Duck and Turner would not be the first men trying to cast off the weight they carried—without understanding how it got there in the first place.

Our evidence tech showed up with a small box. I signed the chain of custody receipt for the contents of Earl Turner's truck. There wasn't much. Two books were sealed in individual plastic bags. Both were about the search for secret silver in the Ozarks. Two other bags contained sheets of paper. One was a wrinkled red copy of the same New American Covenant flier Dando had tried to hide in Johnson Rath's truck. The other was a bill of sale for the truck—listing Tyrell as the seller and Cherry Dando as the buyer. In terms of transferring ownership, it was worthless. As evidence, it was almost perfect. It wasn't an official state of Missouri form. In fact it wasn't official anything. The bill of sale was the kind of generic paperwork you can download from the internet. I was no expert, but I was pretty sure that—for a rebuilt and restored vehicle like the Chevy—the bill of sale needed to be notarized. What it did have were signatures: Tyrell's and Dando's.

Also bagged were a single key attached to a plastic fob, a cigarette butt, and a business card. The card was interesting. The name on it was Landis Tau. It said he was a lawyer with the Midwest Center for Civil Rights Justice.

Was it possible that Cherry Dando and / or my mother were working against Rath and his New American Covenant? I honestly didn't care about Dando, but if there was any chance my mother was more than she seemed. . .

I logged out of the office and got on the road back to Springfield.

* * * *

The offices of the Midwest Center for Civil Rights Justice were downtown—not far from the federal building. I called ahead and asked Agent Birch to meet me. Jurisdiction was always an issue between local cops and federal officers. This time, I wanted him on my side. If you're making a visit to a lawyer who regularly takes on the feds, you want to show you can play on his turf.

That thinking made me feel silly once we were ushered into Mr. Tau's office. Not only was he a gentleman, but he was one of the nicest men you could ever meet. He was less than imposing physically. Mr. Tau was a *little person*—a politically correct term that I can't help but think foolish—not that I have a better idea. At least there was no reason I could see to bring up the issue.

Agent Birch went ahead of me into the office and extended his hand to Tau. His position made it appear that he was bowing. Birch didn't have any kind of reaction to the man's height—and I hoped I could do as well.

"Thank you for seeing us," Birch said.

"Of course." Tau turned to me and raised his hand to mine. "It's not every day I get a visit from the DEA and the Sheriff's Department." His eyes were greenish, and a good match for the red remaining in his graying hair. He kept his pale jade gaze on me and his grip tightened.

"Really?" I asked—surprised as much by the scrutiny as the statement. "I would have thought that your kind of work would at least bring the feds here regularly."

Tau smiled. He grinned, still holding my hand. "I said it's not every day. That doesn't make it rare." His grip tightened and he pulled me closer to him. "I know you."

"You do?" His hand fell away from mine. "How?"

"Hurricane." The nickname was both a statement and an explanation. "Who, in Ozarks law enforcement, hasn't heard of you?"

"Good things, I hope."

He laughed as if I had made a joke. "You are not known for your light step on civil rights." Tau went back to sit behind his desk. "But you're not known for abusing them either. People say you deserve the moniker."

"He's got your number, Hurricane." Birch added.

"Well, we're not here to talk about me."

"Now that's a pity," Tau said sounding sincere. "I imagine you have stories. Please—" He gestured to the chairs in front of his desk. "Sit. Tell me how I can help."

We sat and Birch nodded at me, "It's your show."

"I was hoping you could help me understand what interest Cherry Dando would have in a civil rights attorney."

"Cherry Dando?" Tau laughed again. "Now that's a name. It reminds me of the gun hand in *Red River*. Did you ever see that one? John Wayne. Montgomery Clift." He looked disappointed when we both shook our heads. "Well, it's a great name. But I can't say I know him. Or is it a him? That would be a great stripper name too."

Birch snickered.

I said, "Maybe you know his wife, Carmen Dando?"

"Still no." Tau answered. "Can you say what the investigation involves or what brought you to me?"

I knew without asking that things had gotten even more complicated. "Tyrell Turner." It wasn't a question.

The answer came in the lawyer's face first. Then, "What's happened?"

"He was your client then?"

"Was?"

"He's been killed."

"Those fuckers." The quiet expletive was like a shout. "Those racist, hateful bags of pus."

Tau was reminding me more and more of the sheriff.

"Exactly which racist, hateful bags of pus are we talking about?" Birch asked.

"Ordinarily I would say that's privileged information."

"Ordinarily?" I would have given anyone else a few moments to think. With an experienced lawyer, I thought I needed to keep the urgency fresh.

"That young man would not have wanted me to stand behind legal walls. He wanted the truth out there. In fact, he wanted a big splash. Lots of publicity. Tyrell wanted to pull back all the curtains and stamp his whole life on those people."

"Pulling back curtains can be dangerous," I responded. "And it probably was. But we need to know which curtains exactly."

"Did you know he wanted to go to law school?" Tau took Birch and I in with the question. "He would have made it too. He was the kind of kid who wanted to write *Justice* on the walls in red letters, ten feet high."

"After my own heart." The admiration in Birch's voice was real.

"Do you know about his mother?" Tau asked him.

"I do," I answered. "I've talked with Tyrell's grandfather, Earl Turner. I don't think Agent Birch knows about the abduction or rape."

"Or her suicide?" Tau added.

"Detective Williams and I are working on different but intersecting cases." Birch explained. "Mine is a federal investigation into drug trafficking, criminal racketeering, and. . . uh. . ." His reluctance was clear. Birch didn't know Tau or his clients. He couldn't give too much away. "Interstate gang activity," he finished carefully.

Tau laughed again—like a man who already knows the answers. "You're investigating the local triangle of white shame, the New American Covenant, the AB, and the Ozarks Nightriders."

"How do you know that?" Birch's voice tightened to match the narrowing of his eyes.

"That's what we do here. We track the gangs, the militias, the false front churches, and the lone wolf internet voices who spread hate and peddle race war. We have files on all your bad guys."

I was confused. Or perhaps I had been blinded by my own situation. I had really been thinking the connections were only about Dando and my mother. The search for buried silver and the family connection to Tyrell was how I had been piecing things together. The Nightriders had my vote for weapon of choice: hired thugs to do the dirty work. I may have been wrong. "How does Tyrell Turner figure into all that?"

Tau leaned back in the chair with a thoughtful, storytelling look. Again I was reminded of the sheriff. For the first time I noticed his chair. It fit him perfectly. That made sense I guess. A large office chair might have made him look small. I already had the impression that small was not a definition to Landis Tau's life.

"Tyrell doesn't figure into it so much as it figures into him. And his plans." Tau reached to his throat. He pulled his tie lose and unbuttoned the collar button. "He brought most of it to me. He had files full of clippings and case histories of how the Southern Poverty Law Center had used civil litigation against groups like the Klan."

"He wanted to sue these guys?" Birch asked.

Tau shook his head. "More than that. He had an original idea and wanted to crush them."

"What idea?" I was hooked.

"Tyrell claimed that his mother was abducted and raped by men who were jointly members of the Ozarks Nightriders and The New American Covenant–The Sword and The Word. His claim was that they acted as a group under the direction of Johnson Rath."

"He wanted to pursue civil rights charges." Birch was hooked as deeply as I was.

"More," Tau answered, "he wanted to sue the organizations for paternity and a life time of child support."

"Could that work?" I was amazed at the thought.

"As far as we could tell, there was no reason why not. Corporations and nonprofits are held responsible for their actions every day. If we could show it was an organizational decision to violate the civil rights of Elaine Turner—and that those actions led directly to Tyrell's birth and his mother's eventual suicide—we had a good shot."

"What good would it do?"

"Good?" Tau looked at me and I half-expected him to put dirty boots up on his desk. Or in his case, expensive oxfords. "More than anything, Tyrell wanted to own a piece of them—just as he felt they owned a part of his life. Beyond that. . . Well it depended on what the courts would allow us. We felt pretty sure of the civil rights issue. The paternity thing?" He shrugged. "But any way you look at it—things were going to be very public and extremely embarrassing. That was going to have a big impact on the alliance between The New American Covenant and the AB."

"You think any of them knew about Tyrell's plans?"

"Tyrell was not a leave-well-enough-alone kind of kid."

"You mean he got in the middle of things," Birch said.

"I warned him. . ." Tau looked and sounded like a man regretting things. "Hell, I begged him. Tyrell said he had someone giving him information."

"Who?" I leaned in, eager for a name.

"He never told me the name." Tau answered. "I asked. The kid seemed to think he was protecting sources or something. He didn't think much of the guy, I can tell you that. Tyrell called him a treasure hunter—like it was a big joke."

"*That's* Dando." I looked from Tau to Birch and back. "Cherry Dando is looking for Yocum silver dollars—buried in an abandoned black cemetery. The graves are located on the land owned by Rath and the New American Covenant."

"Yocum dollars?" Tau asked. "I thought those were just a legend."

"Me too," I told him. "But Dando thinks they're real. And he thinks they're buried on that land."

"Johnson said he's getting a lot of pressure from his AB friends to get his compound built." Birch jumped in. "Ever since Waco and Ruby Ridge, the FBI is touchy about getting involved in these groups that cloak themselves in religious freedom."

"I thought the militia movement and separatist groups were a high priority."

"Only if they show up as a domestic terrorism concern." Tau explained. "Your general haters and pure, white, Christian, Nazis are left to groups like ours." He pointed at Agent Birch. "You said the FBI was touchy about it. You're not FBI."

"No." Birch grinned broadly. "I am not." He didn't say it, but I got the feeling that he wasn't touchy about dealing with these groups at all.

I thought things had reached a conclusion. I was about to say so when Tau asked me, "What do you think of what we do here?" He must have seen me trying to puzzle out the motive in his question. "Personally, I mean. Not as a law enforcement professional."

"I think you're trying to empty a lake with a teaspoon. But it's good work." Tau laughed again. It came easy to him. "Right on both counts," he said.

"Why?"

"I think you would make a good fit on our board of directors."

That caught me off guard.

"Me?"

"A perfect fit really. I hope you will think about it."

"Why?"

"We can do a lot of good together."

It was my turn to laugh. "You're evading."

"Every chance I get."

"Why—*me?*"

"There are two kinds of board members for nonprofits. Those with connections and those with cash. You have both."

"I think you overestimate me on both counts."

"Your estimated net worth is 4.5 million. You founded and funded your own charity to help those Peruvian girls caught up in trafficking last year. It's impressive that you recruited Congresswoman Whilomina Tindall to be on the board in that project. But the most impressive thing is that you've never quit your job."

"I need the job more than the money."

"Do more with the money. Then you won't feel that way."

"You know a lot about me."

"I guarantee every worthy cause in a hundred miles knows a lot about you, Hurricane."

* * * *

In the parking lot outside the offices of the Midwest Center for Civil Rights Justice, the first thing Agent Devon Birch said to me was, "Four and a half million dollars?"

"That was the value of the estate my husband left when he died," I told him. Then I winked. "It's more now."

"More?"

"He was an artist. The value of all his work went up. So did the licensing fees and sales of prints, t-shirts, calendars, mugs, that sort of thing. I own a restaurant with a great bar too. You should come have a drink and dinner sometime."

"Oh, you know I will."

I closed the door of my truck and turned both the air conditioning and the radio way up. I drove back to Taney County—bouncing my thoughts off the oldies. I didn't gain any new insights. On the bright side I didn't feel like drinking myself blind or beating anyone senseless—so I was calling it a win.

A few miles outside of Forsyth, my phone rang. Tau's offer to be on the board of the Midwest Center for Civil Rights Justice was on my mind. I didn't really want to set my consideration aside for an unknown caller. Unfortunately, a cop doesn't have the luxury to ignore calls. "Detective Williams."

"You gotta get here," was the instant response.

"Mr. Turner?"

"You need to get here and in a hurry. I can't stop them and I think they sent the wrong park ranger."

"Park ranger? What are you talking about, Mr. Turner? Where are you?"

"I'm at the land. The place where Tyrell was. There's going to be trouble."

"What trouble? What are you talking about?"

"Bulldozers are here and so's the park ranger. It's getting ugly. If those racist sons-of- bitches show up—there's going to be bloodshed."

"Mr. Turner, I'm on my way. Whatever's happening, stay out of it and keep yourself safe."

"I ain't scared."

"I'm not saying you are. And that's not—" I had to stop and tell myself it wasn't the time for explaining. "Just do it." I disconnected, then used the truck communications to send deputies out to the lake plot where Tyrell had been found. I didn't really understand what was going on—but if there were bulldozers at the crime scene—I wanted them stopped.

The scene was even worse than Earl had made it sound. I arrived, bumping hard over broken-up hard pack. It had been chewed down by the semi-trucks loaded with heavy equipment. The crime scene tape was down, and two men were kicking curiously though the burn circle.

Battle lines had apparently been formed. On one side, there were bulldozers and their handlers, bikers, and Johnson Rath. On the other side, two deputies, Earl Turner, and of all people—Cherry Dando. The deputies had hands on their weapons and looked terrified. Dando appeared to be ignoring everyone but Johnson. I had the impression that he was imploring the big man not to stop the treasure hunt. I think the lines would have charged each other already—if it wasn't for a tall black man wearing a US Department of the Interior uniform. Earl was right. There was a Park Ranger here.

The Ranger and the construction crew looked to be actually talking—despite the efforts of Rath and the bikers to provoke something.

I drove my truck right up into the cleared part of the field, stopping between the men and the heavy equipment.

As soon as I stepped out, Earl held up his cell phone. He pointed at it with his free hand and shouted to me, "He's here."

I had no idea what he was talking about. Before I could ask, Johnson Rath tromped straight up to me. When he got close I could smell chewing tobacco and the sweat of more than one hot day. His eyes flashed. His beard flicked in the slight breeze as if each strand had its own life. "You can't stop me," he pronounced. "This is private land."

"Back off." I glared right back at him.

He wasn't the kind of man on whom harsh words and hard looks had much effect. Rath Johnson believed in the physical—the right of arms and muscle. He shook his mane of hair and squared his shoulders. I would have been lying if I said I wasn't scared. The thing is—I've been scared before. It teaches a lot of things—one thing for sure—if I backed down he would consider me the same way a lion considers a wounded zebra. Prey.

I reached back and placed my hand on my service weapon. I didn't let it rest. Without taking my gaze from the big man in front of me, I thumbed the gun's safety and lifted it from the deep seat of the holster. The barrel remained tucked. My 9mm was not technically cleared from my holster. It was as close to free as it could get.

"You going to shoot me?" Johnson raised his hands to present his broad chest. He craned his neck down then spoke softly, making sure only I could hear. "If you do you better kill me. Because. . ." He finished the thought by leering. The look was packed with the threat of pain and of something worse. "But I'm an unarmed man. You can't do anything."

I cleared my weapon and held it down at my thigh. I tapped the barrel against my leg a couple of times to get his attention. When he looked I moved my right foot forward about three inches. Not far. Not obvious to anyone but him. Speaking so he had to lean in to hear, I told Johnson, "Don't worry about being unarmed. I've got a spare for you right here." I moved the toe of my boot. "Strapped to my ankle."

He raised his face and locked his gaze to mine. There was no doubt he was listening carefully.

"If I have to put you down. . . I'll do it without thinking about it—and without tears or bad feelings later. In fact, I'll never think of you again. But one thing I can promise you—an unregistered and untraceable .32 will have been in your hand. And no one will ever question me about it."

I wasn't very experienced with bluffing. There was no drop piece. But Rath was just the kind of guy who assumed everyone played by his rules or they were fools. He bought it. I saw the resignation in his eyes an instant before I saw the flash of new anger. It was the look of an animal tricked into a cage—then regretting.

Regret came too late. Two people approached. Each came from a different angle, but generally from the direction of the heavy equipment standoff.

It was the construction operator who spoke first. "You in charge here?"

"I am now." I answered with a full, loud voice keeping my gaze on Johnson Rath a little longer. After I'd spoken, I returned my weapon to its holster with a firm shove. Only then did I turn to the man in the hardhat. "What's your story?"

"I was hired to clear and level this plot. And—"

"When?"

"What do you mean when? Now. Get it done ASAP."

"When were you called?" I clarified.

"This morning."

"Kind of short notice, isn't it?"

"It was a cash offer."

"Who from?" He didn't say, but he looked squarely at Johnson Rath. "I've got a crew to keep busy. I'm not in the business of turning down work," he finished defensively.

I turned and looked at the man in the ranger uniform. He was a poster child for park rangers. Tall and lean, with a dusting of gray at the temples to match the lines radiating from the corners of his eyes. He looked mixed race; maybe black and Indian. He didn't seem nearly as upset as the equipment operator. "Let me guess," I said. "You're the one who got in the way."

He half-smiled—like a man who had been through all of this before, but always enjoyed the ride. "Not me," he said then he held up an envelope. "This."

"He said he had a court order." The workman made his statement an accusation. "He said we had to stop. So I called Rath, here. This is his land. Who else are we supposed to take orders from?"

"From me," the ranger said without leaving much room for discussion. Then he added, "From the court. From the President of the United States. And, I'd imagine, now you're going to take them from this detective." He turned to me and offered his hand. "You're the Hurricane. I'm Jesus."

"What the fuck?" The outburst came from Johnson.

The construction guy quick-stepped backward, two paces. He looked like he expected the ranger to detonate.

"Really?" I was a bit astonished myself. Even so, I took the hand.

"Jesus Selassie Carter." The grin on his face was joy itself. He turned, once again, to face Johnson. Special Agent Jesus Selassie Carter of the National Park Service, Department of the Interior. You can read that as *Federal Agent*."

"That's goddamned, black-assed bullshit." Johnson pronounced.

Still gripping my hand, Jesus turned the high wattage smile on the huge racist. "Ain't that a kick in the racially pure nads?" He laughed.

I couldn't help but think he made a point of sharing his name for effect whenever possible.

Ranger Carter, I couldn't keep thinking of him as Jesus, turned back to me. He released my hand, but kept the grin turned on. "It was inevitable. Mamma is Mary and my daddy is Joseph. Black militant and Osage Indian, Methodist hippie—what else would they name me?"

"I should wipe that shit-eating grin off your face for you." Johnson all but snarled the threat.

The ranger acted as if he hadn't heard. He kept his gaze on me as he said, "In the envelope, you will find a copy of the court order, a copy of the e-mail ordering me here, copies of memos from Congresswoman Tindall to the Department of the Interior, and the President, requesting this site be evaluated for protection under the Antiquities Act as a National Monument. There is a copy of the White House memo to my bosses to make it happen." Jesus turned to Johnson and the construction guy. "And here I am." He flourished his hands toward the other two men.

Suddenly, I realized that Ranger Carter looked a bit like Sammy Davis Jr. —if he had been a lumberjack. I almost laughed at the thought. Instead, I tucked the envelope into my jacket. "That explains you." I nodded at the construction guy, then Johnson." And you. And you. What about everyone else?"

"Aren't you going to read that?" Ranger Carter asked about the paperwork.

"I don't need to. I was expecting something like it. Maybe not from the President, but we take our wins where we get them."

"You did this." Johnson stared—his pale eyes as hard as the accusation in his voice.

"Not me actually. There were a couple of us who got the ball rolling."

"I'll roll some balls—"

"Watch it." I dropped my voice into a "you-better-take-this-seriously" register and placed my hand back on the butt of my weapon. "I don't care what pull you have, threatening an officer is sure to get you put away."

"None of this shit is legal." Johnson spoke up and over our heads. He wanted the bikers to hear. He raised his voice to almost shouting. "This is my land. You can't take it. You can't do any of this." Then he turned to the construction guy and ordered, "Fire up your bulldozer. No one gets to say what I do with my private property."

"It's not yours though." I said. "Is it?"

"You know it's mine."

"No." I admit I enjoyed telling him. "And it's definitely not private property. The deed is registered in the name W&S Foundation."

"And I run the foundation." Johnson didn't sound quite so sure of himself.

"See now, that's the thing." Ranger Carter jumped in. "You know, before memos and orders like those I gave the detective are ever written up, a whole team of lawyers has a look. Just to make sure, you see, that everything is legal. Or if not completely legal on the face, at least defendable."

"What the hell are you goin' on about?" Johnson was losing his edge and confidence. "You ain't a lawyer. You're a park ranger."

"A man can't be both?" His grin beamed again. It was his personal scoreboard. "We all took a good look at the charter of the W&S Foundation. There was a lot of crap in there about the white race, and a Christian America. But there was one little bit about the preservation of heritage—and some BS about preserving the history of the *real* America."

"Fuck you." Johnson's curse was more a declaration of despair.

"No," Ranger Carter smiled along with the slow shake of his head. "You're fucked. And it's by your own hand. You created and chartered a nonprofit with the stated goal of preserving heritage and history. Then you purchased land filled with both. The government is assisting in that noble goal."

If life were a cartoon, Johnson Rath would have had whistling steam coming from his ears. I was close to laughing—even without the added visual—so I gave my attention back to the construction guy. "So you called Rath. Then what happened?"

"The bikers started showing up first. Then Johnson came barrelin' up the road. That other guy was with him." He pointed over at Cherry Dando—who was stalking around the machines as if he could find some weakness. Shifting his aim over to Earl Turner he said, "Then that guy showed up and started shouting about murder and saying the killer was here."

Earl was wandering through the torn up field staring at Elaine's phone.

"Earl," I shouted. When he looked, up I waved him over.

He ignored my summons and kept following his phone around.

"What's he doing?" I asked not expecting any answer.

Agent Carter surprised me. "Looks like he's tracking something on his phone."

As soon as he said it, some pieces fell into place. Earl had his daughter's phone. She was Tyrell's mother, and worried mothers aren't above putting tracking software on their kid's phones.

"He's tracking Tyrell's phone."

Before I got three steps, I heard a piercing whistle. When I glanced back, following the sound, I saw Johnson whipping his raised arm in a tight circle. I kept running but realized I was too late. All the motorcycles fired up. The Nightriders twisted their throttles and charged from the field—throwing rooster tails of dust behind them.

"No," Earl exclaimed at his phone as I reached him. "No. It's here." He pointed through the dirty haze at passing bikers. I looked. The last to clear the grounds was Roland Duques. "One of them has Tyrell's phone."

Chapter 12

I calmed Earl as the dust settled. It turned out as I had thought. He'd been following the tracking feature on the cell phone to find Tyrell's phone, and, he believed, the boy's killer. He implored me to chase the retreating dot on the phone's map. I explained the rules of evidence and how using tracking on a phone registered to a dead woman, with no warrant, then searching someone, without a warrant, based on the tracking information could do more harm than good. It didn't matter to him. I understood his need. Still I had to say no.

When I asked for the phone to start the warrant process, Earl gave me a sullen stare. "I'll do it myself."

"Mr. Turner, I don't want to have to arrest you for interfering in an investigation."

"Seems to me, I'm the only one investigating."

"Well you're not."

"I'm going to do what I have to do."

"Then let's do it the right way."

"What's that? I give it over to you and it disappears."

"We're the Sheriff's Department, Mr. Turner. Things don't disappear."

"You can't trust the swamp without trusting alligators. And that ain't happenin'."

I had to think that one through. It took a moment. "There's someone in the department you don't trust?"

His stare gave me nothing.

It didn't matter. If there was one thing I understood it was wariness of people in authority who said, 'Trust me.' So I didn't say it. Instead I said, "Look, Mr. Turner, I can't stop you. And I can't help you. But—"

He looked at me expectantly. "If you find the phone—and pin it down to the possession of a single person—I'll find a way to do something." The expression on Earl's face became cagy. I didn't like what he seemed to be thinking. "But only if you don't confront anyone. Don't do anything that puts you at risk. And if you try being a vigilante in any way—"

"I got it."

He ambled off to his car, and I pulled my own phone from my pocket. I called the sheriff to fill him in and get him out to the scene. As we talked, I watched the bulldozer and grader being loaded onto the trailers. The grading crew was leaving.

When the big dozer pulled toward its ramp, I saw the truck behind it. Johnson Rath and Cherry Dando were arguing again. There was something new about the fight though. Outside the jail, they had tangled more out of annoyance than deeper anger. This time, the fire was stoked and teeth were bared. Johnson shoved Dando and shook his bandaged finger at him. Dando swiped at the injured digit. From the distance I could read the pain in the string of heated cursing that followed.

Something else was different. Parked beside the same old car I'd seen at my house, were two big motorcycles. Each bike was mounted by a huge man whose arms were illustrated by blue ink. One of the men I'd never seen before. He was wearing jeans and engineer boots, but no club colors. The other man was familiar. Charlie Lipscomb, the Nightrider's Sergeant-at-Arms.

I was too far away to be absolutely certain, but it appeared that the pair had some matching ink on their right forearms. I hadn't paid any attention to his tattoos when I last saw him at Roland Duques' trailer. Now, paired up with the same symbols on the other man, they were hard to ignore. They looked like jailhouse tats—with the Nazi lightning bolt *SS* matching up over the number *88*. In white supremacist code, 8 can represent the eighth letter of the alphabet, H. 88 is shorthand for *Heil Hitler*. Some also say it's a reference to a passage in *Mein Kampf* that runs eighty-eight words long. I don't know the truth of it, but I know hate when I see it.

I immediately assumed they were representatives of the AB: one inside the Nightriders to manage things, and one here to check on the status of their investment. They were watching the argument, and Johnson seemed to be focused on them more than on Dando. He turned his back on the smaller man and stomped toward the men on bikes.

Dando wouldn't be ignored. He ran forward and imposed himself between Johnson and the other men. As I watched, I caught the rising tone of the exchange, not the words themselves. Dando pointed at the

surrounding ground—then back to Johnson. He barked out something
that sounded harsh—and the bigger man swung his arm out. Dando took
a hard hit to the side of the head and went down.

The men on the bikes joined in and started pointing and yelling too.
Johnson didn't seem so forceful with them.

Dando got up. His shouts and angry gestures took in the bikers, as well
as Johnson. The two men turned even grimmer than they had been. One
at a time they stood, still straddling their motorcycles. I could tell the new
stance was a threat.

Dando kept slinging words, but backed away from the bikers. He made
the mistake of getting back in Johnson's reach.

Johnson grabbed the skinny man in one big hand. His brutal grip
locked onto the meat of Dando's trapezius. He lifted Dando—kicking and
swearing—from the dead grass. Johnson Rath pulled the man, who had
been a friend, close. He spoke very deliberately into Dando's grimacing
face, then he pulled back a meaty fist and punched.

It wasn't until Dando hit the ground that I saw Carmen. She jumped
from the car's passenger side door and came to shield her husband from
further blows with her body.

The two men on the bikes settled back into their seats, but that didn't
mean they were satisfied. Both began pointing again. They looked to be
asking hard questions—to which Johnson didn't have the answers.

I could have waded in and put a stop to things, but I wanted to see
where all of this was going. Besides, I was dead certain Dando would not
cooperate in a legal solution.

"What's going on there?" Ranger Carter asked.

I hadn't seen him approach. At first, I thought the question was coming
from my own head. "You'd need a road map," I answered.

Carmen said something to Johnson who said something right back. He
followed up his words by pointing at his crotch.

"If I had the map, I'm not sure it would show any place I want to
go." Carter said.

"Trust me, you don't. I've been there."

Carmen appeared to be crying, and she was screaming at Johnson. I
heard the words that time, but they were still unclear. Meaningless rage.

"Listen," Carter said to me. His gaze remained fixed, just as mine
was, on the shouting match. "You don't have a lot of time keeping this
place protected. Those documents only go so far. A good lawyer can get
them set aside."

"I don't think we need a lot of time. See those two guys on the bikes?" I glanced at Carter long enough to see his focus shift. "I think they are the bankers for this project."

"They don't seem happy."

"No they don't."

My mother leapt to her feet and took a swing. She may as well have been striking brick. Her fist hit Johnson in the chest. All of its force died there. He responded, waving like a man might at a fly. Carmen was tossed aside and landed solidly, sprawled on her backside.

Before anyone could react further, before I pulled the telescoping baton from my kit and started running, Johnson Rath was in the car. He spun the tires and fishtailed in the dirt following the two bikers back to the road.

By the time the sheriff arrived, Cherry Dando was cuffed and seated on the dropped tailgate of my truck. His tormented nose was flowing blood. Sheriff Benson looked Dando over but didn't say anything. I introduced him to Ranger Carter and gave him the short version. They kept talking as I went to the front of my truck and beckoned my mother over.

She approached without looking me in the eye.

"Where's all this going?" I asked.

"Everything goes to the same place."

"You have to explain that to me."

"Life is lived in one direction."

"I'm not asking about life. I'm asking about chasing imaginary treasure with a man willing to traffic with the worst of people to get it."

"I don't know what you want from me." Her look was both question and challenge and. . . I didn't know. There was more. I couldn't puzzle it out.

"The truth," I responded. I let the word come out blunt. It sat there between us for a silent half-minute before I added, "If not that, how about a plan? A reason? Any bit of sense I can use to get to understanding."

"Do you have a lot of understanding in your life?" She looked right at me—with my own eyes and a backward echo of my own face. "I don't. I have. . ." She looked around as if searching for her words in the ragged, burnt field. "Time. I have a wind at my back that keeps pushing. Place. Person. Thing. None of it holds me." Carmen tilted her head and a bit of thin, frail hair dropped. She pushed at it with a fingertip.

I mimicked the movement but touching instead the scar curling out of my brow. When I realized what I was doing, I pulled my hand away quickly and turned to the back of the truck where she looked. "What about him?"

"He blows with me." She met my gaze, and for the first time I thought I saw something honest and genuinely painful there. "Your father was solid. Clement Williams was a monument—a man carved into any space he occupied. He had no doubt. No rambling. People came to him."

There was no way I could fail to see her longing to be understood. For the first time she was opening up, revealing something painful. For the first time, she put herself in the position to hope for forgiveness. Maybe I don't have that kindness in me. I asked her, "What was I?"

"You are your father's daughter." Even as she spoke the words, something about her faded.

I imagined a wind in sails, blowing a ship from shore. The lights it carried growing dim with irretrievable distance.

I left her with him and went to talk things over with the sheriff. He didn't quite buy my certainty of guilt. He did accept my reasoning, as far as it went, and we agreed to arrest Cherry Dando on suspicion of murder. Arresting Dando gave us time to keep investigating—and to let the threat of the charge hang over him.

Sheriff Benson assigned a deputy to stay on site and a rotation schedule. Ranger Carter promised to remain in contact. We all exchanged contact information, then he departed.

"Now, that's quite a character," Sheriff Benson said with admiration as we watched Carter drive off.

"That first name caught me off guard," I admitted.

The sheriff laughed, but instead of saying anything more about the ranger he said, "It's done."

"What's done?"

"I called Riley Yates."

"And?"

"And I made an official announcement of my retirement."

"Oh." I had known it was coming. I didn't know it would hit so hard.

"You're going to have some things to work out."

"What things?"

Sheriff Benson pivoted and took a solid two foot stand with both hands on his gun belt. "Are you being intentionally dense? Or are you really not thinking about how this is going to change things for you?"

"Both probably. Honestly, I've tried not to think about it."

"Well I know that. But it's done now, and I gave Riley the second half of my announcement."

"You endorsed Billy in the election."

"You got it."

I stared out at the open space. The ground was flat and the cropped foliage dead. In places, you could see where graves or markers had been discovered. There was a deep border of scrub and wood between where the field had been cleared and the lake beyond. I wanted to be out there, past the border and floating, away from complications.

The sheriff, my boss and friend, waited without pushing anymore. He was always understood that I needed to take my own long path—to understand how I felt.

"I bought him a car." I didn't mean it to sound dramatic. The look on the sheriff's face told me it was a bigger deal than I'd admitted.

"An El Camino?"

"How'd you know?" It's funny, but his knowing was somehow a relief.

"People do talk when you're not around." He said it as a gentle admonishment. "And pretty much everyone talks to Billy Blevins."

"I talk with him."

"I know you do. *And*—I know he sees beyond the fact that—mostly— you talk to him about you."

"That's not true."

"I said mostly. Mostly about you or you and him, or. . ."

"There are other things."

"Meaningful things?"

I opened my mouth to answer. Then I closed it. I didn't know what to say.

"If he wins this election, Billy will need more than an old car."

"I know."

"And you. . ."

"Me?"

"If you can't be more, you won't do him any good."

"More what?"

"Be a friend." He looked straight into something inside me. Under his bushy white brows, his dark gaze was fixed on the damaged Katrina behind the hurricane. "Need and love aren't enough."

I looked away. "I told Billy he might not be the man for the job."

"Why?"

"Why did I tell him or why—"

"You know what I mean." I didn't have to look at him—to see the anger or disappointment. "Your reason."

"I said he may not have the right kind of toughness for the job."

"Were you talking about you or him? It's like you don't even know the man."

"I know it takes a certain kind—"

"No." He cut me short then waited for me to look at him. "It takes all kinds of toughness. Not any certain kind. You're the certain kind. You reach for your gun or your baton more than any officer I have. It serves you well. It serves the department at times. And in circumstances that fit your. . . proclivities."

"But?"

"How many times have I had to go to bat for you?"

I didn't answer. I couldn't. I knew there were times the sheriff had been at my back without ever making a point of it.

"Sometimes, it was a hard task to keep you on. You drank. You've made examples of people. You've killed. Worse, you're notorious for your *particular* violence." He paused to let it all sink in. Then, with kindness I didn't feel deserving of, he said, "We try harder for friends. Don't make it easy for the next guy to let you go. Even if it is Billy."

* * * *

Moonshines is a bar and distillery restaurant. For most people like me, dry drunks fighting the cravings every day, it would be the last place to run to at the end of a long day. Most people like me don't own the bar though. When Nelson died, Moonshines was another of the options he left behind for me. It was also a refuge—because of the vigilance of a friend. Clare Bolin was the distillery master and bartender. He was also my personal roadblock. There was not a chance in the world I was getting drunk on his watch.

Again, I was dressed to express the feminine side that I usually worked so hard to hide. I wore a white linen, eyelet, lace skirt and a gray silk top under a light weight black jacket. The jacket was there just to cover up the cuffs, baton, and pistol I had clipped to the broad black belt. Sometimes a lady. Never not a cop. I had ditched both boots and sensible shoes for some pretty heels. They were only two inches though. No point in over doing a good thing.

Even though I had gone home, showered and changed, I dragged the day behind me as I went to the bar.

Dando was in our jail. Earl Turner was doing his own investigating and I had let it happen. That's a lie. I had encouraged it. Johnson Rath and a bunch of bikers were running loose. None of them were in my thoughts though.

I didn't know where my mother had gone. That didn't bother me. At least that was what I told myself. Questions that I wanted to ask her kept showing up in my mind—then the anger flashed behind them. It was two-fold. It bothered me both that she had never been there for me to know, and that I wanted to know.

I didn't know where Billy Blevins was either. I had no more pretending in me to spare for that. It bothered me. I wanted to talk to him. I wanted to be right with him—more than I wanted to be right with anything else in my life. The sheriff was right about me. I dealt better with violence than with honest feelings. What does that say about me? What does it say about who I am—that I had to wonder if honest feelings were worth the fight and worry?

Clare was at the bar. He had an iced tea poured and ready before I sat down. Ours was an interesting relationship. Maybe not so much interesting—as pathetic. Clarence was another old man who thought he was my father. And he was my employee. When Nelson died and left me in control of Moonshines, who else was I going to turn to but an old bootlegger? He had much worse character flaws. I could trust him because his secrets were as big as mine.

"Carmen was here," Clare said as soon as I sat down.

I pointed at the tea. "I'm going to need something stronger."

He nodded thoughtfully before reaching into the garnish trays. In an instant my glass was topped with a lemon and a sprig of fresh mint. "There you go."

"You read me like a book."

"Nope. I've seen the kinds of books you read. Do they sell those in regular stores—or do you have to get them in a plain brown wrapper?"

"They're about romance," I protested but not too hard. "Besides, who buys anything from a store anymore?"

"They have romance, but that's not what they're about. And that's part of what's wrong with the world these days. The loss of the corner store."

"How do you know what my books are about, if you've never read them?"

"I peeked at that last one you left lying around here."

We went around like that for a while. He defended the lost way of life, and books in which people died—but without intimacy. I defended shopping in pajamas and books with strong women who knew what they wanted. It was all place-holding.

Finally, I ran out of small talk and asked, "Did she say what she wanted?"

"I didn't ask." Clare watched me take a long drink of my tea. He looked like a man getting ready for bad news.

"She hasn't gotten much of a reception around here."

He relaxed. I believed he thought he might get a fight from me. He arranged glasses that were already in perfect order. "In my experience—" Clare paused and looked to be thinking about what, exactly, his experience was. When he came to it, he began again. "In my experience, people rarely deserve what happens to them."

"But?"

"But, we all have a way of earning how we're treated."

"That's harsh."

"I'm not talking about crime or random violence. I'm talking about family. Friends. The lack of both. . ."

"Maybe. . ."

I was saved from more of Clare's speculation by Billy. He sauntered through the bar side doors laughing and smiling at the greetings of customers and service people. It wasn't all about his role with the sheriff's department. Some of them knew him as the guy who sings on the summer deck weekend nights. But they all knew him.

He sat beside me. Clare already had a handcrafted root beer waiting. For an instant I thought, we're a fine pair: a teetotaler and an ex-drunk. Then I thought saying 'ex,' was giving myself too much credit.

"Hey," Billy said as a greeting.

"Hey yourself."

He took a deep drink of the foamy root beer, then let the mug thump heavily down. "That's amazing, Clare."

Clare smiled his thanks then moved to the far end of the bar.

"Something I said?" Billy asked.

"He's giving us privacy," I answered.

"Do we need privacy?"

"You tell me."

Billy took another drink and drained his mug. "I filed papers with the county today."

"That was quick."

"It's best when it's icy cold."

"I was talking about the paperwork."

"I know." He punctuated the small joke with an even smaller laugh.

"I thought you were mad at me."

"Not mad." He ran his hands over the condensation on the bar top. "And it's good that you're honest with me."

"Just not so honest?"

He didn't answer. He nodded like it was another tiny joke. I was glad that I had invested in a rusted El Camino. Then, as if he'd read my next thought before it had even formed he said, "I'm working tonight. The sheriff asked me to sit on that field and make sure no one tampers with anything."

That was no surprise. Over the years, Billy had become the go-to guy for the kinds of jobs that required detail and attention. Sheriff Benson had once described the difference between Billy and me. He said one was a watchmaker and one was a bull with a bee on its balls. It was left to me to decide which was which.

"Well, how about I bring you a soda later?" I suggested. "Something tall and cold, to help you stay awake."

"I'd like that." It was a simple, direct statement. The warmth in the smile that went with it said so many things that I wanted, needed, to hear.

After saying goodbye, Billy left and I sat at the bar talking with Clare. For the first time since leaving Billy's bed Sunday morning, I was actually feeling good. That should have served as a warning.

I was working my third glass of tea and thinking about being under the stars with Billy Blevins when the big biker I'd seen with Charlie Lipscomb came into the bar. He swaggered as if on display at some half-assed, white power fashion show. When he sat, he tossed his leg over the back of the chair like he was settling onto his motorcycle.

"You want me to take care of it?" Clare offered.

I didn't know, and I didn't want to know, if Clare was armed. I did assume he was though. That was one reason not to turn him loose. The other was the hot electric current running down my spine. A mutated version of Rick's line in *Casablanca* started repeating in my head, "In all the gin joints. . ." The biker's presence in Moonshines wasn't a coincidence.

I shook my head then told Clare, "Give him some rope."

The biker slapped a hand on the table and demanded, "Bring me something with hair on its nuts."

"Are we talking whiskey?" Clare snapped back. "Or your fantasy date?"

"You're a funny old man. You got a baby in that gut or are you just full of shit?" The biker slapped the table again. This time it was to amplify laughing at his own joke. When the flat of his hand smacked down the last time, the braying died with it. That was when I saw the tattoos again. I'd been right before. On his right forearm there were a pair of *SS* lightning bolts—centered directly over the number *88*.

"I may have a well-earned gut," Clare spoke up as if joking with an audience. "But the ladies like me." Then, quietly, he asked the man, "Want to know my secret?"

"Is it your big mouth?" More table slapping.

Clare looked at me with a bright spark in his eye.

"Don't write that check," I warned him.

He turned back to the biker and said, "No. It's because I'm not a dickless Nazi who smells like road kill washed in piss."

There are times in my life I hated all men for their predictability. There are times I had to love them for their foolishness too. I resolved to decide later which of those times this was. Someone was going to have to pay that bill and I wasn't going to let Clare do it.

There wasn't any more table slapping. The biker stood silently.

I rose from my stool and told him, "You need to get out of here."

"I don't suffer no disrespect." He answered me but kept his gaze on Clare. It wasn't until then that I noticed that the whole building, the bar and the restaurant were silent.

Clare sucked his teeth and it was somehow more insulting than any words could be.

I said, "You're going to have to suffer this." I held up my open badge case and showed my star. "Sheriff's department."

"You think a dyke cop means fuck to me?"

The silence deepened and took on the color of blowing, dirt. It was the same dun shade of wasted earth that covered me as I lay brutalized and bleeding in Iraq. My vision tunneled. Looking at the biker was like staring through the wrong end of binoculars. He was framed in a black-edged circle of haze.

I closed my badge wallet and tucked it away into my pocket. Into the soft black edges of my sight came the welcome throb of red.

Clare saw something he didn't like. It could have been in my face or my eyes or maybe it was my hand under my jacket, holding my pistol. He got in front of me and tried to hold me back. It might have worked. He might have reached me or pushed me. The might haves, stack up in times like that and make dunes over which the tide of inevitability wash.

As he faced me, with hands on my shoulders, Clare took a hard blow to the back of his head. I saw, as clearly as I've ever seen anything, the arcing fist. On the fat, inked fingers were two silver rings. One had a swastika the other had a smirking, goat faced devil. The fallen angel slammed like a shooting star against Clare. It struck at the base of his skull. The impact was red, gouging meat and blood from an opening furrow. I saw also the turning up of Clare's eyes and the instant slackening of his face.

I saw everything, but I couldn't catch him. Clare crumpled to the floor as though his bones had been magically taken away.

I could feel the warm blood on my face. Then I sensed the hot flush of anger creep up under it. Without thinking I had somehow changed my choice of weapon. I pulled my hand from under my jacket and it carried my baton. Thumbing the button, it fell, dragged by gravity to its full extension. We're trained not to use the baton above the waist. It is a weapon for subduing by judicious force. My badge was put away. This wasn't about being a cop. I was a woman facing a much larger man without back-up. There were no rules.

I whipped the baton forward then snapped my wrist. The weighted end hit the biker in the curled lips. His mouth gaped, showering blood and bits of broken teeth.

The strike could have been a kiss for his reaction. He surged forward with flailing arms oblivious to the harm I'd done him.

I ducked his hands and jammed the baton between his legs as I darted to the side. The leverage twisted his feet and dropped him, bloody face first to the floor. Before he finished grunting I was back on my feet.

The biker got his hand under himself and started to push up. I raised my right foot and stomped down with my heel—into the muscle between his shoulder blade and spine. When the heel hit, I twisted it.

He sounded like a steam-powered machine going to pieces, all fury and wind.

After grinding my heel I lifted my foot again and dropped with my left knee. All my weight slammed into his ribs and something snapped.

What breath he had left was caught in his frozen lung then it escaped in a whistling wail of pain.

I thought it was over. It could have—it should have been over. But he reached into a pocket with his right hand and pulled out a tactical knife. He had enough life left in him to flick the four inch blade open. Not enough to avoid the impact of my baton. First I broke his hand and kicked the blade away. Then, just for good measure, I whipped the weighted nightstick down on the back of his thigh.

The biker froze in a rictus of pain.

The colors in my vision evaporated. I turned to Clare, and pressed a damp bar towel to his wound.

"Call 911!" I shouted to anyone who might hear, hoping that it had already been done.

Chapter 13

The bar rag I had stuffed against the wound in Clare's head was saturated with fresh blood and old beer. I retrieved a pair of clean towels and tucked them under him. He moaned and fluttered his eyes.

"Don't move," I warned.

As soon as I said it he twisted his head and winced.

"I told you not to move."

"I'm a tell-me-twice kind of guy."

"Then I'm telling you three times—stay still and wait for the EMT's."

Clare's eyes widened as if he saw Satan himself beckoning. Even with both of my hands holding his shoulders he lurched up, shouting, "Don't."

If he hadn't moved it would have been the end. Clare's motion shifted me just enough. When the big and bloody fist flashed down, it only grazed my ear and edge of my jaw.

The biker, who I had foolishly neglected to cuff in my concern for Clare, was up. He didn't seem to have as much fight in him though. When his blindside punch missed, he pushed me and ran for the exit.

"Get him," Clare grunted as he fell back.

I was already on my way.

Some doors are better left closed. I'd always thought of that expression as a metaphor for things better left unknown. The moment I realized opening a door could be a literal transition into a world you hoped to never see again, it was too late. I had chased my own nightmare and caught it in the parking lot.

The biker who had started everything was standing alone. He wasn't crouched for action or holding a weapon. In fact, he watched me with such a depth of disinterest, that I should have known he wasn't alone.

It was a lesson I learned fast when a hand grabbed me by the hair. It was like running out to the end of a steel cable that was tethered to a mountain. All of my speed and momentum disappeared. My feet left me behind, and kicked uselessly at empty air. I didn't simply fall either. The powerful hand waited for the apex of my swing then jerked me downward.

I hit the asphalt on my back. The air in my lungs burst from my mouth in a gasping bark of pain. As I struggled to recover the lost breath, my eyes washed out from under my bunched lids and slowly focused.

Johnson Rath stood over me. "Time to get some things straight." Then, still with one hand, he picked me up by the hair and punched straight into my left temple.

* * * *

"Your mama had a thing for boys on bikes."

My eyes were open, but still not focused. We were in a car. Moving. I wasn't sure if there were any other passengers. I was in the front but didn't have the strength or leverage to get my head up over the seat.

It was night. Even so, when Johnson Rath turned from the road to look at me, his eyes were glowing ice.

"Did you know that?"

I wouldn't have answered if I could.

"She came sniffing around when she was married to that soldier boy. A woman like that is too bent for a straight arrow like him."

He reached over. The finger I had broken was still splinted. It was thicker and rougher than the rest of his wriggling digits. I thought at first he was trying to get a grip to pull me to him. That wasn't it.

He tore away at the front of my shirt. Two of the buttons popped and fell, dead sentries murdered at their posts.

I grabbed at my shirt and drew the cloth closed. Johnson had already moved on. His squirming digits were under the waist of my skirt. My belt was gone. The linen was frail protection under his assault. The thin string that kept the material drawn up at my waist broke.

His splinted finger, straight and seemingly lifeless was the worst part of his touch. It moved, cold like a dead fish, on my belly as the other digits scrabbled into my satin underwear.

I bolted upright, thrusting my hands out in front of me. There was no plan in the effort. It was instinct and rage. Johnson Rath was unmoved. He shoved my hands down then jerked the back of his hand up into my face. The effect of the blow sent an electric charge of pain from my nose down my spine. What was already a muddy perception, became starry and swirled with sickening motion.

I gathered every bit of will I had—and rose again.

Without turning or looking, probably without thinking of me as anything but a nuisance, Johnson swung his arm to the side. It was as much a horse-kick as a punch. He hit me between the heart and my collar bone. Something inside my chest convulsed. I fell still.

Johnson laughed. "Your mama didn't fight as much as you did."

My mouth filled with coppery wetness. It took all I had to spit the blood out.

Johnson laughed more, like my spit was some kind of great joke. He twisted the wheel and hit the brake at the same time. We swung suddenly off whatever road we were on and bounced hard. The car rattled. It staggered as if drunk. I realized it had to be the same old vehicle I'd seen Johnson take from Dando and my mother earlier.

A stone rattled under the carriage as we skidded to a stop. The headlights illuminated a low roofed shack with a hand painted sign over the door. It read, *The New American Covenant–The Word and The Sword.* The lettering was flanked by a crudely illustrated cross on one side and sword on the other. The building itself was bleached bone-white, but white-power slogans in black and swastikas in red were painted all over it.

From impact or despair I can't say, but at that point I must have blacked out. My next memory is of opening my eyes and seeing myself. The image was faint and indistinct. It was definitely me. I had the same certainty as a dreamer viewing herself in third person as she drifts into slumber.

It wasn't a dream. It was a reflection. I was seeing myself in the windshield of the old car. My body was bent at the waist over the hood. What light there was came from the headlights I was lying between. My shirt was open. Hot metal burned my bare gut. I was grateful my bra was still in place.

I wasn't tied. My hands weren't taped. In no way was I secured. That didn't mean I could move. Volition was stripped from me. Fear can hold us as securely as any rope.

Something moved over my distorted reflection. Johnson Rath was behind me. "You're scarred as shit. Who cut hell out of you?"

Memory, unwelcome but undeniable, settled into my vision. Two men with knives were in front of me along with the blowing dirt of Iraq. They had raped and cut me. They left me for dead beside a mud wall, and let the blowing dust slowly bury me.

It's strange to say how tempting it was to let go. I could have disappeared into that earlier terror—married the Satan who had wooed me for so long—and diminished the current violation. I would have survived. I would not have lived.

Between then and now—between two times of terror and trauma—I think I understood the moments my mother spoke of. She felt herself bound to travel from instant to instant, in fear of the one mistake that had started it all. I felt like my life was one long moment. One in which I was trapped between the grave and the dying.

I knew something perhaps she didn't. Running from the pain gave it a deeper bite.

I tried to rise. A hard arm dropped onto my back.

"That's good," he said.

I didn't know what he was talking about. Was it my attempt to stand? Or was it something he was looking at? I wanted to know—but I didn't. Then the arm was gone. Both of his hands clapped onto my hips. On the right, the splinted finger tapped at bare skin above my skirt. All the other fingers curled under the waist band. The linen material peeled back without resistance, then sagged over my hip. It caught on a bit of the old car's loose chrome.

He pulled. It ripped but didn't give way.

That was the moment I refused the darkness—and took my feet from the grave.

I twisted with a scream.

Johnson was bent over trying to get my skirt pushed down. His head was just above my hip. I led with my left elbow. I caught him with the sharpest point of bone. It struck just in front of his ear, exactly where the jaw pivots on the skull. A satisfying crunch was communicated up my arm.

I didn't stop there.

Johnson staggered, still bent at the waist, clutching his jaw. I tore myself from the car then kicked, aiming for the same spot my elbow hit. I got pretty close. The big man howled in pain. When he released his face to reach for me, his jaw looked lower on the left side.

After I had kicked, I'd resettled my feet in a wide stance ready to use them again. The most powerful muscles in a woman's body are those in the thighs. It is always good to know your strengths.

Johnson charged forward with both hands out, heedless of his defense. He was still underestimating me. It was impossible for a man like him to imagine being beaten by a woman. When his leading leg planted and straightened, I kicked again. That time I went straight in at the knee. It buckled and he fell, too shocked with pain to scream.

I wasn't going to underestimate him. Surging forward, I used my nails to gouge at his eyes. Then I ran.

Johnson had driven off road into a clearing behind thick oaks and walnut trees. I avoided the path and dashed through the dark woods. As I went, I pulled at my torn clothing for coverage.

* * * *

I didn't know about the search for me. I found out about it later—not that it would have mattered to me if I had known. I didn't want to be found.

When I was dragged back into my own life, it was by Billy Blevins. How many more times would he rescue me?

I had lost the rest of that night, the entire next day, and that night. It was another early morning and the bartender, another friend of Billy's, called him when I refused to leave at last call.

Billy got me outside and to his car door. He made the mistake of telling me we were on the way to the hospital. By the time I calmed again, I was lying in the back seat of his cruiser and crying. Billy was driving, and I could see him holding a tissue to his bloody nose. "You're going to be all right," he said. "We're almost there. "You're going to be all right."

I started to answer. I wanted to tell him again that I didn't want to go to the hospital. But when I tried to rise in the seat, I realized I was cuffed.

Billy had restrained me—and that knowledge flushed the words out of my mouth. I rode the rest of the way in silence.

Every few moments Billy reassured me, "Everything will be all right." After the fourth or fifth time I told him, "You said that to me before." Billy didn't answer.

"Do you remember?"

Still no answer.

"It was a long time ago."

He wasn't talking, but he was listening.

"We were in Iraq. You were the medic in the squad that found me by the road. You did what you could to hold me together in the back of a Humvee. Do you remember that?" That time I didn't expect an answer. "You had kind eyes. And you looked sad to have to do the things you did to help me. I remember thinking that you had never seen a woman naked before."

"That wasn't me."

"I can hear you lying."

His silence was that of an old, empty house—memory and time.

Billy slowed the car then pushed the wheel over, aiming carefully. I could feel the change as we rolled, once again, from blacktop to dirt. I experienced an instant of panic and raging heart beat before I caught myself. I was with Billy.

The tires crunched on rocks and packed dirt. They kicked grit up under the car—and it sounded like a hard, slow, rain.

We went like that for a distance. I began to feel lulled. The road was familiar.

Billy stopped and put the car in park. For a moment he seemed to be thinking through what he wanted to do. When he decided, he shut off the engine and got out.

"Come on," he said opening my door. He helped me to slide out.

We were alone on a stretch of dirt road. The rutted tracks curved ahead of us into darkness.

I knew where we were. "Why did you bring me here?"

"Where else should I take you?"

To the left rose a shallow bluff. It was made up of sandstone laid down over ages. In another process of ages, it was being crumbled to dust by junipers and grapevine. To our right was a fallow field, beyond which was a thicket of overgrowth and a stream. Those were the realities. Everything here bent under the weight of things only I could see.

In the middle of the thicket was the spot where a girl was murdered. The spot where the car was parked was where I drank myself to sickness more than once.

"I don't want to be here."

"Tell me one place that you want to be," Billy said looking up at stars. He turned to face me. "I'll take you there."

It was my turn not to answer.

Billy turned back to the stars. "When I was a kid, my father always said there should be no goin' without knowin'. It took me a long time to really get that." That time when he looked back at me, he put a hand on my arm and urged me to turn away from him.

I'd almost forgotten I was cuffed.

Billy released me.

When I turned, he was there. His eyes were waiting for mine. He had more to say. I beat him to it. "Why?"

His expression neither asked nor answered.

"Why did you lie about being the medic who helped me in Iraq?"

"That wasn't me." Billy was not a very good liar.

"*Why?*" I pressed.

"I'm surprised," he said. "You're the strongest person I know. . ."

I pulled the reins in on my need to control the conversation. I needed to see where he was going—more than I needed to hear or say—anything.

"You don't like so show your weaknesses. I mean. . . You don't like to be seen weak at all." He paused, seeming to expect a comment or question.

It was hard for me not to jump in.

"The medic in the back of that Humvee, saw you at your weakest. I don't imagine you would want him to talk about that. And he, I'm sure, would never hold that moment up for scrutiny. Not anyone's. Not even yours."

"Maybe it needs a little scrutiny."

"I bet it does." Billy walked a few steps, creating a distance between us. He looked at stars shimmering over the black band of deep woods. "But it needs *your* scrutiny. Your own time. Your own place."

"Is that why you brought me here?"

"I brought you here to see the stars."

I looked. I stared, actually letting my mind fall into the beautiful fires. I closed my eyes and the constellations were still there. "Just to see stars?" I opened my eyes.

"No," he shook his head without looking back at me. "I wanted to you see the place. Remember it."

"I do."

"No you don't. Really look. Think about it."

"Think about what?"

"Drunks need to see the bottom, Katrina. And this is it."

I'd never felt soft words hit so hard. Billy spoke gently. His voice was kind. I still felt a freight train derail in my gut.

"You never—"

"Do you remember the nights you sat here? Do you remember when I found you and had to take your keys and weapon? What about the time your father sat close while you cried and puked?"

"You don't know what happened yesterday, Billy."

"Then tell me."

I looked away—studying the stars. I didn't even consider telling him. "I don't have to know, to understand it was bad."

"*Bad?*"

"What are you going to do about it?"

"It's not that easy."

"Nothing's easy, Katrina. There is no easy. Ever." Billy, still facing away from me brushed at his eyes with the back of his hand.

I almost asked if he was crying.

Before I could, he turned and pointed at the dirt road. With his finger, he showed the long arc from darkness to darkness. "The road goes two ways. Go forward or go back. But sitting in the middle, with a bottle, serves no one."

"You're an ass."

"If you show up drunk, Sheriff Benson will fire you."

"What? No. He's always—"

"Not anymore. He thinks it will be easier for him to do it. And he thinks it will make it easier for me in the election."

"What do you think?

"You need to tell me what happened."

I did. Some of it. I told some more that simply wasn't true. The basics were there. I told him about Clare and the unknown biker. I told him that Johnson Rath was waiting outside. After that I held back. I told him that Rath got the better of me, then sent me running.

If there was anyone I needed to share the events of that night with, it was Billy. It wasn't about trust. When I began talking, shame kept at my back like a whip guiding my words.

When I finished we were sitting on the hood of Billy's cruiser. He had tried to put an arm around me. I had tried to not to run away from it. We ended up sitting with a foot of open space between us. We were under a silent sky, but the Ozarks called noisily all around us. Cicadas buzzed endlessly. Tree frogs cried for love. I felt a little like I was suspended between the two worlds with different gravities. I had no idea which way I was going to fall.

Without a word, Billy slipped from the hood and went to the back of the car. He opened the trunk and returned—carrying his guitar. The fact that he almost always had the guitar in his car was one of the reasons I worried about him.

He sat beside me, again, on the hood of the car and started strumming. There was no melody. It was the musical equivalent of fidgeting.

"You have something to say?" I asked.

"I have a lot to say. But you're not in a listening frame of mind." Billy said it with a smile and a sad chord. It was hard to hold it against him.

"Are you ever?"

"That's not true, and it's not fair either."

"You know what's not fair?" He strummed again finding the sound and melody he wanted. "Hoyt Axton wrote a song about it."

"What are you talking about?"

"I've never been to Spain," Billy started singing and plucking the strings quietly. He sounded sadder than sad. The song built. He let it come a little faster and louder. It was a strange mix I'd never heard from him. The strumming, the beat, were energetic. The words, and Billy's voice remained mournful.

It wasn't until he was almost finished that I shamefully realized that I was trying to see how the song was about me. If it was, it wasn't how I wanted.

When he finished, Billy sat the guitar aside and looked at me.

"Do you really want to go to Spain?" I asked. As soon as the question was out there, I felt foolish for asking.

"I'm taking you to your uncle's place." His face had become like the stars over us, distant and unreadable. "You can hide out there."

"What makes you think I need to hide?"

"Where's your badge?"

The question was another train—wrecking in my stomach.

"Where's your weapon?" He hit me again. "Do you want to show up at the Sheriff's Office without them after a drunk?"

It had become a night for hard questions.

* * * *

Uncle Orson was waiting at the end of the gangway when we pulled up at the dock. He had a blanket that he draped over my shoulders before ushering me in. Billy didn't follow. Once I was with my uncle, he returned to the cruiser and took off.

"Where's he going?" I asked Uncle Orson.

"You'd know that better than I would," he answered. "Let's get you inside before someone sees you."

"What's it matter if I'm seen?"

"You don't want the attention. Not yet."

"I don't know—"

"You stink, Katrina." Orson opened the shop door then followed me inside. "Your clothes are torn and dirty, you're sweating whisky."

"I can smell you from here." Clare spoke from the shadows on the far side of the shop.

"Clarence." I raised my arms rushing forward. The depth of my relief at seeing him was, in part, a reflection of my shame at having—not once—thought about him since I'd run through that door into the parking lot. "Are you all right?"

"I'm fine. Let's get you cleaned up."

"What's going on?"

"I told you," Uncle Orson said. "You stink."

"It's more than that." I planted my feet and shoved off the blanket. "Did someone tell you what happened to me?"

"We don't know anything about that, sweetheart," Orson said. "And you never have to talk about it if you don't want to."

"Something else happened." Both of the men looked down—like all the truth in the world was sitting on their feet. "Billy talked like I was going to lose my job. You two are acting like I'm a fugitive. The sheriff will be mad, but he's always been on my side before."

"Did Billy tell you about Earl Turner?"

"No."

"Earl called the sheriff's office yesterday." Uncle Orson talked to his shoes. "He said he was doing what you told him to do."

"What I told him?"

"He said he was following his nephew's phone. That you told him to. He said he couldn't trust anyone else in the sheriff's department so he was going to do it alone."

"No." I tried to explain. "That's not what I said. I told him not to—"

"He's dead." Uncle Orson was looking up at me when he said it. "His body was found on another pile of brush—in that old graveyard."

"I didn't tell him. . ." The truth was—I was not completely sure what I'd told him.

I walked through the dark shop and out the dock side door to the houseboat. Neither my uncle nor Clare said anything, or tried to stop me.

In the boat's tiny shower I washed and cried until the water went cold. Even then, I kept rubbing at my skin until the tank went dry. The sun was coming up over a ragged, blazing horizon when I stepped out.

It wasn't until I was dressing again that I took real note of the clothes I had been wearing since that night. They were spattered with blood. Most of it, the big, smeared tracks, was what I had feebly spit out. Buttons were missing from my shirt. The placket was torn away from the thinner fabric. The drawstring of my skirt was broken. At some point I had re knotted it. On the side there was a ragged tear where the lace fabric had hooked on the car. Each bit of damage was a reminder and a blessing.

I turned within the closet-sized bathroom and wiped the mist from the mirror. There on my skin were other, more terrible wounds—reminders were carved into my body like a railroad map of secret spurs. All lines ran to pain, and I was so lucky to have only torn clothing to show for the encounter.

I wanted a drink.

That's the thing about drunks. Harsh words and good advice are no match against the need to drown the internal fires we carry within us. And there is no extinguishing them. The alcohol only banks the coals for a time. The only salvation is to find our own way to live with the flames that gnaw, but never devour us.

Dressed in fresh clothes, jeans, and boots, I returned to the bait shop. The day was already inferno-bright—to match the need in my gut. There was a huge breakfast piled up in the corner booth—my uncle's only table. My first reaction was a lurching nausea. . . then I was starving.

"We started cooking when we heard the water running," Uncle Orson explained.

"You didn't look like you were going to sleep," Clare added.

When he said it, I couldn't help but imagine closing my eyes on cool sheets. It was a foolish thing to do. The nightmares were waiting, reaching for me at the mere thought of sleep.

"No," I admitted. "No sleep." I took a piece of bacon and stuck it into the sun-bright-yellow center of an egg. The meat and yoke went into my mouth, and I chewed slowly, thinking. When my mouth was empty, I said, "I want to talk to my mother."

There was no response—not that I expected one.

"Uncle Orson, do you know where she is?"

He nodded, then he started piling food on his plate. "I'll need a good breakfast first."

Chapter 14

I ate only a few more bites of the huge meal, then went back to the houseboat. If there had been any more water, I would have washed again. I sat on the edge of the bunk and stared at my clasped hands. Despite the rising heat of the day, I shivered.

When Carmen Dando, my mother, came through the door I was curled into a trembling ball on the bed and crying like the child she had left at this same dock.

I don't know what I wanted from her at that moment. I doubt that she could have said what she wanted from me. We had become like magnets, the same poles facing each other. We repelled each other, and I think, each longed to change. It would have been everything—if one of us could have found a way to become something else. . . something with a different charge.

Carmen sat on the floor beside the bunk and rested a hand on mine—that was when I drifted off.

She was still there, her hand over mine, when I woke. It was a small thing that meant a lot to me.

"How long?" My mouth was gummy, boozy, and smelled like roadkill.

"About an hour."

"Thanks for staying."

Carmen looked back at me with my own eyes. I wondered if I looked as sad as she did. She looked like someone with something to say. The hold-back showed in her eyes before she patted my hand. "I've been where you are."

"Where do you think I am?" I didn't invite the distain into my voice.

Carmen took her hand away.

"I'm sorry."

"You have the right." She pulled her knees up and rocked herself gently on the floor. "You can hate me. You can blame me. I drink too, and I drink too much. Bad genes. You didn't get that from your father."

I reached. Putting my hand over hers, I peeled it away from her knees. She let me bring it back to the bed beside me.

"You've been where I am—but this is about more than falling head first into a high ball glass."

"I don't. . ." Her hand squirmed under my own.

"I need to talk to you about Johnson Rath."

She tried to pull her hand away. I didn't let her.

"What about. . ."

"What he did."

"I don't know. . ."

"What he did to you all those years ago."

"No."

"What he tried to do to me." When I said it, the fight was over. Her hand went still. It melted into passivity. I relaxed my hold. Her hand slipped away leaving only a small memory of its presence.

"He's a bad man." Her gaze was pointed to some place I couldn't see. It was her moment, a private pain. I refused to imagine it. When she turned away from the past, my mother looked at me. It was only for a heartbeat of time. She returned to staring at the floor and at something I couldn't see. "He's as cruel as a graveside joke."

I didn't know how to proceed, or exactly where I wanted to go. I simply knew this needed talking about—for me at least. "Why do you spend so much time around him?"

"Cherry doesn't know." She raised her head. Her eyes had ghosts within—and the red swelling of held tears without. "You can't tell him."

"I don't plan on telling him anything."

"*He* wanted to come here. *He* wanted to help Rath with that church. Cherry's not like them. Not a racist. Not exactly. . . He's. . . Well, he's not a good man, but he's good to me. Understand?"

The first rule of interrogation is to let them talk. Silence is often better than a question or prompt for keeping the words coming. That's what I gave my mother, blank silence. It was all she needed.

"With Cherry, it's always about the pay day. He's the kind of man always chasing the treasure. It's why we went to Alaska. We spent almost eight years there—prospecting for gold. We found some too. Put it all together, we worked ninety hours a week and probably made two dollars an hour."

She sat for a while, dwelling in her thoughts. I had to give her a nudge. "If it was about money, where was it coming from?"

"Johnson has a plan. And he needed someone he could trust."

"Cherry?"

"They were friends in the Navy. They met in the brig. Cherry was always in trouble. Johnson protected Cherry once when they got to drinking in the wrong bar. They backed each other up in a hundred scrapes since then. This time's different. Johnson is taking money from the Aryan Brotherhood to build his church and to distribute drugs—covered by religion. But he's working with the DEA too. The idea is to short some of the packages, then make sure that shipment gets intercepted."

"So the AB would just consider the loss part of doing business— and not theft."

"Cherry has friends—out west and all the way back to Alaska. He knows a lot of oil rig workers and tanker hands. He and Johnson think they can move the drugs to those friends without getting noticed."

"What about Tyrell Turner?" My probing was too pointed or too excited. The spell was broken.

"Is that really all you care about?"

I said nothing.

"I'm not talking to my daughter am I? I'm talking to a cop." My mother looked stricken. "I should have known. Cherry made the brush piles to burn old bone and what was left from coffins. He had nothing to do with that kid."

"He tried to pass off a worthless bill of sale. He knew Tyrell."

"I knew Tyrell. It was me."

"What? How?"

I knew the story about the Yocum dollars and his family connection."

"The silver is just a legend."

"The dollars are real. Your father had one. Orson too."

"I've never seen them."

"Just because you've never seen something—doesn't make it impossible."

"Why did you. . ." I couldn't finish. I didn't know exactly what it was she did.

"I was looking for a way to get Cherry away from Rath—or to mess up their plans before my husband got killed. Cherry can't resist the idea of found money. He'll spend his life digging worthless holes searching, but won't take a job in air conditioning. Jobs are for suckers, he always says."

"How?"

"I sent letters to the old man."

"Earl Turner?"

"He didn't answer. His nephew did. The kid had his own reasons—he was looking for his father."

"Cherry Dando?"

"Of course not!"

I decided to ignore the offence in her voice. It was something else I wasn't sure I wanted to know about.

"His name was on a police report the kid had a copy of. His mother had been—" Panic showed in Carmen's eyes.

I read it as fear of even saying the word. "Raped."

"Attacked," she corrected carefully.

"Did you see the report?"

"No. But he asked about several names from back then."

"What names?"

"Cherry, Johnson, Lipscomb."

"Charlie Lipscomb?"

"Yeah. Some others. But he was most interested in Donald Duques."

"Duck?"

"Yes. He got kind of funny when he heard that name. Like Duck meant something to him."

There was a lot to ask about and a lot more to think through. I didn't have the energy after that. We sat in the stifling fiberglass cabin alone with individual thoughts. Carmen moved first, rising after several silent minutes.

"Why didn't you ever come see me?" The question had been lolling around my mouth like a piece of broken glass since she came in. I was unable to swallow it, but afraid of spitting it out. At that moment though, I feared never seeing my mother again.

"Is the interrogation over?" The pain in her voice was impossible to miss. "Are we family again?"

"Were we ever?" It was one of those questions you don't plan and you can't take back.

My mother wheeled about and pushed through the cabin door. I didn't try to stop her.

I did try to follow. It was a failure. Carmen crossed the dock, then dashed through the bait shop. I walked slowly. Reaching the far door, the one that led from the bait shop to the outside world, I was suddenly terrified of opening it.

"You want a soda?" Uncle Orson offered from behind the counter.

I hadn't even seen him there. "No. I. . ." My gaze finished the sentence by shifting to look at the bottles of liquor Orson kept under locked glass.

He walked through my staring and out of my view. The strawberry soda he pulled from the cooler spit when the top popped off. That was when I looked away from what I really wanted.

"I can't talk to her," I admitted. "Why?"

Uncle Orson sat the frosting bottle on the counter in front of me. "You don't even know her."

"She's my mother."

"It doesn't work like that. If it did, no family anywhere would have problems talking. And families are pretty much all about problems communicating."

"I don't think it was her problem." I tasted the soda. Strawberry was not my favorite. When my body was wishing so badly for whiskey, it was a bad choice. I think Orson knew that when he opened it. "I wanted to talk to her. Really talk. I didn't. I couldn't."

"Try another time."

"I'm not sure there will be another time."

"What did you want to talk to her about?"

I returned the bottle to my lips. The liquid was cold and the carbon dioxide bit at my nose. It took two tries to take a swallow. Super sweet, artificially flavored, and blood red, there was no doubt he was punishing me for getting drunk. "I wanted to talk. . ." I shoved the bottle away. "I didn't talk. I questioned her about Cherry Dando and Johnson Rath."

"Did it do any good?"

"Good had nothing to do about it. Is there any tea?"

Uncle Orson drank most of my left over soda as he pulled a milk jug full of tea from the cooler, then poured me a cup. "Did you learn anything?"

"Yes. No. And I don't know." I took a long drink of frigid tea, then rattled the ice at him. He refilled the cup and I said, "There's one thing."

"Yeah?"

"She said something about a Yocum dollar. She said Dad had one. And that you did too."

"I still have it." He reached far under the counter, below the display of clear plastic lighters with fishing flies inside, under the pipe tobacco and pocket knives. From a deep slot, he pulled a shoebox filled with campaign ribbons and medals, the pieces of an incomplete pistol, keys, lures, and even a few rocks. It resembled a boy's treasure box more than an old man's secrets. From under the loose splay of naked lady playing cards, Orson lifted a tarnished silver coin.

It looked like a child's idea of money. On one side, crude raised lettering read, *Yocum Dollar*. On the other side was a dollar sign and the word, *One*.

"That's it?" I asked, astonished. "This is what people go looking for?"

"It's not about the coin. It's about the almost-pure silver it's made from." He placed it in my hand.

"It's heavy."

"Silver is almost $20 an ounce right now. That's a lot of incentive for some people."

I kept drinking tea. We kept talking. It was all space-filler. Uncle Orson did his best to keep my mind engaged. I could say I had other things to think about, but I would be lying to myself. I wasn't thinking.

What was in my mind was more of an absence. I was pulled away from myself, and the space in between was where I really was. It was nothing. It was everything terrible.

I reached for my phone and realized it was gone. Another thing in the possession of Johnson Rath? "I need your phone."

Uncle Orson didn't question me. He pulled an old flip phone from his pocket and handed it over.

I didn't even give him a hard time about the phone. I simply took it with me and returned to the houseboat.

Dr. Kurtz was out of town. She left a number with the service for a therapist covering for her while she was gone. I didn't call him.

*　*　*　*

I don't know how long it was, but the light had shifted to the other side of the dock and I had used up all the good air in the cabin when Billy knocked on the door. The phone was still clasped in my hands.

He knocked again, then came in without my asking.

"I don't feel like—"

Billy held up my gun and baton in one hand, my badge and phone with the other.

"How?"

"I know a guy," he answered as I wrapped my arms around him. He tossed everything onto the bunk and embraced me.

I didn't mean to stiffen my back or pull away, but I did.

Billy ignored my reaction. "You have choices to make."

"What choices?"

"The way I see it, we can call the sheriff. We can ask him to come here. Then, you can lie like a dog on a cheap rug, or you can come clean. The man loves you. You know that."

"He does. That's why I can't lie to him. And I can't put him in the position of protecting me again."

"What do you want to do?"

"Want's got nothing to do with it. I have to get myself back into the world. Maybe I do deserve to lose my job; but I want to lose it doing it—not hiding and crying."

Billy looked pleased. I felt better for saying the words. It would have been a nice moment if he hadn't put his hands on my face and tried to kiss me. I take that back. The problem wasn't his kiss—it was me pulling away.

I saw the hurt. I believe I saw the understanding. I told him I still needed some time alone. That didn't sit well, but he didn't protest. Billy was patient. Kind. He was everything I needed, and at that moment, everything I needed pissed me off.

* * * *

Time again became indeterminate. I was unable to count out the hours. I judged everything by color. A sky so pale and blinding—it was almost white—had mellowed into deeper and deeper blue. Eventually, the far horizon took a beating and turned purple and orange. Thin, wasted clouds looked like sutures on a brutal wound. When the sun slipped low enough, it shone like an open artery on the undersides of the thickening wisps. When the light burnished down to the dull sheen of old blood, I left.

Clare brought my truck from Moonshines. I saw the keys hanging from the hook by the door that morning. Grabbing the keys was the only thing that slowed me. I raced through the bait shop without answering my uncle's questions. Had I hesitated at all, I would have stopped at the door. I sped to a chugging jog down the gangway. The weight of my service weapon and baton pulled at my hip.

While I had waited for darkness, I'd checked my phone. Earl Turner had called me five times. Each message was more excited, but less informative, than the last. He was sure he'd found his nephew's killer. He begged me to come. He never said where.

Even though Earl was already dead, I listened to each recording. As they played, I pleaded uselessly with him to call 911. In the final voicemail he told me, "Find the boy."

I didn't know what he meant by that, which didn't make me feel any less guilty. I may have been wrong when I told Earl about the legal constraints of tracking the phone. I'm a detective not a lawyer. We pull local use data from phones all the time. I probably could have made it work—warrant or not. I took an easier path, and let him go where he shouldn't have gone. That was on me.

I was driving the truck. The twin hands of guilt and revenge were steering. It took over an hour of searching to track the path I needed. I knew the area well. I began to recall my run through, and emergence from, the woods. Even with that, if I hadn't seen the tail lights of a pickup bump their way down the hidden dirt track, I may have never found it.

I spent another twenty minutes finding a place to stop and hide the truck. I had enough sense that I wasn't going to simply drive into the single lane path—without knowing who, or what, was waiting. I passed by the tail lights, and found another break in the barbed wire fencing that led to an adjacent field. It was about ten acres of fallow pasture that had been given over to weeds and scrub. The grass was burned and dry. Junipers were thriving, but none of them were over four feet tall. My big GMC rolled over them effortlessly.

I crossed the field and parked, with my lights out, alongside the overgrown fence row. That line of wire was a boundary—shared with the woods I had run through to escape Johnson Rath.

The fencing was loose and rusty. It spread easily. I pulled it open and stepped through.

It occurred to me that I might end up wandering around in the darkness—looking for the shack that housed the New American Covenant–The Word and The Sword. There was no reason to worry. I heard the rising sound, after only a few paces, through the woods. A minute later, the glow of headlights gave me a beacon to follow.

Crouching at the clearing edge, I counted cars, trucks, and bikes. I gave up at twenty vehicles. Their numbers were not going to stop what I had to do. Most of the people were outside, milling around a fire pit and a half dozen coolers. They were all male. They were all white. Most were heavily tattooed.

A scuffle broke out. Three men were pushing and cursing another near a group of motorcycles, on the far side of the fire. They were all familiar to me as Ozarks Nightriders, but two stood out. The one getting worked over was Roland Duques. The one leading the effort was Charlie Lipscomb, the Nightrider's Sergeant-At-Arms. He was easy to pick out—because of the cigar stub sticking out of his mouth.

I crept around the perimeter of the clearing to get closer. I stopped when I could make out the raised voices.

"So what if I did?" Roland shouted, then pushed back against one of the Nightriders pressing him.

"Club business stays club business," Lipscomb bellowed back at the young man. "You know that. We all know that." He inclined his head, and one of the other men punched Roland in the gut.

They all laughed as the kid bent over and vomited out his belly full of beer. Roland fought to catch his breath. Between wet gasps he defiantly said, "Screw you."

The men laughed again.

"You're the only one getting screwed here," Lipscomb shouted back. He took a long drag from the cigar and blew smoke into the kid's face.

"What about family?" Roland stood, still breathing hard. "What about brothers?"

"It's family business," Lipscomb replied. "And business always comes first."

"You set me up."

"Prospects take the weight." Lipscomb threw a hard punch that nestled hard into Roland's eye socket. The other two men joined in. When the kid was on the ground—trying to cover his head and face—they started kicking. "And they keep their mouths shut."

Charlie Lipscomb pulled what was left of the cigar butt from his mouth, then field stripped it. When the last of his cigar had flittered away into darkness, he walked away. After a few more kicks the other two men wandered after him.

For a second, I thought I should help Roland. There were many seconds during which I told myself that, sometimes, we make the beds we most dread sleeping in. Beyond that, Roland was not who I was there for.

Someone at the shack's front door blew a shrieking whistle.

There was Johnson Rath—at the open entrance waving his arms—drawing the faithful inside. Headlights blinked out. Coolers slammed closed. He kept at it, whistling and waving, until Roland was the only person left outside. Rath closed the temple door.

Chapter 15

I stood with my back against a broad walnut tree to conceal my shape. From inside of the shack, I could hear the pulsing rumble of death metal and the rhythmic stomping of boots on wood. At one place in the old wall, there was a gap through which a beam of light shone and flickered as bodies entered.

I was ready. Each moment I wasted chilled the fire that I allowed to flare in my heart. I wasn't so far gone that I could completely ignore Roland. Had he been quiet, I might have convinced myself that he was dead. That would have been easier. I could have let him lie. After I'd done what I came to do, I would have sent deputies to pick up the three men who had beaten him.

He wasn't dead. He was sobbing. That was harder. Men don't want to be rescued by women and they definitely don't want to be caught by them—crying after a losing fight.

I gave him a little time. Then a little turned into too much for me. As I approached, careful to stay low in high grass and skirt the line of motorcycles, Roland sat up. He stood up brushing dirt from his filthy clothes. It was wasted effort.

"Roland." I kept my voice low and soft.

He froze. "Who's there?"

"Roland. It's Sheriff's Detective Katrina Williams."

"Hurricane?"

I almost told him not to call me that. "Yes."

He returned to brushing away at his jeans and denim jacket with the sleeves sliced off. "What do you want?" His question was sullen and angry. I thought it was simply because I'd witnessed the shame of his beating.

"Are you all right?"

"Of course I'm all right. What do you care? You're the reason I got my ass kicked in the first place."

"I don't understand."

"You got your gun don't you?"

Billy had said, *I know a guy*, when I asked him how he got my weapon and badge back. He was talking about Roland Duques.

"I'm sorry it caused you problems." I was sincere. I'm not sure Roland was interested in apologies. "Why did you help?"

He slapped at his jacket again—then pointed at the vibrating shack. "This place—none of it—none of them—nothing is what it was supposed to be."

"Did your father tell you it was something to be admired?"

He turned to face me, straight on, for the first time. In the firelight, I could see the damage to his face and the boyish anger couched within. "Why don't you get out of here? Cops aren't very welcome."

"What's going on inside?"

Roland kept his stare aimed at me.

"Is that something you believe in?"

"Is what something I believe in? You don't know anything about it. Or me."

"I don't know about you."

He kept staring. "You don't know shit."

"I'm trying to help you."

"That's why you're here?" Roland let the question dangle—like bait. When I didn't rise to it, he pressed. "You're going to help me? Skulking around in the dark—asking about what's happening in there? How are you going to help anyone but yourself?"

"You're right. I came here for something else."

He huffed loudly.

"I came here for my own business. Is that what you want to hear?"

"At least it's honest."

"You want a little more honesty? Maybe I don't know a lot about you, but I'm clear on what's happening in that Mein Kampf church. I know enough about both to say you're in trouble."

"Who says I'm in trouble?"

"These are the deep waters, Roland. There's no little bit in. Either you're drenched or you're dry. Right now, you think maybe you can sit on a dock and dip your toes. You think maybe, just *maybe*, it can be like you want it to be." I paused to let it sink in. "You're drowning. This whole thing is a weight taking you down."

"I already helped you. I took my lumps for it."

"Everyone takes lumps in life, Roland. It's up to you to decide who you take them for."

"I'm out of here." He walked straight at the small fire, then stopped and looked back at me. "If you go in there, you're dead. They'll kill you then dance on your bones."

"You can help me."

"No, I can't."

"You don't have to keep walking the straight line. Turn. Get off the road."

"Is that what you're doing?"

"Talking to some people is like chewing barbed wire."

"You said it, lady. You had the whole speech about deep water—but you got it wrong. I'm standing in a boat on choppy water. You're telling me to fall in the boat. Someone else is telling me to fall in the water. The thing is, everyone wants me to fall." Roland Duques turned his back on me and trudged right though the campfire and into the darkness on the other side.

I went to church.

The music was dead by then. All the stomping was over. One voice was occasionally punctuated by shouts of agreement.

I crept up the sagging stairs. There was no door kicking entrance, nothing so dramatic. My gun wasn't even drawn. My hand was on the butt and ready. I pushed and the door opened. No one turned. All faces remained turned to the riser at the far end of the room. Johnson Rath stood there within the blaze of a single spotlight. His cold eyes caught light and reflected it back, cold. There were fresh scratches around them—where my nails had dug in. His bold beard caught in the stream of a fan. It writhed like a living thing. For his sermon, Johnson was shirtless. He was in his sixties, at least, but he looked much younger and stronger. His chest was broad and hard—even if his gut lapped a little over his belt.

Johnson raised his arms in a mockery of the crucifixion. In each hand, he held an open book. One was obviously a bible. The other had a red cover.

"Children," Johnson exclaimed.

"Yes," some voices answered.

"The children," others added.

Many of the voices raised in reply were female. I looked around and noticed several women who I hadn't seen earlier. They must have been inside while the men socialized outside.

"Children," Johnson called out again.

Again he was echoed by the crowd.

"White children born to white families—" Johnson pointed into the gathering with the bible. He raised the red book over his head. It had a black swastika on the cover. "In a world gone brown."

There were hallelujahs and shouts of praise. Someone even said, "You're goddamned right."

"Where is their place? Where is our place?" Johnson lowered his hands and put the books down on a table beside him. "Where will the children of the light and the grace live—in a world of mud? Make no mistake— not only is the world being taken from us, the forces of the dirt are doing everything to lower our progeny to their level.

"So much of that has been our fault. For years we misunderstood. We called them—and I mean *Them*, with a capital T, the Jews, the nigger races, the sand dwellers, all the Mohammad followers—we called them stupid. We believed them ignorant breeders. But they are more than that. They are not wise, but they are canny.

"They use the Jewish banks and the Arab oil—they use lawyers and nigger music—not to raise themselves, but to bring us down."

"Fuckin' A!" a voice chimed in. It was followed by applause and more shouts of agreement.

I'd heard more than enough of that crap. I pushed my way into the knot of National Socialist nonsense and used my fists and elbows to clear a path forward. Hands grabbed at me and I could hear the name, *Hurricane*, spit out in both surprise and anger. The hands I slapped away or twisted off me. The voices I ignored.

Before I made it through the mass, it thinned. A bloated brute of a man, shirtless and wearing red suspenders to hold up tent sized jeans, lumbered into my way.

"Where you think you're goin'?" He tried for a snarl but only managed a slur.

I kicked him in the crotch and went around—as he collapsed.

"Come back for more?" Johnson Rath's big voice boomed down from the riser.

Some voices raised again in laughter.

"Taking on all comers this time?"

The laughter, cruel in sound and intent, swelled up to fill the space. It was a good time for me to pull my weapon.

From behind me, a woman shouted, "You got what was coming to you."

I turned around and hunted for any smirk of admission in the mob. There were some good candidates, but none of whom I was sure. The woman and I were both lucky. Had she shown her laughing face, I would have killed her without a thought.

I turned back with my pistol targeted on Johnson's chest. "You're under arrest."

He, and the crowd, laughed.

I ignored it all and stepped up onto the riser. "For kidnapping, sexual assault, assault on a police officer—"

He raised a hand, reaching out toward me.

"Give me an excuse." I warned him in a voice so quiet—only he and I could hear. "The only way you're going out of here alive is in cuffs."

"What are you going to do?" Johnson waved the hand out to the assembly and invited their outrage. "Arrest us all?"

They laughed. Someone grabbed at my pants. They let go when I kicked. Johnson laughed louder than anyone.

I darted in between his open hands, and whipped the butt of my weapon into his mouth. His blood sprayed. The mob went silent so quickly—I heard one of Johnson's teeth rattle on the bare board floor.

Before he could recover—before anyone could react—I shoved the barrel of my pistol down the front of the big man's jeans. I cocked the hammer.

He wasn't laughing anymore. All of his quiet attention was on me. So was everyone else's.

"You can't do that," a woman protested. "You're a cop. We have rights." She was probably the same one who had said I got what I deserved.

With my free left hand I pulled out my cuffs. "Give me your hand."

He twisted. I jammed my 9mm deeper into his pants. Judging from the look in his pale eyes, I hit something important.

Johnson held up his right hand.

I slapped the cuff on. "You do the other hand. Behind your back."

He complied. I heard the ratchet of the bracelet. That didn't mean I trusted it. I reached around his body to check the cuffs were secure.

"You think they'll let you out of here?" So close, his eyes were halogen bright and glacier cold. "Take a step and you're dead."

"I don't think they want to risk the source of so much white pride." I wiggled the gun in his pants. "I don't think you do either. You'd best take your chances with a lawyer. I hope he's Jewish."

"Fuck that. Birch will kick me loose."

"We'll see. Walk."

Leading Johnson by the pistol in his crotch, I took him through the quiet mob and out to the clearing around the shack. Several men dashed ahead and stood between us and the dirt road. Some climbed into trucks which they pulled around to form a road block. They left the high beams on, illuminating us in hard glare.

I turned my back on the light—pulling Johnson around with me.

"Where are you taking me?" For the first time, Johnson Rath sounded less than confident.

I didn't answer.

The mob followed behind as we trudged through the clearing. The grass and weeds were so dry they crunched under our feet. We reached the edge of the cut, where the smoke and hawthorn trees were wound with poison ivy and poison oak.

"I'm not going in there." Johnson planted his feet. "Someone get in here and take this bitch."

I pulled the pistol from his pants then jammed it back into his crotch and fired a round into the dirt between Johnson's feet. Before anything else could happen, I returned the smoking barrel to its nest within his jeans.

Johnson Rath didn't quite scream. The sound he made was more like a growling moan. He sounded like a wounded bear and was just as dangerous. I worked the pistol in deeper and shook it around making sure the hot opening and the sharp-edged gun sight made plenty of contact with bare skin.

I pulled the hammer back again. "Do you believe I'll do it?"

He didn't respond, at least not in words. He shut up. When I walked into the woods, he followed. No one else did. The mob crowded up to the edge of the clearing and stopped.

It didn't take long before all sign of them was lost.

Darkness, woody and deep, swallowed us. Our path was by touch, each foot reaching out and finding solid purchase before the next lifted. The ground shifted, roots caught, and rotted wood gave way. Several times, one of us stumbled. Each time, I could hear Johnson take a hard breath anticipating the discharge that would take his manhood.

We reached a shallow gully. In a normal season it would have held a trickle of water draining the green space down to the lakes. That summer it was dry. There was a layer of sandstone exposed by earlier waters. It was as good a place as any.

"Kneel here," I told him.

Even Johnson's unnaturally bright eyes were invisible in the forest dark. I didn't need to see them to know his reaction. I felt it the way you feel tragedy when you walk by an open hospital room.

"You're a cop." The argument was as feeble as the sound of his voice. I think he knew it.

"You're a rapist." The hope that drained from him was a physical thing. Cold air leaking from the refrigerator on a hot day. "You're a sadist. And a Nazi. And a murderer."

"I've never killed anyone." The refutation was a small gesture. Judas throwing away the silver.

"Kneel."

He did.

As his legs bent, and his body sank, I turned my pistol so the sight was against his belly. I pulled the weapon quickly, gouging a line of revenge up his skin. He hissed a quick reaction then returned to silence on his knees. I had the gun to his head by then.

We remained like that, locked together in the moment, stretching it out over hundreds of heartbeats. No matter how I counted time, I realized it was one moment. I understood my mother. I understood how easy it would be to live an entire lifetime right there, in that one segment of uncountable time.

It wasn't until I was there, in that moment, that I realized the degree to which I had been living in another one.

"You don't have the guts." It wasn't bluster or bravado. Johnson was making a simple, grateful, statement.

"You think it takes courage to kill?" I brought the barrel of my service weapon from the back of his head to the swelling of bone behind the right ear. I pushed. I pushed hard, grinding the pistol against skin and skull. I didn't stop until his head was bent over as far as it would go. He appeared to be praying. "You had better hope I have the courage not to kill you. Because I'm not sure I do."

That moment, elastic and terrible, stretched into an eternity. Sweat rolled into my eyes and I brushed it away. My right hand, and with it, the gun, shook.

I don't think I was breathing. I do know I was ready. I tightened my finger. Time slipped into increments of pressure on a trigger.

"Please." Johnson spoke so quietly I almost missed it.

Maybe I imagined it. It didn't matter. Salvation comes in small words. His and mine.

I holstered my weapon.

Together, we waited in the darkness for time to find us again. The moon was out. It beamed bands of light that flitted in the trees and showed like silver stepping stones on the ground. Any other time, any other darkness, and I would never have seen it.

Chapter 16

"You did what?" The sheriff's question burst out at me.

I told him again that I had arrested Johnson Rath and put him in our jail.

Sheriff Benson thought about it for a moment. Then he asked how I was. He was calm and kind, the man who was my friend.

I tried evading the question, and he became my boss again.

He cursed and pointed fingers at me. He jabbed them in all directions—punctuating his points.

For my part, I stood quietly and took it as deserved. When he settled enough to tell me to sit, the boss was spent. The friend returned. He asked me what had happened. Anyone else would have meant that as, why had I disappeared for a day? I didn't have to tell him I had been drunk. And I couldn't hide it from him either. So I told him. Everything.

My friend the sheriff was one of the few people who knew exactly what had happened to me in Iraq. He knew about the problems I had with the Army—after reporting my assault and rape at the hands of two superior officers in a war zone. If anyone was going to cut me slack when I allowed violence and my distrust of protocol to raise their ugly heads, it was him.

"I should have your badge." There was no slack in his voice.

"I'd heard you're already planning on it."

"You're goddamned right, I am planning on it." He kicked back in his chair and put dirty boots up on his desk. "And not just for my sake."

"For Billy's."

"For yours."

"Mine?"

"How long do you think it can go on like this?"

I had no answer for that.

"The only reason I don't take your gun and badge—the only reason I don't pin a pink slip to your chest right now—is it would probably be a free pass for Johnson Rath. He's had enough of that. And I've had enough of that son-of-a-bitch to last a lifetime."

It went on like that for a while: the sheriff cursing and railing against a world that had people like Rath in it.

"You should get out," he finished up. "Leave this awful business."

"I'm a woman with options."

"You are that. More than that. You have a life ahead of you. One that does not need to be so full of heartbreak and gunfire."

"Why do I get the feeling you're trying to tell me something more?"

"Birch will be here in the morning."

"Who's to say the DEA has to know? Maybe Agent Birch can find out in the newspapers like everyone else."

"I'm saying it. I can't say I like it, but there's the way things should be done—and the way things have to be done."

"What about Earl Turner's phone?"

"What about it?"

I gave him a synopsis of what I had discussed with Turner, and my fears of using the tracking feature.

"I'd say you were right about the legal issues. With no one to give consent, it seems murky to me. I'd say you were as wrong as fur on a frog to let him keep using it himself. And, I'd sure as shit say you were wrong not to just pick up the phone and ask for a warrant."

"Things got a little busy."

"Don't they always?"

"He called me several times."

"Yeah, well that's something you're going to have to live with."

* * * *

At home I showered again. Then another few times.

Night became early morning as I was sitting on the big leather couch in the living room. Light from the dropping moon passed through the lakeside wall of glass. It rested easy on my eyes—not so easy as to let me close them.

The knock came after 1 a.m. Billy was at the door. The gentle rapping called without demand. A request I couldn't honor.

When he left, I was both lighter and heavier inside.

* * * *

My phone rang not long after the sun rose—like a hot rocket into a sky so heated and lifeless—it seemed like blank paper. I was already awake and dressed.

"Devon Birch is on his way here," the sheriff said, without any greeting.

"I'll be there."

I skipped breakfast that morning. I did not go straight to meet the sheriff and Agent Birch. Instead, I went to the jail. Duck was already there.

"You're here early," I said.

"I figured you'd get a quick start on things." He didn't want to meet my gaze directly.

"How's that?"

"You got Dando sitting in there with no charges filed. You got Rath wrapped up in everything but the flag. Still, he keeps talking about being out for lunch."

"Is that it?"

He got a look, but turned it to the floor before I could read anything. "Thanks."

"What?"

"Thanks." He looked at me, then away. "For trying to help Roland."

"He told you?"

"He's not a bad kid."

"I'm not sure that has anything to do with it anymore."

"He's in trouble?"

"You're not that stupid, Duck."

"Okay. I know he's in trouble. I know he thought he was a big man. He wants to do it all his way. And he wants the privilege of being ashamed of his daddy—while asking for my help at the same time." Duck still didn't look right at me. His face was showing pictures like a drive-in movie screen. Fear. Shame. Desperation.

"You know what he's gotten into?"

"It more what has his hooks in him. Or who."

"The Nightriders?"

"Not that easy."

"I don't know what that means."

"The Nightriders aren't independent anymore. They tucked themselves under the wing of the AB."

"I know that. You still could have shared it earlier."

"Hey, I'm walking a line here, and my balance ain't so good." Color flushed up his jowls and under the big Elvis sideburns he'd probably worn since he could grow them.

"Then help me out, or join the circus."

"He's my kid, Hurricane." Duck dropped his defenses like a man throwing off a heavy yoke. His wide, flabby body merely sagged. His face crashed. "He's my kid. And everything I say to you about it puts him at risk."

Suddenly a connection sparked in my brain. "He's your kid. Maybe he's *the* kid."

"What kid?"

"What has all this got to do with the old days?"

"I'm not talking about any old days. I'm talking about my son and these days. Right now is his time. Ancient history has nothing to do with him."

"We're going to talk a lot more about all of this." I pointed down the corridor of cells. "Open the door and kick Dando out. When my mother comes to pick him up, maybe the three of you can talk about how the past has a way of coming home to roost."

* * * *

"Put him out." Agent Devon Birch made the mistake of letting it sound like an order.

"The hell you say." Sheriff Benson shot back.

"I mean it. This is bigger than whatever the hell you think you can pin on the son-of-a-bitch. Things are rolling. Big heavy things that will sweep up a lot of trash."

"Maybe you want to listen to what's going on—before you make statements about what's big and what isn't."

"I don't." Birch stood his ground. "I don't want to listen to anything. Because I don't care. Just get this done."

"That's the whole problem with feds." I stood at the door talking past Birch. "They try to big picture everything."

"You got that right," the sheriff answered.

"That's hardly a fair assessment—"

"Save it. Maybe *I* don't want to listen."

"Who says it's about you?" I didn't answer. The sheriff didn't answer. The weight of our silence was too much for Birch. "What?" he asked, looking from one of us to the other then back again, "What's going on?"

"Detective Williams. . ." The sheriff let his voice become soft to match the slump in his shoulders. "Maybe you would like to leave us alone?"

"No." I made it a hard pronouncement. "I wouldn't."

"If you two are finished putting on your one-act drama, maybe we can get some work taken care of."

"Yeah, maybe we can." Sheriff Benson sat behind his desk. He did not put his feet up. "Sit down." He gestured Birch to a seat.

"I don't plan on staying."

"Sit the fuck down, Agent Birch." The sheriff has a way of turning a hot conversation cold real quick.

I actually felt a little sorry for Birch. He was expecting a familiar dance. Feds and locals always did a give and take over jurisdiction and charges. The federal government usually wins. They hold a lot of purse strings. And the big picture is. . .well, the big picture.

"What's going on?" To his credit, Birch didn't get defensive and he had the sense to know it wasn't personal. He sat.

"Johnson Rath is in our jail charged with multiple counts of assault on an officer and sexual assault." Sheriff Benson gave me a look that was part apology. The other part was the same professional sympathy I've seen him give to other victims.

"You mean. . ." Birch followed the sheriff's gaze to me. "You?"

That was all I could take. I've become all too familiar with a certain facial expression. It is the way good men look when they're confronted by women who have been sexually assaulted. It is sympathy, welded to an instant cataloging of guilt—for every laugh at every joke—for each backward, appraising glance as a woman passed—for every time they saw a pretty woman and had the inevitable thought. It is a look that shows a broken heart and an understanding of their own flaws.

It's a terrible way to be looked at.

They would talk straighter without me, I realized. So I left.

Work, the routine work of digging through files, making phone calls, and returning e-mails did little to occupy my mind. In fact, it made things worse. The demands were so light—they left a big part of my brain to dwell on the darkness. In the darkness, a bottle of whiskey was always waiting—claiming to have all the answers.

Someone laughed down the hall. Another voice spoke cheerfully, and the same someone laughed again. It was Doreen, our daytime dispatcher, laughing. The voice that had her going belonged to Billy Blevins.

I rushed to close my door. I didn't make it. Billy stepped into the frame. I pretended like I hadn't known he was coming. He pretended I wasn't closing the door.

"Hey." Billy took a drink from his ever-present thermal cup full of soda.

I tried to smile but the expression didn't feel right on my face. "Hi, Billy." I inched the door a little more closed. It stood between us, a barrier that I hid behind. "I don't feel much like talking right now."

"Oh."

"I'm sorry."

"No problem," he answered in a way that refuted the words. "The sheriff's waiting for me anyway." He walked.

"Sheriff?"

"He called me in for something." Billy kept walking without looking back.

I closed my door and stood behind. Hiding lasted only a few minutes. I went to the sheriff's office and went in without knocking. The sheriff and Birch looked at me. Billy didn't.

"Detective Williams," the sheriff said too formally. "Not now."

"If this is about me—"

"Not everything is about you." He stared at me after he said it. Waiting. I backed out and closed the door.

Billy came out about twenty minutes later. My door was open, waiting for him. He didn't even glance in. He walked quickly by and left the building. There was no denying the feeling that I had missed some chance. . .

When Billy had gone, the Sheriff's Department building was too small and brightly lit. Everyone inside looked at me like they knew something. I skipped out.

Without much thought, my truck took me to the place where all of this had begun. Along with the deputy's cruiser, there were several other vehicles parked on the grass—alongside the dirt road that led to the clearing.

Everything was different. The burn circle where someone had tried to incinerate Tyrell Turner's body was staked out with rebar. The thin posts were strung with a combination of crime scene tape and pink plastic construction markings. Dotting the cleared field were tiny yellow flags. People in hard hats were moving through the brown weeds on their hands and knees. When one stopped, she poked a new little flag into the ground before moving on. At the far end, men with chainsaws were cutting down junipers and opening up the remaining overgrowth.

"Hurricane."

I hadn't even noticed the pop-up awning perched on the nearest edge of the field. Within the shade was Ranger Carter. He waved and called my nickname again.

The first thing I said when I stepped under the canvas was, "Don't call me that."

"Hurricane?"

"Yes."

He smiled and bobbed his head, considering. "I get it. Nobody calls me Jesus. In fact they work hard to avoid it. It sounds like we have the same kind of problem with names."

"Different sides of the same coin, maybe."

"Did you come to check on your tax dollars at work?" He pointed to the table in front of him. It was spread with huge sheets of graph paper.

"Actually, I came out to think about the recent crimes committed here. I thought I'd be alone to do it."

"We didn't expect to have much time with this place. Like I said, the legal legs we're standing on are lame. The history is too rich. And it doesn't deserve to be buried under some kind of half-assed Reichstag. We got a team of grad students to do the work."

"Who's we?"

"He means the Park Service. But it's my team." A petite blonde woman walked into the shade from behind me. She was wearing khaki shorts that—despite their color—showed the fresh ground in dirt. Her knees were covered with hard shelled pads. My first thought was that she was, maybe, twenty. She pushed the boonie hat from her head. Her face was softly lined. Her eyes were beauty-pageant blue. She offered her hand. "Dr. Janice Carter."

"Carter?" I couldn't stop my eyes from shifting to Agent Carter.

He grinned proudly. "My wife."

"Jesus." At first I thought Dr. Carter was cursing. It took a moment to catch the familiarity. She was chastising her husband. To me she said, "He always makes it sound like he has the prize hog at the county fair."

"A man can't be happy with his own good fortune?" he asked.

As we shook hands, she smiled. "Don't worry. It's not a race thing. It's the doctor thing."

"Janice has her Ph.D. in cultural anthropology," Agent Carter offered.

"See?" she asked. "You're the one they call 'Hurricane'."

"She doesn't like that nickname," her husband jumped in, before I could say anything.

"Why?" She beamed blue eyes at me. "You look like a force of nature. You're six foot without those boots."

"Close enough," I answered.

She leaned close. In a conspiratorial whisper asked, "You know what advice I would give any woman?"

I shook my head.

"Be the hurricane." She smiled warmly, then slapped dust from her shorts. "I've got something for you, by the way."

"For me?"

"Oh yes, for you." Janice lifted a notebook from the table. It was stuffed to overflowing with loose papers and photographs. She rifled through, then pulled several pieces and handed them over. "I checked out the scene over there." She pointed to the taped off burn circle. "I didn't go in. I know what kind of trouble that can be. But I gave the outside a good going-over. We were doing the survey anyway so. . ."

I scanned the first page. It was a drawing over a grid—showing the burned area and the ground around it. "That's amazing." I meant it. I reached into my pocket and produced my own notepad. Opening it to the sketches I made Sunday morning, I passed it over to Janice.

"You do good work," she said, "but you need scale for real clarity."

"It's not for evidence. It's more to help me see."

"We get down to a little more detail."

I looked at the next page, another drawing. "What's this?"

"Look at the photos."

I did. There was a black and white photo of a cigarette butt. There was another of a tire tread pattern in the dirt. The third was something that just looked like more dirt. "What's this last one?"

"See this?" Janice ran a short, ragged nail along the edge of a barely visible pattern. "Something was spilled here. It soaked into the dry ground. The spot still smelled of gas."

I looked at the photos again, then turned back to the drawing. "This isn't part of the burn area."

"No." Janice pointed over to the far edge of the clearing where we had found open holes. "Over there—" Then she used the same finger to show the spot on the drawing. "Is this open grave. Nothing has been touched and they are flagged. It might not be anything but. . ." She shrugged broadly.

"That's a motorcycle tread," I said. "I don't think I'll have to work very hard to find a match."

"What about the cigarette? Will you get DNA?"

"We're a county sheriff's department. Spending that kind of money is a last resort."

"Janice watches too many of the cop shows with ten minute forensics, and every speck of dust getting the third degree." Agent Carter said with good humor. "Never her husband."

"My husband is no fun."

They had everything I needed. I picked up the cigarette butt with tweezers. It got sealed into a zipper bag. I even scooped a bit of the soil where Janice said there had been a spill—to make her happy. She enjoyed playing a part in the investigation.

"I have a question," I said, as I tucked the bags away. "You said, 'cultural anthropology.' This looks like archaeology."

"Lines blur," she answered. "The kids out there, clearing trees and marking things, are grad students—both archaeology and anthropology. If this was an Indian mound or a Civil War battlefield, a real archaeologist would take the lead. Something like this. . ." Janice walked to the open grave and looked inside. "Well, I was interested and available. May I ask *you* something?"

"I guess."

"Fair warning. It's a favor not a question."

"Okay. . ."

"We have a daughter. She's in the fourth grade. They have parents come in all the time and talk about their jobs." Her look turned hopeful. "It would be pretty amazing for her. . ."

"You want me to come talk to her class?"

"They have moms come in—nurses, a lot of nurses, some work at factories, or banks—good jobs. But all the cops, or firefighters, surgeons, utility line workers, are dads."

"I don't imagine that there are many moms who are anthropologists."

"I'm her mother. Nothing I do is cool."

"I'd be glad to."

"Great. I can't wait to tell her. It can be hard—mothers and daughters."

"Tell me about it."

I don't know if there was something in my voice or my eyes. I would not have wanted there to be, but Janice caught something. Her face changed. Her gaze shifted down into the open grave. "It could be worse you know."

"What could?"

"Mothers. Families." She squatted and used the side of her hand to draw some loose dirt from the edge of the hole. "We can lose them all. To time and history. This poor woman—"

"Woman?"

"Henrietta Patee."

The name struck me. Patee. The first stone I found had the name Freeman Patee engraved on it. Earl Turner had said his family was buried here, the Turners and Patees. "How do you know? I haven't seen a stone."

"No stone. It was a board, rotted off at the bottom. Whoever dug the body out tossed the marker aside. We found it there." Janice pointed out the pile of dirt taken from the grave.

A breeze, slow and hot like fevered breath, walked over us. It had just enough strength to bend the tips of the tallest weeds. Movement caught my eye. Color held it. The dry dirt was wasted and pale. The surrounding plants were scorched to a wan yellow. Caught on a desiccated thistle, was a ribbon of rich, dark, brown.

I walked around the pit to the side Janice was on. Getting down on my hands and knees I put my nose as close to the little strip as I could without touching it. There were smaller flakes of the same color all around it. I breathed in the scent of the ribbon. Tobacco. It was the same cheap cigar tobacco I'd smelled when Charlie Lipscomb was smoking at Roland's trailer.

I bagged it. As I labeled the plastic with a few notes, I said to Janice, "I have a favor to ask, too."

"Anything."

"From your notes, are you able to tell me the family names on the graves that have been opened?"

"I don't need notes. We've only found two families included in the desecration."

"Turner and Patee." I finished for her.

Chapter 17

I tried Roland's mobile home first. The door was again standing open. No one was inside. With the mess inside, it was hard to tell if he had moved out. There was a bed but no sheets or blankets. In the kitchen there were dirty dishes and bugs. In a corner, there was an empty trash can and dozens of empty beer bottles sat on every flat surface.

On my way out, I noticed a cheap cigar sitting on the edge of the counter top. Its front end was nothing but sagging ash. The butt was chewed ragged. It was the same kind I'd seen Lipscomb smoking. I was certain of it. I was just as certain that Charlie Lipscomb was the provenance of the stripped down tobacco I'd seen by the grave.

I left there, and drove to The New American Covenant building in the woods. It was the closest thing I knew to an organized, gathering spot for the Nightriders and their Nazi friends.

I arrived to find the building all but gone. The fire was out, but the bones of the old shack were still smoldering. There was a volunteer fire unit spraying the ashes. I made a quick inventory of faces, but Cherry Dando wasn't there. I checked with the truck captain to see if they needed anything.

They didn't. I called in and asked dispatch to send a deputy. I used my cell phone to call Agent Birch. I assumed that he'd want to know about the fire. He didn't pick up, so I left a message.

From the shack, I went right to our jail. Duck had reported himself sick and checked out for the day. He wasn't the only one missing. Both Cherry Dando and Johnson Rath had been released again.

There was a hollow in my chest, right behind the sternum. It was diffuse as a cloud, reaching from my heart to my stomach. A swallow of whiskey would have been the perfect size to fill it. If I knew one thing at that moment, it was that I was either going to drink or find some answers. It took all I had to opt for answers.

Duck lived in a hundred year old farmhouse with lap siding that had been white, once. The house clearly hadn't been painted in my lifetime. I knocked on the screen door, letting the rattle of it in the frame amplify the sound.

"What are you doing here?" Duck walked over from a dilapidated barn. He was wiping his hands on a dirty shop towel.

"Sick day?" I asked.

"What's it to you?"

"Where's Roland?"

"Again. What's it to you?"

"He knows something."

Duck stopped at the bottom of the porch stairs and looked up at me. "Roland's my son." He kept working his hands thoughtfully. "But what that boy knows wouldn't fill a shot glass."

"I need to talk to him, Duck."

"Good luck with that. He ain't much for sharing. And before you ask, I have tried."

The big door of the barn flopped slowly open as if caught in a wind. There wasn't any wind. An engine fired up.

I moved to the stairs but Duck blocked me.

"Get out of my way, Duck."

Roland, on his motorcycle, burst through the open barn door and tore up dirt getting to the road.

"Duck!"

He didn't fight me. Duck simply let his bulk block me—and looked shamefully after his son. "He's my boy, Hurricane."

The sound of the bike's loud pipes faded in the distance. There was no chance I would catch him. "Why?"

"I told you, he's my boy."

"You're not helping him."

Duck stepped out of my path and sat on the porch step. "That's not the way he sees it. Wrong or right, he sees me on his side. Right now that seems better than anything. How many chances do you get to show someone you love that you're in the fight with them—no matter what."

"Are you so sure it's his fight?"

"What do you mean?"

"I mean, whatever this is, wherever it goes, I think it started a long time ago."

"Of course it did." Duck looked at me with sad, rheumy eyes. "This is the Ozarks. The oldest feuds are the only ones that really matter."

"Tell me about this one."

He did. For two hours, Duck talked and told me secrets from the past. He alternately enraged and devastated me. One generation, it seems, always keeps their secrets from the next one, even as they lay the terrible burdens on their shoulders.

We could have talked another two hours—if my phone hadn't rung, we might have. It was the sheriff calling. Cherry Dando was badly hurt and in the hospital.

* * * *

Dando was in surgery. Outside in the waiting room were the two people I needed to talk to most—the sheriff and my mother. Carmen was crying. When she saw me, she rushed forward and threw her arms around my shoulders. She buried her face in my neck. Her tears rolled in fat drops under my collar. I didn't know what to do. After a long, one-sided embrace, I put my arms around her. I wasn't prepared for how much I needed her touch—even in tragedy—maybe especially then.

"What happened?" I asked, to hold back the sting of tears.

"Rath," the sheriff answered, "He uh. . . he hurt Mr. Dando pretty bad." His speech was careful. Sheriff Benson always had a good presence with victims. He lost the vulgarities, and the colorful idioms. It reminded me just how professional his tenure had been, despite having me as his loose cannon. This is the part Billy would be good at, I thought.

"Why?"

Carmen released me and backed away. "It's my fault."

I waited.

"Because of what happened," she added, "and talking to you. I told him what had happened so long ago. . .what Johnson had done to me."

"Cherry confronted him?" I asked.

She nodded, then dabbed her running nose with an already soggy tissue.

I retrieved a new tissue from a box on a table. Waiting rooms are all the same. So much pain can be summed up by bad magazines and tissues sitting on a table.

She took it, then wadded the tissues—old and new—together to dab again.

"Did Rath admit to it?"

"Admit it?" Carmen shook at the thought. "He laughed about it. Johnson told Cherry everything. He pushed the shameful details in his face. I told Cherry, but Johnson made him see it. Then he beat him simply because he could."

"Why was he free?" My question went to the sheriff. It got no answer. Then I turned back to Carmen and asked her, "Did he tell Cherry why it happened?"

"Johnson Rath never needed a reason for cruelty."

"But he had one. Or he thought he did, didn't he?"

My mother lowered the tissue from her face and looked at me with my own eyes. It was like looking into a broken mirror. "You want all the secrets don't you?"

"There's no reason for secrets." I intended it kindly. "No reason for shame."

"It was a different world, even a few years ago. It's always a different world and always the same down deep."

The sheriff was listening carefully.

"Earl Turner told me about that land and the history of white jealousy." I was talking to him. "He never mentioned the name *Rath*. But they were one of the families that tormented the blacks. It was about money and power and race. Cash had the power to raise one over the other. The Rath family was one that could not accept being less than any blacks for any reason."

"I never knew." Sheriff Benson had a belly-punched look. I'm sure he was thinking if he knew more, things would have been different.

"That had nothing to do with me." The way my mother said it—it could have been warning or imploring.

"It had everything to do with family, though. Didn't it? Your family."

"Yours too." Definitely a warning that time.

I almost laughed, but there was nothing funny. "You have no idea how little that shames me."

"Please?" Her request, small and fearful, reminded me of the same word from Johnson Rath, when he thought I would kill him.

"My mother's maiden name is Patee," I told the sheriff. "Funny, I never knew that until Duck told me." I filled him in on what I learned from Janice Carter.

Carmen wouldn't look at me.

"Over a century of hate—all to bring us here," the sheriff said, shaking his head. It looked old and fragile without the hat.

"I'm going to bring Johnson Rath in." I informed him. "Since we can't prosecute, I can't promise what shape he'll be in."

Sheriff Benson snapped his head up, suddenly alert. Not just alert, wary.

"What's wrong?" I asked.

"I should have told you."

"What?"

"Johnson is in custody. Two deputies are with him here, in this hospital."

Before I could ask anything more, or begin to understand, Billy walked into the waiting area.

He was bruised and bloody. On his temple was a thick bandage that ran into the hair line. There was a hitch as he walked—as if he was trying to hide what should have been a limp. There was no insulated cup of soda in his hands. They were cut and ragged looking—with visible stiches on two fingers. Every knuckle was an open wound.

"Billy?" My feet remained planted. The only thing keeping me from running to him was myself—and I hated knowing that. The only thing worse was the feeling that he knew it as well. "What happened to you?" As soon as I spoke it, my question felt like another wasted chance.

Billy smiled shyly, then looked at his hands. When he looked back up, it was to the sheriff. "If you don't need me anymore. . ." He approached the older man, then handed something over. The exchange was hidden by their bodies.

"No, go on," Sheriff Benson told him. He put a hand on Billy's shoulder. "You did a job of work—and did it well."

"Thank you, Sheriff." Billy turned and nodded to Carmen. "Ma'am."

"Thank you for saving my husband," she said to him. "Thank you for stopping Johnson Rath."

"Billy?"

He looked at me and gave a slight nod. I thought for a second he was going to call me ma'am, too. He passed me—headed for the door.

"Billy." That time I whispered.

He stopped. But he didn't turn or look back. Just as quietly as I had spoken, he said, "I don't feel much like talking now." Billy left.

I turned around. My mother was pulling more tissues. Sheriff Benson was staring at his boots.

"What happened?" I asked the sheriff.

"Billy offered a solution."

"What solution?"

Sheriff Benson looked sideways at Carmen. "I don't guess it matters who knows now. Johnson is staying in jail this time. Then prison." He drew himself up and took a deep breath. "The informant problem. Billy suggested someone who might be an asset to the DEA."

"Billy knows a guy."

"Yeah. It wouldn't be the same. Not like building a compound the DEA can wire. But Birch was getting a little burned out on Johnson Rath and his big plans."

"So why didn't Rath stay in jail?"

"Billy had the name. He had the relationship. He had the plan to set things up."

"What does that have to do with anything?"

"Billy also had conditions."

"Conditions." The word caught in my throat, a hard and bad tasting knot. "What did he hand you?"

"You know what."

"Show me."

Sheriff Benson put a gnarled old hand into his pants pocket and pulled out brass knuckles.

"The old ways," I said, accusing.

"It's an old feud. You said so yourself."

"There's something neither of you know. Carmen?" My mother was sitting beside the tissue box and staring at the one in her hand. "Carmen?" I asked again, gently.

"Yes?"

"You were there that night, weren't you?"

"I don't know what you're talking about."

"Yes you do. You set everything up. You wanted Cherry looking for silver. Doing anything really but working with his old friend, Johnson."

"I already told you that."

"You said then you knew the story of the silver coins being buried there. You didn't say how."

"So what?"

"Did you tell Tyrell how you knew?"

That time she didn't defend or deflect. She dabbed at the snot dripping from her nose. Then she sniffed it back and stared at me.

"Did you offer to trade the information? For his uncle's truck? For an introduction to his father?"

"Nobody knew which one was the father. The whole club had his mother. A son shouldn't know that, but he wanted to know. He wanted to meet them. I set it up—in exchange for information about the graves. But he lied. There was never anything."

"How many of the Nightriders showed up?"

"I don't know. I made Cherry take me out of there. Tyrell said he wanted to meet them and talk. But he started saying things about DNA and finding the real father."

"You thought there would be violence."

"You tell some of those men they have a black son—and that you're going to make it public—there's sure to be something. Mostly, I was afraid it would come out we were related. I was ashamed."

She and I looked away at the same time. My gaze met the sheriff's. "I'm sure Roland Duques was one of the bikers that showed up. I heard him talking about being set up."

"Roland is—"

"The guy Billy knows."

Chapter 18

Billy didn't answer my calls. He wasn't at home either. There was one other place to look. The drive gave me time to think about all the ways I'd let him down.

Billy had never held back or made me wonder about what he wanted from me. He was the kind of a man who presented himself as exactly as what he was. At the same time, he accepted me for who I was—even if who I was—was a drunk or a victim.

I didn't—couldn't—do the same for him—not in the way I presented myself—not with the support I gave him.

Golden hour was blooming on a wilted world when I found the farm road I needed. I took the turn a bit too fast, but never hit the brakes.

At that point I wasn't clear on who I was trying to save. I wanted my own guilt assuaged, yes—for pushing Billy away—for accepting his help as a drunk—then for hiding what had driven me to it from him. More than anything, I felt guilty about the violence he'd done to Johnson Rath. It should have been me. More than anyone, I know how violence changes someone.

The road turned to a series of low, sharp hills. On the second one, my big GMC launched. For a few moments I was in the air with no control. It was exhilarating. The sensation of freefall was a release. Then came the reality. My truck returned to Earth in the rising trough of the next hill. The impact was hard. Tires crunched into loose rock and dirt—that turned to brown smoke on impact. There was no traction. I spun the wheels one way—then the other—looking for any measure of control.

As my truck's rear end slid around to the left, and the front end headed for the weedy ditch on the right, the tires finally bit. I steered into the skid.

My back tires swerved into line just as I topped the next hill—and missed a tractor by inches.

Every flight has consequences.

And that was what I was afraid of. It took a near-fatal accident to make it clear to me. Like everything else in my life, my fears about Billy were really about me. I told him that he wasn't the right kind of man to be sheriff. I said it because I wanted him to remain what I needed. The worst thing about it was—I may have driven him to violence—to be more like me.

I didn't stop for the frightened farmer. I did drive more carefully for the last mile. The fields on the driver's side of the truck transitioned from hay to natural scrub. I steered through a gap in the fence, and followed tracks of beat down weeds to another gate. The gate was a string of barbed wire—strung and held in tension between two posts and a board—tucked into a wire loop.

Billy wasn't there. I went through anyway. It had been a long time since I had come here. Billy owned this land. At the back of it was a wall of limestone—a remaining piece of an ancient sea that had covered the Ozarks for millions of years. The land held a secret—a cave hidden behind a screen of honeysuckle and vines. It was in the darkness of that cave that Billy had kissed me for the first time.

What do we give up when we choose to fly alone? How do you control a fall?

I was sitting on the hood of the truck, staring at a cave opening that—I knew was there but couldn't see—when my phone rang.

It wasn't until I heard it that I knew I'd been listening for contact. I should have checked the display. "Billy?"

"Hurricane, it's Duck."

Try to imagine my disappointment. "What do you want, Duck?"

"You need to get out here."

"Here? Where? And why?"

"My place. Ro's back."

"I'll talk to him later. There are other things happening."

"Things are going to be happening here."

"Call the sheriff."

"I'm calling you because Billy is on his way over here."

"He's meeting Roland?" I slid off the truck's hood. "I'm on my way."

"You need to hurry."

I was already racing across the uneven field when I asked, "Why, Duck? What's going on?"

"I don't know. Roland looks desperate. He talks about making a deal. But he's afraid."

"Is he armed?"

"I don't know."

"Go talk to him, Duck. Take any weapon he has. But more than anything, just talk to him. Keep things calm."

"How?"

"He's your kid. You know how to talk to him. Make him remember how to listen."

I disconnected and concentrated on driving. When I came to the serpentine hills, I flew over them at dangerous speeds. I passed a tractor and waved—as I left the driver in a cloud of red dust.

Roland Duques was the kind of person who didn't want to be dangerous—but he was willing to make himself a party to other people's danger—and it had gotten him trapped. Being trapped *was* dangerous.

I didn't know exactly what Billy was expecting from the meeting, but I had a feeling it wasn't the same thing Roland was planning.

* * * *

I parked alongside Billy's truck in the lot between Duck's house and his barn. Duck and Roland were inside the barn. Bill was standing outside of the open door. They all turned to look as I got out of the truck. The tension in the air wasn't only about me.

"What are you doing here?" Roland asked as I approached.

"I wondered that too." Billy looked more curious than bothered. Either way, he didn't look happy.

"I called her," Duck answered. "Thanks for coming, Hurricane."

"You don't need to be here," Roland said.

"We're working a few things out here," Billy told me. "It might be best—"

"You're working things out. Are you sure Roland here, is working through the same things?"

"What are you talking about?" Billy looked from me to Roland.

Roland looked from Billy to me. "This doesn't concern you."

"Sure it does, Roland. I think both of you are dealing—without knowing all the facts."

"Keep your facts." He managed to sound like he was sneering and whining at the same time. "The only thing that matters is what you do."

"And what you did."

He froze.

"I didn't. . ."

"Then you have nothing to be afraid of." I gave Billy my attention. "Roland was there Sunday morning. He's feeling bad about what he did."

"They made me," Roland blurted.

"You killed Tyrell Turner?" Billy asked him.

"No." Roland's eyes rimmed with tears. "No. But. . ."

Donald Duques put a meaty hand on his son's shoulder. The squeeze he gave was soft encouragement for hard things. "It's time for the truth, boy." He looked at me and added, "All of it."

"I didn't kill him." Roland slumped under the weight of his father's hand and his own guilt. "They made me fight him. They said I had to." Tears spilled over from the corners of his eyes and dropped in rolling tracks. "It wasn't a fight. It was a beating. They said I had to protect their secrets. They said I had to do it because he was black. And I did it because I was afraid not to. They took pictures. They even took my shirt with his blood on it. It was all evidence to hold over my head. To keep me loyal."

Duck's hand slipped from his son's shoulder. The fall looked like it was a thousand miles. "Tell him," Duck said. "I can't."

"Tell me what?" Roland sniffed and wiped his snotty nose with the back of his hand.

"Tyrell was looking for his father," I said.

"I know. They said the whole club raped his mother. That's what they wanted to stay secret. Tyrell was talking about lawsuits."

"Did they tell you that your father was involved in the rape?"

"He was already kicked out by then. Rath said my father was a race traitor."

"She was the one." Duck spoke quietly. He didn't look at his son. "Elaine showed me I didn't have to be a stupid, racist, fuck—just because I had been raised that way. It was because of her that I tried to raise you without that foolishness."

"What are you talking about?" Roland looked genuinely confused. "Who's Elaine?"

"Tyrell Turner's mother," I said. My answer didn't seem to lessen Roland's confusion so I said, "She was the one your father committed 'race treason' with. She was the one they gang-raped to make the point."

"I don't. . . No. No. I. . ." Roland looked from face to face—looking for denial of the truth. He found none. He turned to his father. "Dad? Daddy?"

"When the DNA gets looked at, I'm betting that you'll find Tyrell was your half-brother." I spoke to Roland, but I looked at Billy. "But there's more truth isn't there?"

"More?" Billy asked.

"Who actually killed Tyrell? And who killed Earl Turner when he was following Roland?"

From out beyond the barn and the long drive, on the road behind the trees, rose the sound of engines. Loud pipes spit the roar of angry bikes.

"He did," Roland said. "Charlie Lipscomb killed them both."

Lipscomb and five other bikers rolled up the gravel drive, and stopped at the edge of the lot. The man right beside Lipscomb was the AB biker who had drawn me out—and into the hands of Johnson Rath.

Chapter 19

Lipscomb pulled and lit one of his cheap cigars, as he approached. He didn't come too close. "Come on, Ro." He said. "No reason for any mess. The Club has your back."

"You called them?" Duck asked his son.

"I'm sorry," Roland answered.

"Hey, Duck." Lipscomb took the cigar from his mouth. He tucked his thumbs in his armpits and flapped. "Quack, quack, quack." Then he laughed—like it was the funniest joke ever. He was the only one.

Roland took a step forward.

Billy stopped him by putting one of his torn up hands on Roland's chest. "If you go with them now—you're never coming back."

"I guess maybe we do get what we deserve out of life."

"Deserve has nothing to do with it," Billy told him, earnestly. "It's a long song. No one knows all the words. But you can change your tune anytime."

"That's the dumbest thing I've ever heard," Roland said, but he stayed where he was.

I looked across the lot at the man I'd fought with in Moonshines. "Why don't you ask your friend to come over here?" I said to Lipscomb. "I'd like to have a word with him."

"I bet you would." He puffed a blue cloud up over his head. "I-just-bet-you-would." He laughed. "Look at you. The big-assed *Hurricane*. But you're still just a bitch in a man's world."

Billy turned to face Lipscomb. He eased forward with his hands on his belt. The bloody knuckles and stitches were a clear sign.

"You took on Rath." Lipscomb said. "He's a tough old bird. But old is the word, ain't it?"

"I'm not going to fight you, Charlie." Billy put a hand on his weapon. "I'm going to arrest you."

I stepped forward. "But if it's a fight you want, Charlie."

The other bikers got off their motorcycles. The AB guy pulled off the dark sunglasses he wore. He stared right at me with a second round look in his eyes. "I'll dance if you want, sweetheart."

"You've got no one to run to this time." I took a few more steps forward. "Really think you're man enough, *sweetheart?*"

"Man enough to break your back, bitch."

I stepped forward again.

Charlie wheeled around and shouted to the other man, "I'm handling things here, Gordon."

I laughed. "Gordon? Your name is Gordon?" Two more steps brought me in line with, and in reach of, Charlie. "Not, Adolph?" I laughed again. "You look more like an Eva to me."

Charlie grabbed at me. He got his hand in my collar, then pulled. "I think it's about time you shut your mouth."

I'd taken a risk and invited Charlie's violence. It paid off exactly as it should have. While Charlie's focus was on me, Billy moved closer.

Billy took hold of the hand that gripped my shirt. His knuckles were so close to my face I could see the tearing of his stitches—as his fingers flexed and twisted. He pulled the hand. The force of his action turned Charlie and I inward—like spindles attached to the same lever.

Billy had Charlie's arm locked in his right hand. As he pulled, he also pivoted. His left arm was raised and the fist pulled tight to his shoulder. All of Billy's weight and twisting force met Charlie's elbow at his forearm. As soon as contact was made, Billy angled the forearm down, leaning into it. At the same time, he pulled up with his right.

Charlie screamed. It wasn't loud enough to cover the sound of his elbow snapping.

Charlie Lipscomb, the Ozarks Nightriders Sergeant-at-Arms, hit the gravel, face first, wailing like a lost calf.

Billy had his knee in the center of Charlie's back. He still held the arm he'd broken with one hand, as he pulled his cuffs with the other. When he had the bracelets snapped tight, it looked like everything was over. It should have been.

A gunshot boomed from the doorway of the barn behind us.

Roland Duques stood with a huge, blued .44 revolver in his hand. It was smoking and still pointing at the splintered hole it had torn through the barn wall. He turned it to Charlie Lipscomb, and pulled the hammer back.

"Get away from him," Roland's bellow was still thick with his tears, "I'm going to kill him."

Billy instantly stood with his weapon drawn. He kept himself between his prisoner and Roland.

I pulled my own weapon. At the same time I looked for Duck, hoping he could calm his son. He was gone. As far as I could tell he wasn't in the barn. A quick look around told me he wasn't in the lot.

"Get back," Roland ordered again.

"We can't do that, Roland," I explained gently. "He'll go to prison."

"It's not good enough." Roland's tears were flowing freely. He had to wipe his eyes with the back of his free hand.

He looked so much like a scared child, I wondered again where his father had gone. "Where's your father?"

Roland took his eyes from Charlie—long enough to glance around the barn. He looked confused and hurt. "Dad?" When he looked back it was with a new, harder resolve. "Get out of the way, Billy."

"I can't." Billy looked stricken, but his aim never wavered. I knew for a fact it was set, center mass, right on Roland's heart—just as mine was.

"Roland." I saw his eyes shift to me and back to Charlie. "Roland, this won't fix anything."

"There is no fixing." Roland took a step forward.

Both Billy and I tensed even more—if that was possible.

"But there is ending it." Roland said. His voice was different. The tears were gone replaced by a chilled resignation. "That's what I'm going to do."

"Lower your weapon," Billy shouted in a command voice.

"Roland, don't," I pleaded with him.

I saw the focus in Roland's eyes change again. I realized that Billy and I had both focused on the danger in front of us and neglected the one behind. Before I could turn to see what was happening, there came the pop of a 9mm and Roland's chest flowered with crimson. He slumped to the barn floor.

As I turned. I saw Billy spinning as well. We both had our weapons out in two handed grips. Before we could bring them around, a second bullet fired. That one ripped through Billy's ankle and he toppled awkwardly on top of Charlie Lipscomb.

I took an instant's worth of satisfaction in knowing the pain that had to cause Lipscomb. When my weapon came to bear on Gordon, the AB biker, he was close and marching closer. His gun was already aimed at me.

He fired.

I fired.

The other four bikers, all advancing on us, fired too.

I felt—as well as heard—the wasp buzz of Gordon's bullet passing close to my neck and just under my ear.

My aim was better but only marginally. A spray of blood misted up over Gordon's shoulder—where my bullet nicked him. I kept firing as I dove for the ground.

Gordon ducked sideways still shooting.

Bullets splashed in the gravel around me—like pebbles tossed in water. From behind me, I heard more shots. Billy was shooting.

The air filled with metal, jacketed rockets as the Nightriders poured fire on Billy. The barn echoed with the impacts. From the corner of my eye, I could see flakes of old wood, sawdust blood, falling from the weathered walls.

I also saw Billy moving. He crawled quickly to Roland's body. He fired back twice then tried to pull the kid out of the line of fire.

I rolled to my right. The whole world kaleidoscoped around the axis of my weapon. I fired at Gordon as I moved. He fired at me as he crabbed in the opposite direction.

My gun clicked on an empty chamber.

My next heartbeat was cold, as though the muscle had only the frozen run off of all my hopes to feed my body.

Gordon stopped scrambling and stood. He loomed with a hateful smile. The arm that extended his pistol at me was covered in blue jailhouse ink. The lightning bolts and 88 were mixed with skulls and the body of a naked woman. I had a second to understand that hate and misogyny were going to murder me.

A shotgun blasted. The guns firing at Billy and Roland stopped.

Gordon turned.

I looked as I kicked my feet and scrabbled my hands in the gravel. As I got to my knees I saw Duck with the smoking twelve-gauge. One of the bikers, with most of his right arm and shoulder missing, hit the ground.

Duck racked a new shell into the chamber, and fired at the closest standing biker. The man's chest exploded.

Gordon had his pistol up and aimed at Duck. I released a handful of driveway gravel at his face. He fired. I didn't see what happened. I was looking only at Gordon by then.

I hit him low, thrusting my right shoulder into the short ribs.

Gordon's pistol cartwheeled into the sky.

I heard more gunshots, and the shotgun fire at least two more times. I couldn't see what was happening. Gordon and I hit the ground together. He tried to hold me as I tumbled over him and clear.

I made my feet and turned.

He was up and ready.

Gordon charged high. His thick arms closed engulfing my shoulders. He squeezed.

Through my body, I could hear the shifting of my bones as he crushed my chest inward. The constriction pressed the air from my lungs and allowed no breath in. The pain was excruciating. My vision tunneled down to a tiny hole of perception. The black edges of closing consciousness sparkled with stars.

For some reason my mind went to the stars that Billy had taken me to look at. Would I ever see them again? Is it possible that I could become a part of them?

That was the terrifying thing. Not the pain or the threat, it was the acceptance that scared me. The longing.

Without waiting for thought, I lunged forward with my head. Leading with my forehead, I crushed Gordon's nose.

He flinched. His grip lessened. Lessened but remained.

Still, I caught a small breath. It was enough to inspire a harder fight. I kicked my feet.

Gordon arched his back, lifting me.

I kicked harder.

He squeezed again. Then he lifted me higher. He pushed me up, and let me drop into an even tighter grip.

Something in my ribs popped. Searing pain shot though my side. Again, there was no breath and no breathing.

I didn't wait for darkness that time. I reared back and head-butted his nose again.

That time he was ready. He barely acknowledged the impact. In fact he grinned at me. The blood flowing from his broken nose stained his teeth.

That told me what I had to do.

I opened my mouth, stretching my lips back in a silent snarl. I bit his nose.

Gordon screamed, but that was his only concession to the pain. His grip around my body tightened.

I bit harder, digging my teeth deep into the flesh of his already damaged and bloody nose.

Another pop in my chest.

I almost opened my mouth to gasp. Instead I screamed through clenched teeth and twisted my neck.

His skin ripped. The cartilage gave way and split away from bone.

Gordon dropped me.

I hit the ground on my back.

He stomped backward, cupping his hand over the gushing wound that his nose had become.

I stole a second to wipe the blood from my face with my sleeve. I charged to my feet. It hurt a lot more than I'd anticipated. Instead of running at Gordon, I limped with an arm clamped around my ribs.

I managed to get my foot up, and thrust my boot heel into the front of his extended knee. It crunched into hyperextension. I could almost hear the ligaments tearing.

Gordon released his nose to reach for the new source of pain. When he did, I saw the dangling meat and the hole in his face.

I fought the urge to feel proud.

Chapter 20

It took time for my vision to open fully. It took longer for my hearing to clear from muted roar, to actual sound, to understanding.

Duck ran past. In his wake, he'd left two men definitely dead. One was still writhing on the ground—apparently missing a foot.

I didn't make the same mistake I'd made in Moonshines. I cuffed Gordon. That time though, I was sure it was overkill.

Billy was kneeling over Roland's body keeping pressure on the wound in his chest.

Duck dropped his shotgun to sit beside his son. I could see him whispering to Roland. I hoped that they were finally able to talk honestly.

I did not reflect on my own failings in honest communication. Not then. I pulled my phone and called dispatch.

* * * *

It took hours, long into darkness, to clear the scene. If the sheriff hadn't put his foot down, every deputy we had would have been at Duck's farm to help. Honestly, I think that was more because of Billy than anything else. I couldn't begrudge him the care of so many friends. It was clear how wrong I was—even if my own reasons for thinking so weren't clear—Billy Blevins would make a great sheriff.

Over the next few weeks, things about the case shook out. Duck was right. It's the old feuds that carry the most weight in the Ozarks. DNA showed that Duck was indeed Tyrell's father. A pile of letters that Elaine Turner had written, but never sent him, detailed her pain and fears after the assault—by men who claimed what they did to her was for the good of their own race.

She had been in love with Donald. In the letters, she never called him Duck. Not only her body, but her spirit was damaged. She needed Donald, but never found the courage to tell him the truth. She never sought counseling. She never told anyone but her father, a man who shared the fear and damage inflicted by the same men.

It was a miracle that Tyrell had grown up as strong and normal as he had—which spoke volumes about the tenacity of that family.

Cherry Dando recovered from the beating that Johnson had given him.

Johnson, however, wasn't as fortunate. Someone, I believe it was my mother, Carmen, passed word to the AB about his scheme to defraud them of drugs and inform to the DEA. The Aryan Brotherhood is, at heart, a prison gang—with a long reach behind bars. Their justice is not that of courts and lawyers. Johnson Rath was murdered in prison.

Johnson's death made things even murkier for the standing of his Nazi church. Landis Tau stepped in. Making a deal with the federal government, he took over the nonprofit organization upon which The New American Covenant–The Word and The Sword was built. It was expected to be essentially valueless, with the graveyard as its only asset. It turned out that the AB had deposited some cash to fund the compound construction. To protect themselves, it had been listed as an anonymous donation. The "donation" was a good start at funding the work to preserve the graves. Doctor and Agent Carter remained with the organization. They turned— what had once been—a place of desperate burial into a monument to forgotten lives.

I visited their daughter's school. I thought I went to talk to the girls. In my mind, I had it all planned out. I would tell them to be anything they dreamed of, and to dream big. I did say that. I did talk about being a woman in the military and law enforcement. At the end, however, I realized I was there to talk to the boys. I told them to forget everything they had ever been taught about being gentlemen, or treating girls special. I told them to remember everything they learned about playing fair. I asked them to treat everyone with kindness. I informed them about the many ways they shape the world, and the many chances they had to make it better—not by treating girls as different or even better—but simply by understanding the equality of all people.

I don't know how much good I did, but I felt a lot better for it.

Agent Darion Birch caught hell from the DEA about the implosion of his operation. I understand he gave as good as he got.

Roland Duques survived. It was no miracle. It was Billy. He applied pressure to the wound—even while bullets were still winging past him. He maintained pressure and soothing words until the kid was loaded into the ambulance. It turned out that Roland was the one who burned the shack in the woods. He'd also been the one to call and tell Charlie Lipscomb he was waiting at the barn. He'd planned all along to kill the Sergeant-at-Arms, and escape the Nightriders. It just wasn't a good plan.

Duck still looked like two fat Elvises stuffed into one sheriff's department uniform, but he looked like a different man to me. After that day, he was my friend. I made a greater effort to be his friend.

I didn't get away with my sins—not that we ever do. The sheriff added another full year requirement to my mandated counseling. For the first time, I didn't see that as a punishment.

While Cherry Dando was in the hospital, I went there to visit my mother. It remained tense, but I thought we were making some progress. I guess I was wrong. Cherry was released one morning. I understand Carmen picked him up in that old beater of a car—loaded with boxes and clothes. That time, she didn't even bother to say goodbye.

My relationship with Billy Blevins was damaged. I had done that. Problems don't magically repair in the euphoria of surviving life-threatening situations. Every action movie ever made—that ended in a kiss and the promise of future happiness—is a lie. I never told him the truth about what happened when Johnson Rath took me to that shack.

Roy Finley made great progress on the El Camino. Billy never came to see it. He said he couldn't accept that kind of gift from someone who would work for him if he won the election. It was sound reasoning, but Billy Blevins was never a very good liar.

The heat finally broke one evening—with the arrival of a cold front from the Rockies. Black clouds exploded with lighting and rain—as if taking vengeance for crimes the Ozarks kept secret. I watched from behind glass walls. My body was surrounded by a home and art created by my dead husband. My heart was surrounded by my longing to be with Billy. It was a moment of my life that seemed to be everything.

Meet the Author

Robert Dunn is the author of the Katrina Williams series, as well as the novels *The Red Highway, The Harrowing,* and *Dead Man's Badge.* He can be found on Facebook at https://www.facebook.com/RobertEDunnAuthor or on Twitter at @WritingDead.

A Living Grave

The first in a gritty new series featuring sheriff's detective Katrina Williams, as she investigates moonshine, murder, and the ghosts of her own past . . .

BODY OF PROOF

Katrina Williams left the Army ten years ago disillusioned and damaged. Now a sheriff's detective at home in the Missouri Ozarks, Katrina is living her life one case at a time—between mandated therapy sessions—until she learns that she's a suspect in a military investigation with ties to her painful past.

The disappearance of a local girl is far from the routine distraction, however. Brutally murdered, the girl's corpse is found by a bootlegger whose information leads Katrina into a tangled web of teenagers, moonshiners, motorcycle clubs, and a fellow veteran battling illness and his own personal demons. Unraveling each thread will take time Katrina might not have as the Army investigator turns his searchlight on the devastating incident that ended her military career. Now Katrina will need to dig deep for the truth—before she's found buried . . .

Printed in the United States
by Baker & Taylor Publisher Services